UNDERGROUND

by

Niels Aage Skov

Booklocker.com, Inc.
2007

Courage in danger is half the battle.

- Plautus

In the following narrative, background events and some of the story line are strictly authentic in time and place. The details of Abramek Blum's ordeal in escaping Gestapo's grasp are fictional, though enacted many times over during the years when the Nazis held sway in occupied Europe.
I am indebted to Professor Lorraine Hale Robinson, whose meticulous editing and thoughtful advice have invaluably enhanced the manuscript.

Commando Order

From now on all men operating against German troops in so-called Commando raids...are to be slaughtered to the last man...whether they be soldiers in uniform, or saboteurs, with or without arms; and whether fighting or seeking to escape; and...whether they come into action from Ships and Aircraft, or whether they land by parachute.

Should individual members...such as agents, saboteurs etc., fall into the hands of the Armed Forces...they are to be instantly handed over to the S.D.

(Signed) A Hitler

HEADQUARTERS OF THE ARMY
SECRET

No. 551781/42G.K. Chefs W.F.St/Qu. F.H. Qu. 19/10/42

The enclosed Order from the Führer is forwarded in connection with destruction of enemy Terror and Sabotage-troops. This order is intended for Commanders only and is in no circumstances to fall into Enemy hands.

Chief of Staff of the Army
(Signed) Jodl

Note: After the war, German officers who carried out the illegal executions under the Commando Order were found guilty at the Nuremberg Trials. The Commando Order was one of the specifications in the charge against Field Marshal Alfred Jodl, who was convicted and hanged.

Chapter 1

The darkness on the railroad embankment was far from total, just the Northern spring night's ghostly semi-darkness. In another half hour the moon would rise and illuminate the scene, but he hoped to be gone by then. Svend Lund crouched on the embankment north of the station yard, waiting for his breath to return to normal after the dash to pick up the Suomi pistol at the apartment. This was a totally unexpected opportunity, and yet the kind of thing a saboteur always hoped to run into. Through the night air came the sound of the locomotive, wheezing plaintively in the station as if impatient at having the journey interrupted. Obviously, the driver was keeping up steam, ready to continue.

Lund had just graduated from the Polytechnic Institute in Copenhagen, at the age of twenty-seven an electrical engineer at last. The war had caused interruptions and delayed his final studies, as he had started some Underground resistance against the German occupiers, well before the option of such activity had occurred to anyone else. At the moment he was visiting his grandparents in Ribe, a small provincial town of ancient origin on the Danish North Sea coast. The unstated but more important reason for his presence was to train a local Resistance group he had recently formed. It was not easy to find young men both willing and capable of engaging in sabotage against the Wehrmacht troops. The Danes were such thoroughly civilized people, recoiling from the prospect of risking freedom and maybe life by acting contrary to their government's exhortation to behave with restraint. "To act in a dignified manner," as the old King Christian had admonished. Thanks a lot. That was also how Hitler hoped people would behave in the countries occupied by the Germans, for that would put the least strain on Germany's manpower. Norway, Denmark, Holland, Belgium and France were now under the German heel, a sizable handful to administer and monitor. If only these nations would be quiet and cooperative, producing food and industrial goods for the Reich, a minimum of military forces would be required to control and monitor them. That would leave most German strength to be deployed on the Eastern Front, where Hitler's titanic struggle with the Soviet Union was hanging in the balance.

A few determined people, Lund among the very first, saw this clearly and had resolved to do what they could to obstruct the German plans. He had worked mostly in Copenhagen, recruiting and training saboteurs, but two months ago, he had formed a six-man group from old school chums in Ribe, the town of his birth. He had given them some minimal basic training during a couple of hurried visits. This time he had brought a collection of German handguns, eleven in all, from the hodge-podge of side arms carried by German soldiers and by personnel of the Sicherheitsdienst, or SD, the notorious German secret police. He had also brought the Suomi M/31 machine pistol, thank God. He felt its reassuring presence under his wind jacket. Its rate of fire, almost one thousand 9-mm bullets per minute, put him on a par with an average infantry platoon in firepower.

In the distance the engine was still intermittently letting off steam. He had taken a walk after dinner. The night was balmy with all the unmistakable scents of spring flowers, mixed with the earthy smell of composting plants on the banks of the small river. The unceasing west wind also carried hints of the North Sea, just three miles distant. This was spring in Denmark, a lovely season, harbinger of the brief northern summer. The storks were arriving, soon they would be hatching their young in nests balanced on the ridges of red-tiled roofs. In late summer they would be practicing formation flying every day, getting ready for their migratory trek to Africa, and by

September 1st they would be gone, like clockwork. Lund was born in Ribe, and he loved this flat, west coast land intensely, felt at home here, although he had lived in Copenhagen since he was sixteen.

The town lay dark and silent, but on his walk he had heard distant sounds announcing that a train from the south was pulling in to the railroad station. It sounded like a freight, and out of idle curiosity he had turned toward the station to see what it might be. The station was deserted except for two employees working in the office behind blackout curtains. He went through the building to the platform where the train was standing, and became instantly alert. It was a freight, alright, but a military one, about three dozen flatcars loaded with Wehrmacht vehicles in camouflage paint, and without any guards in sight. A prime target! He had returned through the station building to the unlit street and started running for his grandparents' apartment. How he wished there had been time to get a couple of the guys from his new local group, for there was enough work here for all of them, but he was afraid there wouldn't be time to rouse them before the train left.

A sudden release of steam announced that the locomotive was trying to get its load moving. Chooo......chooo.... chooo..chooo. The train was slowly pulling out and he could see the light on the engine drawing nearer. He moved back from the embankment to be out of the sparse beam from the hooded lantern, and when the locomotive had gone past, he jumped without difficulty onto one of the flatcars. The vehicles, largely trucks and armored cars, were strapped down securely; most of them were diesel powered, but he located a *Kübel*, a small scout vehicle which had a gasoline engine, and punctured the gas tank with a small screwdriver. By the time he was ready to ignite the gasoline, the train was rumbling along at moderate speed, and as he was digging in his pocket for matches, a bullet smashed through the *Kübel's* windshield. He ducked behind the vehicle and tried to figure out where it had come from, for the noise of the train had drowned out the report of the gun. A second bullet solved the problem, for this time he saw the muzzle flash. The shooting came from a small wood brake house on a flatcar three cars farther back. Some of the flatcars on European trains had such brake houses, two-by-three-foot structures, five feet high, mounted high at one end of the car, open on one side and having one-foot-square, glassless openings facing front and back to give a man overview to manipulate the mechanical wheel brakes during switching operations. Offering protection against inclement weather, it was the perfect vantage point for someone guarding the freight, and evidently a soldier was holed up in this one, obtaining some shelter from the wind.

As he lay on his side close to the *Kübel* his thoughts flashed to other occasions, when he had been less adequately equipped, and he felt grimly grateful for the Suomi under his jacket. He readied the gun, rolled over onto his stomach to bring the target into view and squeezed off a burst that stitched a lethal pattern across the full width of the brake house. He felt the chatter of the recoil, and he tried for an instant to visualize what it would be like inside, when the wood wall in front of his unseen adversary suddenly erupted in a shower of splinters and bullets. *Sorry, Nazi soldier, but your rotten government should not have sent you to my country.* Then he put the thought aside. They had tried to kill each other, but it was his good luck to be better armed for the contest. Even in the hands of a marksman a rifle was a poor weapon on a rattling and lurching freight car, but the Suomi was absolutely perfect for this situation.

Without waiting to investigate further, he stepped back from the *Kübel* and threw a match into the accumulated gasoline. As it caught with a whoosh, he jumped off the flatcar onto the grass embankment, holding the Suomi well clear. The train proceeded into the night as if nothing had happened, the fire building slowly but surely, like a cheerful candle. Apparently the engineer was not looking back at his freight, or perhaps there was no instruction for dealing with this sort of occurrence.

While the train receded into the distance, he started to walk the opposite way along the railroad track, back toward town.

x

The old steamer *Pride of Dundee* was pulling away from the quay in Mombasa, meeting the welcome coolness of the sea breeze that came every evening at this time. The gentle wind arose an hour after sundown and blew until almost midnight, relieving the heat and odors of the city and its hinterland in an ancient ritual governed by the immutable exchanges of heat energy between the ocean and the landmass.

Elizabeth van Paassen stood at the railing, looking back at the town and at the land where she was born, her home until the war and her own circumstances now conspired to force a change. Her father had been Dutch, of Walloon Huguenot stock, ancestors who had fought the Spanish for the sake of freedom of conscience in another war, one that had lasted eighty years. He had settled in Kenya just before the Great War in 1914-18 and had married a nurse from the British contingent, so that Liz had grown up speaking her mother's English and her father's Dutch with equal ease. After her father's sudden death three months ago, her mother had insisted that they return to Britain in this, the Empire's critical hour of need.

The time since her father's death had been crowded with activity. The farm had been sold together with most of their belongings, for mother and daughter both recognized the merit in traveling light, when the future was uncertain. The last week had actually been hectic, when the shipboard opportunity had unexpectedly appeared. The Mediterranean was deemed too risky for an old tub like *Pride of Dundee*. Furious fighting between Eisenhower's forces and Rommel's Africa Corps was inexorably spelling the end of Hitler's North African venture, but in the closing stages it still compelled civilian traffic bound for Britain to take the longer route around the Cape of Good Hope.

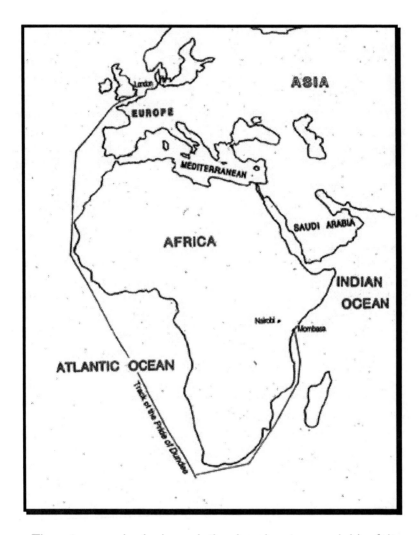

The steamer had cleared the breakwater, and Liz felt a barely perceptible motion, as the ship met a lazy swell from the southeast. She tried to visualize their future after arriving in London, but no images came to her mind. Instead, she saw her childhood at the coffee plantation in the Ngong Hills. In the scrubby grass patches beyond the Kikuyu shambas she used to shoot spurfowl, a relative to the partridge, and to perfect her marksmanship, her father had bought her a 20-gage shotgun. It reached farther than the 12-gage but also required greater precision. It had forced her to discipline herself to make every shot count, and the spurfowl had taught her speed. Once they broke from cover, you had just two seconds, no more, before they were out of range.

When she closed her eyes, she was making the trip from the farm in the Ngong Hills to Nairobi, fifteen miles distant. Nairobi held the Government House and the administrative offices, from which the country was ruled. It was a motley place, some fine stone buildings amid quarters of old corrugated iron shacks, and a few rows of bungalows along dusty streets lined with eucalyptus trees. In her mind she could see the fine ball room in the Government House, where her parents had taken her to parties on the King's birthday and on other official occasions.

At twenty-one she was in excellent physical shape, slender, slightly under average height and strikingly attractive. Her shoulder-length, bronze-red hair, pale complexion and grey-blue eyes bespoke her North European roots. No man had ever told her she was beautiful, for there had been no boy friends in Nairobi, and the visitors to the farm had almost all been of her parents' generation. She wondered what London would have to offer under war time conditions. When they had visited her mother's relations there four years ago, it had been an exciting experience. Would her contemporaries all be in uniform now?

She tore away from her reverie at the railing and went below to their cabin, where her mother was unpacking and hanging clothes into a tiny closet.

"Mum, where will we stay in London?"

"Oh, when I get a nursing job at some hospital, we'll find a flat nearby. Your occupation will be more important. Have you thought any more about where you'd like to serve?"

They had touched on the subject, inconclusively, as neither could quite imagine what the options might be.

"I think I'll apply to the Special Operations Executive. It's a new branch, and I read somewhere that they are looking for people who speak a foreign language. Maybe my Dutch will qualify me."

x

In the café at Amsterdam's main railroad station Viggo Hansen looked across the small table at his girl friend, wondering when he would see her again. Sophie Harring was the first woman he had seriously considered marrying, *was* considering marrying, he corrected himself, but he was not in a position to entertain such plans at present. His job as aircraft mechanic with KLM, the Royal Dutch Airline, had gradually petered out. The German occupiers had requisitioned most of the planes and equipment, forcing the airline to lay off more and more staff until even Hansen's skeleton crew had been let go. After three years in Holland–three very enjoyable years–he had decided to return to his native Denmark, where work was slightly easier to obtain.

Sophie was chattering nervously, trying not to cry at his departure. To understand her in her own language had been his main motivation to perfect his Dutch, rather than to compromise by conversing in German or English. She was now talking about a girlfriend whose wedding they had both attended a week ago. The bridegroom was a civil engineer, employed by the government on the draining of the Inland Lake, an immense operation that would go on for decades. That meant future employment security, something a woman could appreciate these days. Hansen was only half listening, watching the play of emotions on her expressive face, silently envying the civil engineer's desirability as a marriage prospect. He also knew that Sophie would immediately accept his proposal, job or no job, but that would not be fair.

Hansen was a strapping six feet, strongly built, with the grey-blue eyes and medium blond hair that conferred on most

Danes a non-descript look, making each invisible in a crowd simply by blending in. At thirty he had no illusions about love as the sole requirement to make a happy and successful marriage. He would have had a supervisory job by now, had it not been for the war and the interruptions it caused in untold lives and careers, including his own. He was by nature thoughtful, deliberate in plans and actions. His present move of returning to Denmark did not hold much promise but was better than staying in Holland.

He glanced at the large clock suspended overhead in the hall outside the café.

"My train leaves in five minutes, Phie. We have to go down to the platform."

He picked up his suitcase, and they descended, arm in arm, with Sophie leaning against him, forcing back tears and pretending their separation would be of short duration. She worked in the accounting department of a large shipping firm and made a good salary, though not enough for two. Anyway, that was not something he would ever contemplate. Hansen kissed her one last time and got on, one step ahead of the conductor who was slamming the doors shut. The train started moving and she waved and smiled through a blur of tears.

Damn that war.

x

Marek took a quick glance through the glassless window. Below him, Franziszkanska Street was dark and quiet except for the nervous chatter of a German machine gun a couple of blocks to the north. He looked at Mordechaj who was wrapping the papers in oil cloth and trying to seal the bundle with wax. Their eyes met, as Mordechaj handed him the slim parcel.

"Keep it close to your body so the wax stays soft; I think that will help keep it watertight. Remember, the fight of *Zydowska Organizacja Bojowa* deserves to be known to the rest of the world. We owe it to the many who have died."

He did not add, "and to ourselves," for they would all die very soon. Marek knew and understood. Since the ZOB was formed in January, its fifty battle groups had been in constant action and had earned the admiration of the entire Polish Underground outside the Ghetto wall. The leaders of *Armie Krajowa*, the Polish Home Army, had sent fifty pistols and fifty hand grenades, a welcome addition to the primitive arms produced in the Ghetto's small workshops and the German weapons occasionally taken in street battles. The uprising, always a hopeless fight but better than being freighted passively to the killing centers, was slowly, inexorably being ground down by the Germans. Spotted fever, tuberculosis and hunger were aiding the SS, leaving only the youngest and strongest still able to lift a weapon. It had been an epic struggle, fully as worthy as Eleazar's suicidal defiance of the Roman Tenth Legion on Masada nineteen hundred years ago.

The two men, both twenty-three years of age, had known each other since they were yeshiva students. Mordechaj was in command of the ZOB, such as were still left, and Marek had led one of the battle groups. Now he was tasked with taking to the outside world a record of immortal valor in the struggle against the Nazi scourge. Marek had been chosen in part because his uncle, Abramek Blum, had found a temporary haven in Amsterdam, a beacon of hope if Marek could make his way across Nazi occupied Europe, including Germany itself. Word had filtered back to the Ghetto that his uncle was working under the assumed name of Voigt. It was all somewhat confusing, but Marek was concentrating on the immediate problem at hand: extricating himself and getting away from the slaughter in the Ghetto.

As he handed the package to Marek, Mordechaj added a final reminder.

"This has to go all the way to England, somehow, and now it depends on you."

Marek took the parcel and slid it into a pocket on the inside of his shirt, under his left arm pit.

"I'll do my best."

They went downstairs and stood for a moment in the stairwell. The door to the street was missing, and they peered into the choking, pasty darkness beyond the empty opening, listening intently. They were both of average height, dark haired, and would in normal circumstances have been considered handsome. As it was, strain and hunger gave them a haggard, almost scrawny look, but in their eyes burned a determination that had defied two thousand years of persecution.

They embraced, knowing they would not meet again, and Marek mumbled a Hebrew phrase, *hazak ve'emats* (be strong and of good courage). Then he left, silent as a shadow. It took him almost half an hour to reach a point in Lezno Street where a pile of masonry debris was stacked against the wall of a burned-out building. He began cautiously to shift the material and slowly uncovered a manhole to the sewer. When he was able to lift the cover aside, he lowered himself into the vertical shaft and slid the cover back in place. Descending the iron ladder, his nostrils were assaulted by the fetid stench of the sewer, mixed with a chemical smell reminiscent of ammonia, the remnants of a German gas grenade dropped some place in the system a couple of weeks earlier. This particular sewer line had been unused and blocked off for decades, and in some places the Germans had placed booby-trapped obstacles. Several days of painstaking work by ZOB had made it passable, but it took him almost an hour to reach the outfall on the Vistula River. The exit itself was blocked by an iron grate, one bar of which had been cut the previous night. He fumbled to dislodge the bar, squeezed through the opening, and lay silent in the grass, listening and breathing deeply of the spring air. The outfall was set in a steep slope, at the top of which Warsaw loomed silent. He sensed the agony of the city he knew so well. Like an animal wounded by the hunter, it lay prostrate under the heel of the invader.

His plan was to let the river carry him downstream concealed under some of the flotsam that dotted the river's surface at this time of year. Poland was heavily forested, and in the spring when the mountain snow melt swelled its tributaries, the Vistula carried bushes, windfalls and all manner of forest debris all the way to the Baltic Sea.

There was just enough light to perceive objects close at hand, and he made a cautious survey of the nearest surroundings. A seven-foot chunk of timber, stranded and half out of the water looked to have enough buoyancy to keep his head above water. That would have to do, with some additional camouflage. A further scan revealed two uprooted bushes. He crawled over and ran his hands over them; they seemed to be forest vegetation of some kind he didn't know, but they would serve. He unwound a thin rope coiled around his waist and lashed the bushes and his shoes to the timber. With a last look around he pushed the contraption into the stream and followed in a crouch that immediately soaked him to the skin, making him gasp. The spring sun had raised the river's temperature some, but not enough to invite swimming. Hoping to stave off some of the cold, he had put on the few clothes he owned. On land he had felt like a stuffed bear, but now he felt submerged in ice water.

Holding on to the timber while hiding his head in the largest bush, he stroked with his legs until well away from the shore. The current took over, and he rested, feeling suspended in time and space, vaguely wondering how long his emaciated body could stay alive in water at this temperature. He closed his eyes and spoke an ancient Hebrew prayer.

"*Yehi ratzon skeekhye*" ("Let me live.")

Chapter 2

There were just three of them, Lund plus two men he had chosen with care from his Copenhagen group. Together they had planned tonight's action with a dual purpose: putting a small supplier to Hitler's war machine out of business, and at the same time testing an explosive furnished by the British.

A week earlier they had been in northern Jutland as part of a group receiving a parachute drop of sabotage material sent by the British to kindle resistance to the Nazis in occupied Denmark. The operation took place in a remote forest clearing, and the Halifax bomber had appeared exactly as programmed, a brilliant feat of navigation without electronic aids. Rumor had it that the pilots selected for this delivery task came from remnants of the Polish Air Force, intrepid fliers who had eluded German prison camps to join the RAF. The receiving group had spirited the stuff away in a motley array of vehicles: a couple of milk trucks, a country doctor's car, an ambulance, and a lone taxi, all of whom still had licenses to operate on generator gas. The men unpacked the containers in a barn belonging to a farmer in the group and marveled at the contents. There were two kinds of explosives, several Sten submachine guns, a large quantity of fire starters, four Albion revolvers, a selection of timing devices and detonators, all with instructions, and a supply of ammunition. Lund had brought some of the stuff back with him to his apartment in Copenhagen and was intent on field testing it without delay.

It was near ten in the evening and pitch dark, for their purposes a perfect night, and they felt this was going to be an order of magnitude better than anything they had done before. With nothing better than matches to work with, their only means of destruction so far had been fire, and not everything will burn.

But now, in possession of the coveted explosives, they had elevated their sights and chosen the Ruko factory. Located in the northern part of the city, Ruko had been a peacetime manufacturer of door and window hardware, locksets, hinges and such. It was now producing miscellaneous small items for the German military, and it was protected by *Sabotagevagter*, Danish armed guards, who had recently appeared on the scene to protect installations the authorities deemed vulnerable. To avoid dealing with them, the trio had devised what they thought to be an elegant artifice rather than a heavy-handed frontal assault. Some very discreet reconnaissance had established that the factory's heating plant was shut down for the summer, and also that it was located in the same building as the power plant. They had decided therefore to lower a bomb down the chimney stack and into the heating unit, aiming to blow the entire powerhouse to bits. To do this, they needed to get onto the powerhouse roof, which was accessible via the factory roof over a fourteen-foot wall from the city street. Using a ladder from a nearby yard, the three climbed quickly, swung themselves over the wall and onto the flat roof of the factory building, and hauled the ladder up to prevent a passing pedestrian from seeing it and getting nosy. They proceeded to climb onto the adjacent powerhouse roof and reached the chimney stack which rose eight feet above the roof surface. Lund carried the bomb which was the size of a basket ball, wrapped in burlap with a line attached. He activated a twenty-minute delay detonator, jabbed it through the burlap into the explosive, and his two collaborators boosted him onto their shoulders. Reaching the top of the chimney, he slowly lowered the bomb down the stack. When it reached bottom, they made their way back, lowered the ladder to the street again, and climbed back down. One man returned the ladder to the yard where they had taken it, while Lund went to the nearest public telephone booth and called the plant with a warning for everyone to get out.

As the nightshift workers left the factory through the main gate on the opposite side of the block from where the saboteurs had made the approach, the three sat down in a beer joint several blocks away counting down the remaining couple of minutes. On time a powerful WHOOMP shook the building. The barmaid and the few patrons rushed to the door to look and listen in the darkness, while the little team quietly toasted the removal of one tiny supply source of the Wehrmacht, marveling at the ease of doing sabotage with the help of modern technology.

x

The Vistula swept in a gentle curve westward, causing back-eddies along the western bank. The sun was half visible on the eastern horizon, weakly illuminating the area on both sides of the river, deserted, marshy land with patches of brush. Marek kicked feebly to move his floating debris pile toward shore, but with no discernible result. Conveniently, an eddy in the current took over the task and slowly carried him into shoaler water. Some thirty yards from shore he suddenly felt the river bottom, detached himself and his shoes from the debris and waded toward dry land. Staggering to some bushes, he thought he had never been so cold in his life. Teeth chattering he took off all his clothes, wrung as much water from each garment as he could, and laboriously pulled each item back onto his shivering body. Toward the west, some sparse forest could be seen in the distance. Feeling certain that he could walk at most a mile or two, he willed his emaciated body to move in the direction of the forest, starting his trek across Europe.

It seemed an eternity, but by the position of the sun on his left, he judged it to be mid-morning, when he crossed the tree line. The flat landscape was rising slightly, the marshy area yielding to firmer ground, easier to walk over. Most of the trees were coniferous, but here and there stood groves of beeches close to greening, and where the beeches ruled, anemones covered the forest floor with pale shrouds. He stumbled onto a path, perhaps a hunter's trail or an animal track, and he followed it, both fearing and hoping to find human settlement. It was about midday when he encountered a dirt road that ran southeast-northwest. Marek followed it toward the northwest, away from Warsaw, and after another hour he saw a small farmstead off to the right. Smoke was rising from the chimney, and in response to his knock, a woman opened the door slightly, two small boys behind her pushing to glimpse the stranger. She eyed him suspiciously, as Marek explained that he was on his way to a cousin in Poznan, but did not have a travel permit. To avoid German checkpoints, he had swum across the river and kept off major roads. Would she let him dry out a bit by the fire? Reluctantly, she let him in, and he sat down on the floor by the stove with the two boys standing by expectantly.

The warmth met him like waves emanating from heaven itself, as the woman gave him a mug of herb tea and a piece of black bread. Her name was Alicia, and once she got past her initial apprehension, she chatted volubly. Her husband, Geremek, had gone to barter chickens for flour in the nearby village, because the partisans yesterday had taken what flour they had. What kind of partisans, and where were they, Marek asked. She didn't know much about them, only that they were camped somewhere to the north. Did her husband know how to find or contact them? She thought so.

The warmth overcame Marek with irresistible drowsiness. Leaning against the wall, he closed his eyes for a moment. Within seconds, he was asleep.

x

It was ten in the evening as Lund's group converged from various directions on the portal of an elegant apartment house in Bredgade, a quiet street of the inner city near the old citadel. Lund arrived one minute early, carrying besides his gun a small fire starter. Tonight would see the second field test of the British material, this time the fire starter. It was an object the size of a Havana cigar but larger around the middle. It had a dab of sulfur at one end, enabling it to be lit like a match by rubbing on a matchbox striking surface.

Lund had chosen a German marine administrative center as the target for this action. It was located on the third floor of the apartment building, and the reason for this particular choice was a piece of incidental intelligence one of the group had picked up from a fishing skipper plying the Baltic fishing grounds. The man had reported that the Germans were conducting submarine exercises of some sort in the eastern Baltic. Scuttlebutt had it that this was where Hitler's submariners were being drilled to join the Battle of the Atlantic, which was being fought tooth and nail. It was well known that Admiral Dönitz was determined to cut the British life line of supplies from America. The group was therefore unanimous in wanting to aim this small effort at the German navy, Hitler's Kriegsmarine. Besides, a German action had recently precipitated the scuttling of most of the Danish navy, and that still rankled. They ascended the stairway silently to the third-floor landing.

While the team was getting tightly into position behind him, standing in twos shoulder to shoulder, Lund stood with his nose almost touching the door. It flashed through his mind that variants of this situation surely were being played out untold times and in untold places in the occupied countries around the perimeter of Germany: random groups of determined civilians making war on what was perhaps the best military machine since the Romans. Could they hope to make a difference? Was their effort merely symbolic, maybe even counter-productive in the larger scheme of history? Were they learning anything to be used in future human conflicts, or would governments and military establishments continue mindlessly to prepare for the previous war, too preoccupied to prevent the next one? Surely, if even one percent of Denmark's modest military expenditures had been devoted to prepare for this sort of thing, the results could have been a thousand times more effective.

The quiet shuffle behind him had ceased; everyone was in place and ready, guns drawn. He looked at his watch and pushed the doorbell button. They could faintly hear the sound of the bell, then footsteps from the apartment and into the entry hall. When the door opened, Lund glimpsed a German marine guard, his face turning in a flicker from sleepy unconcern to acute surprise, then to horror, as the team behind Lund in accordance with his instructions fairly lifted him, like a human wave flushing him over the doorstep, bowling over the startled marine and pouring into the office beyond. Lund stopped in the main room from which four doors led to other parts of the apartment, one man rushing through each door to cover the entire layout instantly, leaving no time for any occupant to think twice.

Searching the place took but seconds, and they all gathered in the main room, the working center. There were only four Germans in all, two of whom like the guard turned pale and speechless with fright, thinking their hour of doom had struck. Only one man was unimpressed and put up a defiant scuffle, but he was quickly subdued, and the Germans were hustled into a side room and locked up. The center room was lined with file cabinets, and the team rushed to grab file drawers and dump their contents in the middle of the floor.

Lund checked his watch: two minutes had expired from ringing the door bell. While the paper pile grew to impressive size, he waited another thirty seconds before calling out.

"That's it!"

He lit the fire starter and planted it in the middle of the paper pile, while the six departed, this time without worrying about making noise. He lingered a few seconds to observe the fire starter, which was rapidly creating a vigorous blaze. From the street came the distant sound of a police car with its horn wailing. Evidently a tenant had been alarmed by the commotion and had called the police.

Lund descended quickly, and while the police deployed in the street, he departed through the end of the portal that led to a small garden, the getaway route he had reconnoitered and planned on.

x

Marek had walked behind the farmer for almost two hours, following a dwindling trail that from time to time seemed to be petering out altogether. The vegetation was getting denser, with undergrowth of blackberry, hazel, wild roses, snowberry, and several species he didn't know. The trees had also gotten larger, with deciduous larch, beech and alder dominating the evergreens. When Geremek, Alicia's husband, returned to the farmstead, he had quizzed Marek in detail before agreeing to guide him to the partisans. Knowing the anti-Semitism endemic among farmers and peasants, Marek had stuck to his story, keeping mum about his ghetto origin. In the end, Geremek had agreed to put him in contact with the partisans, a sizeable group–Geremek guessed about 150–that harassed German transports on the main road between Warsaw and Gdansk.

As they vaulted the trunk of an alder windfall, they found themselves suddenly boxed in between two young men in tattered Polish uniforms, partly camouflaged and both holding Schmeisser machine pistols. The sentinels knew Geremek and sent him back after explanation of Marek's identity. One of the partisans turned to Marek.

"I'm staying here, while Kristoff takes you to Captain Buchacz. He will decide what to do with you." He spat reflectively. "He'll probably decide to shoot you."

Kristoff motioned Marek to continue on the trail, falling in behind him with the Schmeisser ready. They walked in silence for a while, Marek estimated they covered almost two miles, until his guide ordered a halt by a tall beech tree. The partisan went off to the right of the trail and suddenly vanished into a hole masked by brush. Moments later he reappeared and motioned Marek to come. The hole led into a long dugout where two dozen men were resting or occupied mending clothes and cleaning weapons. They were all wearing at least remnants of uniforms, and Marek recognized them as members of *Armie Krajowa*, the Polish Home Army that had come into being as an Underground force after the German invasion.

A man wearing a captain's insignia sat on a box behind a desk improvised from two planks. Captain Buchacz' bearing and easy authority marked him as a career officer despite the ragged uniform and primitive surroundings. When the war broke out his company had stubbornly fought General List's spearhead, only to be taken prisoner as the German pincer snapped shut on Krakow in the fall of 1939. When the treatment of the POWs demonstrated that civilized rules of war would not be observed, he managed to escape with a few of his men; they had established themselves as roving guerrillas, and had in time become organized as the AK.

For a thousand years, Polish land had been coveted by German and Russian kings and dictators, of whom Hitler and Stalin were but the latest. Like hungry wolves they tore Poland asunder in a secret agreement that became a prelude to the Second World War. The Poles stoically organized themselves for this, the latest fight imposed on them. From remnants of their forces they created the fourth-largest of the Allied armies, and they were to fight Hitler longer than anybody else. Smaller army remnants took up the fight in the Underground and as guerrillas.

Marek was partly and dimly aware of this, as he stood before the primitive desk. Captain Buchacz told Kristoff to get back to his post; then turned to the newcomer.

"So what's your story?"

Marek thought quickly and decided the truth would hold up better than anything else.

28

"I come from the Warsaw Ghetto. The SS has encircled the last remnants of ZOB; I was tasked with taking the written record of the uprising to England."

Buchacz' eyebrows came together in a frown.

"That's not the story you've told before."

"The peasants don't like us Jews. I couldn't take a chance on being turned over to the Germans".

Buchacz pondered the answer.

"Show me the written report you're carrying."

Marek dug the parcel out of his coat lining; Buchacz peeled the oil cloth off and studied it for several minutes before returning his glance to Marek.

"Tell me about the uprising, starting at the beginning."

Marek took a deep breath and related a synopsis of his own experiences. It began with the selections for deportation to Treblinka, the rumors filtering back of mass murder of men, women and children at the killing center, followed by the formation of the ZOB fighting organization under Mordechaj's leadership, the fifty pistols and grenades from the Underground Army to augment their small store of home-made weapons, their devising methods of fighting armored cars, trials and deadly errors.... Buchacz listened in silence, and as the story unfolded, those of the group who were awake rested tools and sewing needles and cleaning rags and silently crowded around. They had enough experience fighting uneven battles to fill in what Marek left out for brevity's sake.

When Marek finished, Buchacz cleared his throat.

"We have been in touch with a group of Jewish partisans west of here, in the direction of Konin. They may know how to help you get to England. I'll have two of my people take you to their camp; it's about a day's walk from here. For now, we'll give you some food and a night's sleep. Jerzy will take care of you."

He pointed at a young soldier in the small crowd of listeners.

x

At the office of Special Operations Executive in Baker Street Brigadier Ansley McKinnon checked the schedule on his desk. Just a few items left, but he believed in clearing his desk completely before departing. He stretched, wishing he could take a short jog, or at least a good walk. This excessively sedentary life definitely did not agree with him. At sixty-two McKinnon was still in good physical condition, of medium height with graying hair and a neatly trimmed mustache. He sometimes walked with a slight limp, when a piece of shrapnel in his left foot acted up, a memento of his service in Flanders in the Great War, now a quarter century in the past. The pain was weather dependent: early winter could bring it on overnight. He was not a military man but a professor of Indo-European languages until Hugh Dalton, the Minister of Economic Warfare, had chosen him two years ago for the SOE. Surprisingly, McKinnon had shown a supreme aptitude for the work. Every hour, sometimes every minute, brought its problem, and his resourcefulness never failed. He had, too, that intuition which is independent of experience or skill, and is at the root of genius. The military rank was a bureaucratic stratagem to give him some clout in military circles.

It was almost three hours later when McKinnon picked up his hat and umbrella and walked downstairs to the street level. The night crew was busy perusing a pile of signals brought by messenger from Bletchley, probably more of the German radio traffic about the fighting in the Warsaw Ghetto. They were still intercepting that.

A very select team of British code breakers from the Government's Code and Cipher School was holed up in an old estate at Bletchley Park in Buckinghamshire. They had succeeded, with the help of Polish Intelligence, in cracking the backbone of German military and intelligence communications, the Enigma cipher. They were able to read German military and other radio communication, and SOE was one of many beneficiaries from this eavesdropping.

The intercepted signals had enabled McKinnon to study the German tactical direction of the war effort, and he had noticed a gruesome quirk in the overall pattern of Hitler's orders: that the Jews be made to suffer especially when Wehrmacht reverses occurred at the Front. The defeat at Stalingrad last January had received too much publicity to be hushed up, and immediately after Field Marshal von Paulus surrendered the pitiful remnants of the German 6th Army, Hitler furiously issued orders that the Warsaw Ghetto be destroyed.

McKinnon could quite well visualize the suffering of the nearly defenseless civilians at the hands of the SS, which used flamethrowers, armor and gas. It seemed incredible that the poor buggers could still be holding out. He shook his head and shuddered, as he walked out into the gathering dusk.

X

It was mid-afternoon when the forest trail the two AK soldiers and Marek were following intersected yet another country road. The rain in which they had been walking for more than six hours had finally stopped, but they were soaked to the skin. They had used small country roads and wagon tracks nearly empty of traffic, except for an occasional peasant with a farm tool over his shoulder, and the rain had kept most of those home. Much of the way they used hunters' trails that crisscrossed the forest in irregular patterns, and all seemed known to Tadeusz, one of the two soldiers who had been assigned to take Marek to the Jewish partisan camp. He wore a corporal's stripes, had come from Konin, and knew this area intimately from hunting here before the war.

"We will take this road for about two miles, then we branch off onto a trail the rest of the way," Tadeusz said. "Now, you go ahead of us, Marek, we'll follow out of sight. There could be German checkpoints, and if we run into one, you just delay with chit-chat, and we'll handle them." He patted the Schmeisser that hung in a strap from his shoulder. "And try not to be in our line of fire."

Marek nodded agreement, wishing he had a gun himself, and started walking. The road cut through the trees, winding around hillocks and large rocks. As he came around a sharp bend, an order rang out.

"*Halt!*"

He stopped and turned toward the voice. Two German soldiers emerged from a makeshift shelter, one of them walking out toward him, holding out his hand.

"Your ID," he said in halting Polish.

Marek started fumbling in his pockets, temporizing an excuse about having left it at home. When the German was halfway toward him, Tadeusz' Schmeisser coughed a short burst behind him, and the impact of the bullets flung the German to the ground. Marek spun away from the shelter and ran. To keep a clear line of fire between Tadeusz and the shelter, he went to the opposite side of the road, and as he dove into the ditch, a rifle shot from the other German caught him in midair. Another burst from Tadeusz tore through the side of the shelter, silencing the rifle shooter, and the two AK soldiers arrived at a run where Marek was lying. Tadeusz bent over him, while his companion went to check out the shelter. Marek was holding his left thigh, trying to staunch the blood oozing from a wound above the knee. Tadeusz called over his shoulder.

"Make a drag litter while I put a tourniquet on him."

The AK soldiers worked feverishly a few minutes, then bundled Marek and the German weapons onto the litter and started with their burden. With one end of the litter dragging on the ground, the two AK soldiers lifted and pulled the other end. They shortly branched off onto the last trail segment, where they lightened their load by stashing the German weapons under a bush, to be picked up on their return trip.

For the next three hours, they struggled over the uneven ground, sweating under the strain while almost keeping up their previous rate of progress. Marek was gritting his teeth, every bump sending a lance of pain through his leg. A wan light was filtering through the trees, and the setting sun was reddening the clouds overhead, when the trail they were using bent around an oak which had been disfigured by lightning long ago, the remains of the trunk resembling an inverted V. The AK soldiers stopped, sat down, and above each of them a cloud of steam rose in the evening air from their wet garments. Tadeusz cupped his hands over his mouth and hooted three times, producing a good imitation of an owl. One minute later, he repeated the signal. Shortly, a man carrying a rifle at the ready emerged from the underbrush and looked them over from a distance of some twenty feet. Tadeusz greeted him impatiently.

"Shah-lohm, Ari, put that gun away before you hurt someone. We are bringing you a Jew." He pointed to Marek.

Ari's rifle and attention swung in Marek's direction.

"Und ver zeit ir?" ("And who are you?")

Marek smiled despite the surging pain. The Galician Yiddish flowed over him like sweet music.

"Marek Blum, from the Warsaw Ghetto."

Ari stuck two fingers between his lips and produced a piercing whistle. Behind them a second sentinel with a rifle stepped out of the bushes onto the trail. Ari waved him closer.

"Aron, come and see someone from the ZOB, a killer of SS."

Without changing his grip on the rifle Aron approached gingerly and looked at Marek with unconcealed curiosity.

"Good, we can always use somebody with combat experience, but he doesn't look to be worth much just now."

Ari laughed. "Maybe the doctor can patch him up. Run up to the camp and get four men down here to carry him."

When Aron departed, Ari shared the sentinels' food with the two AK soldiers. They ate quickly and left while there was still some light in the sky. Marek thanked them, but Tadeusz waved his hand in deprecation.

"If I had been a little faster, we could have gotten you here without any bullet holes in you."

After the AK soldiers had left, Ari became more talkative and willingly told about the Jewish group and its brief history. He explained that they were primarily refugees from the last massacre in Poznan, a rather pitiful group of some seventy families, mostly old people and children. They had found temporary shelter in an abandoned hunters' camp, where they repaired roofs, shuttered windows and made the tumbledown shacks livable again. Over the winter, frost, malnutrition and disease had eliminated the weakest, and the survivors had been joined by a roving band of young Jewish partisans harassing German communications and supply lines. Like Marek, Ari was of Ghetto background but had quickly adapted to the life of a forest guerrilla, and he described eloquently the potential of a daring and resourceful group who possesses intimate knowledge of every track and path, who operates in small bands, travel light, and moves rapidly. Marek had gone through similar adaptation, when his ghetto existence called for tooth and nail fighting in an urban setting, and he immediately saw the immense advantage rural guerrillas have over an enemy who clings to beaten tracks, and moves slowly in large bodies.

The two groups--the families and the roving band--had melded, finding their respective skills and abilities in some ways complementary, with the younger contingent more adept at handling security and foraging for supplies, whereas the older members possessed skills of equally practical value, notably medical and administrative. The elected leader was Samuel Panowicz, a recognized eye surgeon in Poznan before the war.

Ari's chitchat was interrupted by the arrival of bearers from the camp, and with four to handle the litter, the transport became relatively comfortable. The ground sloped down, where they approached a rushing stream; they struck off on a tangent and followed its course to the north where, suddenly, they came upon the settlement and were challenged by another sentinel, this one a young girl. Marek judged her to be no more than fifteen. She greeted them cheerfully, viewing Marek with open curiosity, as one of the bearers addressed her.

"Esther, where do we find the Doctor?"

"I think he is at the Perlzweig's cabin, seeing Rachel."

They found Dr. Panowicz attending Rachel, a young girl with a broken leg. He listened briefly to Marek's report and examined the wound.

"The bullet passed through without striking the bone or the main artery. Very fortunate. It will be a while, though, before you can walk on that leg." He turned to the bearers, "Take him to my cabin."

Chapter 3

Elizabeth Van Paassen parked the ambulance under the shed roof along the side of Westminster Hospital and turned off the engine. She rested her forehead on the steering wheel for a moment, trying to summon enough energy to walk to the apartment she shared with her mother. God, she was tired, and by official reckoning air attacks were at a two-year low. She could hardly imagine what it must have been like during the peak of the Blitz. After the first week she had hurried to a hair salon where they reduced her shoulder length mane to a pageboy. She had gone back the next week to have them trim it still further. No time for primping. She let her thoughts drift back to the coffee plantation in the Ngong Hills outside Nairobi, the farm where she had grown up. She realized now what a virtual paradise it had been. The windows of her room faced north toward Mt. Kenya, but in all directions the views were expansive, particularly toward the Rift Valley.

Once in London they had both volunteered, her mother taking up her old profession as a nurse, while Liz had applied to serve with SOE, the Special Operations Executive, a new hush-hush outfit that was seeking recruits with foreign language abilities. While waiting to hear from them, she was working 12-hour shifts as a lorry and ambulance driver.

A powerful knocking roused her with a start, and a hospital guard opened the door and shone a torch in her face.

"Sorry, Miss, didn't mean to startle you."

"That's quite alright, I didn't mean to doze off."

She picked up her bag, locked the vehicle, and took the keys to the hospital office. Sarah, the night clerk, read her condition in a glance.

"Look, Liz, you'd better have a cuppa before leaving. And I've also got a letter for you here somewhere."

Sarah poured a mug of tea, strong enough to etch a silver spoon, and handed it to her.

"Thanks, yes, I guess I do need it to keep me awake until I get home. What was that about a letter?"

Sarah rummaged in the mail basket on her desk and handed her an envelope, plain government stationery. She tore it open and read its three-line content. In reply to her application, SOE summoned her to an interview two days hence at its headquarters in Baker street. Good. Whatever SOE might want from her, it had to be better than ambulance driving.

x

It was 5 p.m., the time indicated in her summons from SOE, when Major Jack Hawes, McKinnon's aide, led Liz into his office. Hawes was a soft spoken, professional soldier, a graduate of Sandhurst with an encyclopedic memory, whose field service had ended on the beach at Dunkirk, when a Stuka bomb had removed his left arm at the elbow. After introductions, they all sat down; McKinnon spoke first.

"Miss van Paassen, you have applied to serve with the Special Operations Executive. Are you aware of the kind of work SOE does?"

"I believe it is in the realm of intelligence." Liz sounded vague, for she had actually applied to SOE on the spur of an impulse rather than based on much in the way of concrete information.

"Well, let me give you some idea." McKinnon paused briefly to light his pipe before continuing. "We have been set up under the aegis of the Minister for Economic Warfare to stir up trouble in the countries the Nazis have occupied. That involves many functions such as training local people as guerrillas or to do sabotage, and we supply them with weapons and explosives and other paraphernalia to give Hitler's war machine as much trouble as possible. Needless to say, agents we send to do this sort of thing endeavor to melt into the local Underground; they live on a razor's edge, in constant danger of their lives."

He went on to elaborate on the training and typical uses of SOE agents dispatched abroad; while he spoke, he kept his eyes on her face, trying to read her reactions. Liz did not reply but met his glance calmly.

"Now, we do not employ many women in our service, but in certain special situations, women can be very effective. Does it sound like the kind of service you would be interested in?"

"Yes. Tell me where I might fit in." Her voice was steady.

McKinnon smiled. "Let me ask you a few questions first. Do you speak Dutch without an accent?"

"My father said so."

"Tell me about your last visit to Holland."

"We spent a month there, visiting family, four years ago. Most of the time we stayed in Utrecht, where I have an aunt, and in Amsterdam; we also spent a week at a beach resort on the island of Texel."

McKinnon listened attentively, as Liz described her vacation activities in Holland, and Hawes jotted notes on a pad strapped to his artificial left arm. Both men realized she had the qualifications needed to work in Holland. How would she handle herself in the emergency situations that all too often got in the way of the best laid plans? That was always the key question, and in that regard McKinnon could only rely on his judgment and intuition.

"Thank you Miss van Paassen." He rose from his chair and shook her hand. "Would you kindly wait in the outer office, and Major Hawes will see you there shortly. He will explain what to do next."

When the door closed behind her, McKinnon sat down, swiveled his chair toward Hawes, who wore a thoughtful expression.

"What do you think, Jack?"

"Well, sir, I am not fond of sending pretty girls to do a man's job, but I must admit she sounds good."

"I also recoil at the idea of using females," McKinnon averred, "but she seems heaven sent at this particular moment, when we don't have enough locals to rely on just now, after the affair last month."

He was referring to an SD raid that had killed four and arrested a number of local saboteurs. An informer had provided the information to enable the Germans to intercept a parachute drop, capturing most of the group receiving the stuff from across the Channel. An SOE agent had been among the dead, as he had used his L-tablet, a cyanide poison provided as the ultimate avoidance of capture.

"Yes, sir, I quite agree. I have told the screening office to notify us of any Dutch speakers they may find. Should I send her to Arisaig?"

He was referring to SOE's training facility, situated in the Scottish lake country, where SOE personnel learned the basics of dirty tricks, mostly how to handle explosives, and how to kill quietly and efficiently, the latter having more variants than most people realized.

"Yes, but send her first to Mac at the firing range. Make sure she can learn to handle guns, before you go any further."

"Very well, sir, I will take her there tomorrow morning. Is there anything else, sir?"

McKinnon shook his head.

"No, Jack, and I won't need you any more today."

McKinnon watched Hawes leave. What a stroke of luck to have a super efficient aide to rely on. He put on his glasses, turned to a stack of papers that still needed his attention, and settled down to work.

x

In addition to an elaborate training facility at Arisaig House in Invernesshire, SOE had set up a simple firing range, improvised in a basement below a bombed-out warehouse near the Thames. It was sufficiently equipped to familiarize SOE operatives with just about any of the multitude of weapons they could expect to encounter in German-occupied Europe. Hawes left Liz with the armorer, a dour Scot by the name of McMillan. There was no other instruction going on at the moment, so that she had McMillan's full attention. He started by going over the different targets propped up against sand bags, mostly life-size cutouts of human silhouettes, some in German uniforms with the characteristic steel helmet.

McMillan turned out to have definite opinions about the art of marksmanship.

"Major Hawes wants us to concentrate on hand guns. You're not likely to have to use rifles, and I understand you have experience with shotguns. If you come up against one of these buggers," he jerked his head in the direction of the German cutouts, "don't try for any fancy pistol shooting, like going for a leg to cripple the bastard—begging your pardon, Miss—always aim for the center of the body, it gives you the best chance for a hit. We practice using the full length of the range, twenty-five yards, but out there," he jerked a thumb over his shoulder to indicate the world at large, "don't try for that with a handgun. Even with a rifle, close is better than far. And with a hand gun, always get in close."

"How close?" Liz wanted to know.

"Just as close as you can get. Poking the muzzle into his back or stomach when pulling the trigger is a very good idea, if the circumstances permit."

McMillan led her into an adjoining room that reeked with the smell of gun oil. Several counters stood side by side, carrying guns of every size and description. He went to a row of hand guns laid out on a counter.

"The Germans have some very good hand guns. This here is a Walther PPK 7.65mm, handy little weapon, magazine in the grip. It's a favorite of German police and security services. This is the Walther P-38, larger and heavier, as you can see, with two hammer positions, the safety works like this." He showed her. "It is extremely reliable, preferred by Wehrmacht officers. Next to it is the Luger, also a very popular gun. We will do some shooting with these three, starting with the PPK."

They returned to the range, where he let her load the pistol and showed her a two-handed stance.

"Always use both hands, if there is time and room."

He fitted her with a headset of hearing protectors, pointed to a cutout of a charging German.

"Shoot the whole magazine."

Liz fired eight shots in rapid succession, as McMillan watched her carefully. He liked what he saw. This girl was all business, no hesitation.

"Let us look up close."

They walked to the target and examined the result. The cutout has three holes in the body, one in the left arm, one in the knee.

"I would guess these to be your first five shots; after those your aim began to wander. Now reload and do it again with half a breath between the shots. Take the target on the left."

Liz did as he told her, squeezing the shots off in a slower, steady cadence. McMillan looked on approvingly. Inspection of the target showed five body hits, two in the left leg, and one in the left shoulder. They repeated the exercise with the P-38 and then with the Luger, after which McMillan switched her to revolvers.

"You are not likely to encounter any of these on the Continent, but we'll do a bit of practice, just in case. Now, here is an Enfield Albion, and this is a Smith & Wesson."

He brought out the two revolvers and slowly demonstrated their features.

"The trigger action is different, as you can see, and no two guns are identical in that regard. They take some getting used to after handling the semi-automatic pistols. Let's see how you get along with them."

The drill continued until McMillan called a halt.

"You are doing very well, Miss. Tomorrow we'll get to automatic weapons. With one of those you can take out a whole squad of Gestapo, if need be."

Liz said goodbye, and as the door closed behind her, he shook his head with a worried look, mumbling to himself.

"And I'll bet those fuckers will be after you the moment you land."

x

The ferry across the Belt Sea between Funen and Zealand was nosing into Korsør harbor with the midday sun glittering on the wavelets and on the vessel's gleaming white superstructure. Lund stood at the railing enjoying the sun and the breeze and the elegant flight of more than a score of sea gulls, circling the ferry while screeching for a handout. He was returning from another trip to Ribe, training the six whom he now thought of as his Ribe Group. They had become quite proficient in the use of explosives and firearms, and Lund felt confident that they would hold up well in a scrape with the Germans. Not that any militia or other volunteer force could ever be expected to hold its own against regular troops, but in a brush with the SD or Gestapo, that would be a different matter. He had designated Valdemar Nielsen, a stone mason, as leader of the group, instructing them to start arming themselves by taking weapons from the German soldiers billeted in the town. So far, they had acquired two rifles and two Schmeisser submachine guns, together with enough ammunition to start a minor war of their own. Lund smiled, thinking of the enthusiasm they had displayed when they showed him their well-hidden depot.

This time his weapons had been packed in two suitcases and from the Copenhagen Central station checked directly to Ribe. The Germans had recently taken steps to guard against train travelers transporting such contraband, so that passengers now had to open hand baggage for inspection at the Belt Sea ferry. But the Krauts ignored—or had forgotten about–baggage not carried by the traveler but checked through to the destination. Sometimes you wondered whether they had any sense at all.

Two hawsers around power-driven capstans pulled the ferry snug against the pier, and two streams of passengers sluiced across two gangways. Those going to Copenhagen were queuing to have their baggage searched by four Wehrmacht soldiers at an improvised counter before boarding the train. The soldiers were slow and somewhat clumsy; the thrill of riffling through the belongings of strangers had long since yielded to boredom. Emerging from the ferry, a baggage handler was pulling a four-wheel cart loaded with bags and parcels past the line of queuing people toward the waiting train. This particular load was baggage checked through to Copenhagen Central, and Lund noticed one of his own suitcases perched precariously at the back of the cart.

The handler was keeping an eye on the baggage pile, as he maneuvered the rattling cart across the uneven concrete between ferry slip and train platform. He had reached the head of the queue where the four soldiers were working, when a bump tipped two suitcases off the back of the cart. Lund's was one of them, a cheap wartime product of imitation leather, actually cardboard, and not intended for heavy use. It hit the concrete with a crash and ruptured at one end, spilling a Walther automatic pistol onto the pavement with a metallic clunk. The handler, half a dozen of the nearest passengers, and the four Germans all saw the offending object simultaneously. With eyes fixed on the Walther, each observer stood momentarily frozen, like a bird staring at a snake. Then one of the soldiers started on a dead run toward the guard office. Some twenty feet back, Lund inconspicuously stepped out of the line and blended into the stream of people walking through the station and into town. He found a window seat in a nearby cafe, ordered lunch and pondered his situation.

This was damn bad luck, no question about that. Already when the German attack came on 9 April 1940, he had been one of a handful of men—a very small handful, actually—who had without hesitation decided to resist the Nazis. For two years he had methodically trained himself with that in mind, living the normal life of a student finishing his engineering studies while practicing sabotage as chance might allow. He had volunteered for military service in the token force the Germans permitted the Danes to keep under arms, going through instruction at the Kornetskole, a preliminary training facility for field officers, just to learn combat tactics and gain proficiency in the use of infantry weapons. It had paid off; he had earned the small silver shield identifying a regimental Suomi marksman. And then there had been a brief stint of real combat, when he volunteered to help the Finns repel the Russians. That was while Stalin and Hitler were friendly allies, the short period that ended abruptly in June 1941 with Operation *Barbarossa*, when three million German soldiers in a mighty wave flung themselves eastward, driving toward Moscow.

Lund had long felt a gnawing frustration at being relegated by circumstance to piddling sabotage when world history was being writ large, almost within his reach. In a recurring dream he saw himself in a Spitfire, making a real contribution. Through the window he could see a German platoon heading on the double for the railroad station. Well, they could have his handguns, each taken from a German soldier. More important was the fact his cover was now blown for good. In Ribe his real identity was known by too many people, so that his suitcases of necessity bore his real name and address, not his undercover alias. Perhaps this was the finger of fate, pointing him in a new direction. Yes, it had to be. It was time to get himself to England.

Chapter 4

Hansen fished a rag out of the box and wiped his hands. One thing about work on aircraft engines: it was cleaner than any other mechanical repairs. Not that there was much aircraft work to be done these days at the small Kramme & Zeuten factory in Hellerup, a suburb in the northern outskirts of Copenhagen. The firm was bravely trying to keep a skeleton crew busy on developing an ambulance version of the KZ-3. The small firm's flat refusal to work for the Germans had necessitated branching into other fields such as automotive parts, gas generators, and domestic charcoal cookers. It was unexciting work. Still, he had been lucky to get this job after his return from Amsterdam.

The thought had struck him that there had to be work galore for an aircraft mechanic in England, because the Brits were surely stretching all resources to keep the Royal Air Force flying. But so far he hadn't thought of a way to get himself to England and put his skills to use in the Allied cause.

Hansen's three years in Holland had been the most agreeable period of his life, in part because he had met Sofie there. It had been love at first sight before the war broke out and put all private plans on indefinite hold. He had left Sophie with a firm promise to return, though with a vague time line. So, here he was, still single at thirty.

His daydreaming was interrupted as Mr. Zeuten appeared at the door to his office and motioned for him to come. Inside, the old engineer just pointed to a chair. Zeuten had designed the firm's aircraft, of which the two-seater KZ-3 had met with modest pre-war success. He studied Hansen for a moment before he spoke.

"You remember the KZ-3 that belongs to Mr. Feldsted at the Steensholt?"

Hansen nodded. The plane had been delivered just before the war and was sitting in a barn in southern Jutland, not far from his home town of Haderslev. After the Germans arrived, he had been sent there to put it into storage condition.

"Well, it is being confiscated by the occupation authorities, and they want to make it flyable again and to add a long-range tank. Do you think you can handle that?"

Hansen's heart leaped at the thought of such an assignment at company expense. So, the company would make an exception and undertake this job for the Krauts. That was slightly puzzling.

"You understand," Zeuten continued, "that you should use some judgment in preparing this fine little plane to be turned over to the Germans."

Automatically, Hansen nodded again, as he tried to divine what the older man meant. Zeuten handed him an envelope.

"Here is some travel money, two hundred kroner. We'll ship the long-range tank tomorrow. Take with you what tools you think you'll need."

Two hours later, he was on the train to Esbjerg. It was a beautiful summer afternoon, the fields of Zealand burgeoning with crops almost ready to harvest. Watching the landscape flow by, he carefully recalled every word Zeuten had spoken. He should use "some judgment" in preparing that fine little plane to be turned over to the Nazis. "Some judgment?" Zeuten must have meant that he should sabotage the plane, render it somehow useless to the Nazis. That would not be difficult, of course. Perhaps a bit of carborundum in a bearing, or a partial blockage of the fuel supply. Should he devise something that was likely to kill the pilot in the same process? He let his mind play with three or four different ideas but decided to wait and see what condition the plane was in. There was plenty of time to come up with a foolproof scheme.

X

After returning to Copenhagen Central by train–a slow milk run that arrived late in the afternoon–Lund went to the counter for stored items and retrieved a small parcel he had deposited there for emergency purposes. In the station's pay-toilet he unpacked the contents, a .32 Colt automatic in a slim suede holster, which he slid inside his belt. Then he walked to a bar in Vesterbro, the downtown section west of the station. The establishment was two steps down from the street level, dimly lit, and smelled of beer and stale tobacco smoke. He took a chair in a corner near the door, where he could overlook the room with his back to the wall.

A young woman waited on the few customers, and she eyed him approvingly while asking for his order. Lund smiled at her, "Give me a Carlsberg Hof. Is Anna around?" She shook her head. "No, but I expect her back any minute." He looked at her, smiling again, "When she comes, please let her know that Aage is waiting for her." Now that he was back in Copenhagen, using his cover name came naturally. She brought the beer, and Lund relaxed in his chair, reviewing his situation and his plans.

He could not return to his apartment. There had already been enough time for the SD to get there and post somebody to ambush him. He had now decided to leave Denmark, get himself across the waterway known as The Sound between Denmark and Sweden, and go directly to the British embassy in Stockholm, where he would volunteer for military service, hoping to get into the RAF. Sweden was neutral, and while the Danish coast along The Sound was under total blackout at night, the Swedish side glittered with lights from streets and buildings, a peacetime beacon in a Europe languishing in the gloom of war. It was not unusual for people who ran afoul of the Gestapo to take the "Swedish solution" by means of passage in a fishing boat or other craft across the few miles of water. At Copenhagen, The Sound was some 28 miles wide between the two countries, but the north end narrowed to a mere two miles at Elsinore. A few Underground transport lines had come into being under pressure of necessity, as the SD was trying to throttle the embryonic Resistance. Some people broke down under the strain of being hunted, while a few thrived on the excitement. He was glad to be of the latter variety, but he was also cautious, not placing himself in the hands of others.

The Underground, a clandestine network that sprouted spontaneously, unpredictably, irrepressibly, had come into being in many places in occupied Europe under the pressure of the new concept: *total war*, the actual physical involvement of civilian populations in hostilities that hitherto had been the exclusive province of the military. There was no prescription for Undergrounds. They varied from country to country and from one location to another, thriving, being rooted out, sprouting anew. Wherever the cold hand of unwanted, arbitrary, illegitimate power imposed restraints, the drive for freedom and self-determination that is innate in the human psyche would assert itself, somehow. Even the Danes—civil, law-abiding, averse to violence, respectful of the individual—even they could not for long abide Nazi overlordship without resisting. People found ways to express their resentment. Printing and distributing Underground news sheets came first, for censorship is galling, an insult to human intelligence. Tentative forms of sabotage came next, and the organizing of channels of escape to Sweden then began in a natural response to a pressing need. How information circulated through the Underground was something nobody could describe or quite fathom, but word about who, where and when mysteriously filtered to those in need of information.

From the start, however, a few individuals had taken a harder line, vaulting the timid beginnings and right away aiming for the German jugular. Lund was one of those.

He had almost finished his beer when a middle-aged woman entered from a door behind the counter and motioned him into the back room. Anna was of unassuming appearance. Her husband had been a fisherman in the Baltic and had been among the first to set up an escape route to Sweden. He had been killed in a firefight with a German patrol boat in one of a few incidents that marred the early trials, before the organizers realized that only stealth could succeed, not firepower. The result had been greater caution and secrecy, but no cessation of efforts. On the contrary, Anna had picked up the threads and carried on her husband's work with a vengeance. She looked at him inquiringly.

"Aage, what brings you here? More passengers to Sweden?"

He shook his head,

"Not exactly, Anna, today just myself."

She looked surprised.

"After all this time? You must have stumbled into bad luck."

He nodded.

"You could say that. What do you have functioning at the moment?"

She paused, lit a cigarette and slowly brought out a bottle of Cherry Heering and two liqueur glasses from a cupboard. Then she sat down and poured two drinks, still thinking. She hefted her glass.

"*Skål!* You are my only customer who prefers this."

They sipped the sweet liqueur in silence. At length she spoke again.

"There are a couple of boys running an old, souped-up Chris- Craft out of Nivaa. They are fairly new on the scene, but they have succeeded in turning their boat into the fastest thing afloat on The Sound right now, and therefore the safest. I will phone them and tell them to meet you at the S-train tonight at 8:10. Then I'll give you recognition instructions."

X

McKinnon was on the phone when WAAF Lieutenant Ann Curtis knocked on his office door, entered without waiting, and

49

placed a mug of tea on the desk before him. It was steaming hot, very dark brown, no sugar, just a drop of milk; it was a Bangalore variety, pungent but not perfumed with flower petals. This morning ritual helped McKinnon to start the day at eight o'clock in an agreeable manner, to maintain his unruffled exterior despite the pressure of work, and to reinforce his unwavering courtesy toward his staff in the face of the coming day's intractable problems. The result was a harmonious atmosphere in which SOE's work flowed expeditiously. Organizations were like individual people in having distinct personalities, and he was aware that SOE certainly did, but he wasn't sure just what it was. That was the trouble with having shaped it from the beginning and being part of it himself.

The telephone call from the Minister's office came just as McKinnon was reaching for his tea. Ann Curtis turned to leave, but he motioned her to wait.

"Yes, Minister...an American colonel?...of course...do we know the purpose or problem...I see...of course, Minister."

He put down the telephone with a sigh.

"Ann, would you ask Major Hawes to come in."

What on earth could the Americans be wanting? As if he didn't have enough to worry about, trying to find suitable recruits to fill SOE's unorthodox training program with the Minister breathing down his neck. SOE had been created only three years ago, and they were still grappling with plans and procedures no other organization had ever touched before. Thank God they operated under the aegis of Minister Hugh Dalton, and not under some agency staffed by career officers looking for ways to impress the Prime Minister. Dalton had built SOE, not from scratch but sensibly from pieces of the intelligence establishment. The main one was Section D of MI6, known in the profession as the dirty tricks department, of which McKinnon had been placed in charge. Major Hawes entered quietly and closed the door behind him.

"Jack, an American Colonel by the name of John Howard is on his way here to see us about some project on which they need our help. It is rated top priority, with Howard reporting directly to General Marshall in Washington, so the Minister wants us to give him all the assistance we can. He is being routed to Biggin, ETA tonight at 23:40. Would you meet him, book him in at the American compound, and bring him here tomorrow at 08:00."

While McKinnon was speaking, Hawes had been taking notes on the pad strapped to his artificial arm.

"Yes, sir. Do we know anything about his mission?"

McKinnon shook his head.

"Only that it is urgent and in our bailiwick. It could be anything."

"Yes, sir. I'll have him here at eight in the morning."

X

It was still daylight, when Lund got off the S-Train and walked into the Nivaa station building with *Ekstrabladet*, a Copenhagen evening newspaper, in his left hand. He was carrying a sea bag with a parka and the rest of his personal armory, retrieved from another locker, a 12.7-mm Belgian Browning, and two hand grenades, Danish army issue.

A young man in work clothes, Lund guessed him to be still a teenager, stepped away from the departure schedule posted on the wall, took off his glasses, and left the station, walking toward the harbor. Lund gave him a hundred-foot head start, then followed behind. The Nivaa harbor had been home port to a small fishing fleet before the war, but now there were only pleasure craft left, and not many of those. Sailing on The Sound had been severely restricted by the German occupation troops, as they attempted to clamp down on the illegal traffic to Sweden. Lund followed his guide into a storage shed, where another man stood at a window and checked whether anybody had been following behind Lund. At length satisfied, the two introduced themselves as Per and Ole (cover names), brothers, seventeen and nineteen years old. Ole, the elder of the two who had waited at the window, looked straight at Lund.

"How good a swimmer are you, just in case that should be necessary?"

Lund suppressed a smile.

"Competition level."

"Are you armed?"

"Yes."

Lund could sense the other recoiling.

"You must leave your weapons here, otherwise the Swedes will confiscate them, and we cannot fight a German patrol, anyway. Our only safety lies in speed."

"I realize that, but I cannot allow any patrol to take me alive."

The brothers exchanged glances.

"That puts all of us at maximum risk."

Lund thought for a moment. The brothers had a perfectly sound point. If the possibility of a firefight were to be contemplated, they should all be armed and trained for it, as he was. On the other hand, getting caught would for him mean execution; he would not consider being quietly picked up and taken to SD headquarters at Dagmarhus in Copenhagen.

"Alright, you should not be saddled with extra risk because of me. In case we should be stopped, I will quietly slip overboard and swim the rest of the way. And by the way, when I step ashore in Sweden, or start swimming, you can have these, of course." He nodded toward the contents of the sea bag.

They left him alone and went outside to discuss the matter. Lund respected their reservations; you did not last long in the Underground by being casual about planning. For all their youth, these two impressed him. A few minutes later they returned, and Ole gave him their decision.

"Okay, we'll take you, but be prepared for a long swim. Show us your hardware."

Lund extracted the Colt and demonstrated the on-off safety latch. Then he opened the sea bag and pulled out the

Browning. Per was visibly impressed. "I've never seen a pistol of that caliber."

Lund smiled. "There aren't many around, but the Wehrmacht has the motliest collection of any army in history and has scraped the bottom of the European supply of handguns."

"What else do you have?"

The brothers were as excited as school children, and Lund agreeably extracted the two hand grenades, which prompted another comment from Per.

"I know these, they're the Danish Army model, but I thought the Krauts had stolen them all."

"Nearly so, but I saved a few, for they are more powerful than the Wehrmacht model, although you can't throw them as far."

"With this armory we can damn near take on one of the new four-man patrol boats," Ole said. When he saw Lund nodding, he added quickly, "but of course, that won't be necessary."

Two hours later they were ready to leave for the Swedish costal hamlet of Råå. The brothers had put a labor of love into the old Chris-Craft, a 1931 Upswept Runabout, 24 feet overall. The original power plant, a Chrysler Royal 8-cylinder engine had been moved to starboard, and a Ford V-8 had been installed in the port side. It would never win any show prize, but the two young builders had contrived to boost the speed to something they were pleased to describe as "flying low."

The night was overcast with a slight breeze from the southwest, when they nosed out with both engines at low RPM, Per at the wheel and Ole monitoring the engines. A sea fog was settling over The Sound, almost immediately blotting out the Danish coast in the gray darkness astern. Nothing could be seen of the lights on the Swedish side. Ole leaned toward Lund and spoke quietly.

"There is no reason for us to burn more gas than we have to, and the engines can be heard for miles if we open up, so we prefer to amble along like this, making about ten knots. It'll get us where we want to go in just over an hour."

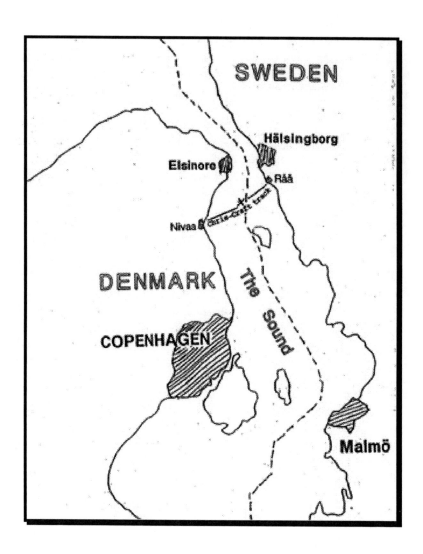

Lund nodded. As they motored along, the fog thickened, and after half an hour the horizon had moved close all around. Ole pointed ahead, whispering, "Channel marker," and Lund saw the buoy, an iron barrel with a super structure holding an unlit beacon, that in peacetime had been blinking a clear light in a slow sequence. He estimated the visibility to be less than two hundred feet. Abreast of the buoy, Ole turned off both engines and motioned the others to listen. They all strained to hear, and Ole stood up, cupped his hands behind his ears and slowly rotated a full turn in the center of the boat. Then he looked at the others.

"Do you hear an engine?" They both nodded.

"Where do you think it is?"

Lund shook his head and whispered, "Impossible to say. It seems to be in whatever direction I'm facing."

Ole tried another complete turn with his palms behind his ears to catch every bit of sound, in the end shaking his head and keeping his voice low.

"That's what I get too. It has to be a Kraut patrol boat, nobody else is out here. If they have heard us, they're probably as uncertain about direction as we are. I think our best chance is to open up and run for it."

Lund nodded. Per took the wheel, while Ole bent over the engines. Lund handed the Colt to Ole, unlimbered the two hand grenades attached to his belt, and readied the Browning. Per signaled Ole with a raised thumb, snapped a quick "Hang on" at Lund, as both engines caught instantly. Their quiet murmur rose to a roar in seconds, as they reached maximum power, and the boat surged ahead with a rooster tail fifty feet behind. Almost simultaneously a powerful searchlight on their port bow stabbed through the murk and bathed the fleeing craft like a deer caught in the headlight of an oncoming car. Per swerved to the right, as a machine gun opened up and raked the stern end of the Chris-Craft's left side, shredding the thin wood planking. The Ford coughed and died, the Chrysler sputtered, and they fell back from the step on the bow wave, making barely steerage way. A German loudspeaker was bellowing an unmistakable order.

"Halt, Motor abschliessen!" Stop, cut your engine!

Out of the side of his mouth Lund mumbled to Ole, "When we get close enough, I'll use the grenades. By then you'll have an easy two-handed shot with the Colt at the searchlight. Remember, they won't expect us to be armed and resist."

This was true, of course, but disciplined soldiers take nothing for granted. He wondered if Ole's hands would be steady enough. Well, this was the time to find out. The German skipper was maneuvering the patrol craft alongside, its higher coaming momentarily shading Lund, who had picked up a boathook to pretend cooperation by helping to pull the two craft together. In a swift motion he armed one of his grenades and flipped it into the German's cockpit.

"Down boys!"

They ducked instantly and just in time, for the Danish grenades had a shorter fuse than the German and British models, and his timing was perfect. The explosion ripped through both cockpit and engine compartment in the patrol boat, and stunned the searchlight operator and machine gunner on the foredeck. Ole rose to his knees in the cockpit with the Colt aimed, and calmly squeezed off three shots that broke the searchlight and killed the operator, casting the scene suddenly in absolute darkness.

Browning in hand, Lund swung himself onto the German's foredeck and glanced into the cockpit where two Germans lay dead. The machine gunner was scrambling toward his weapon and, slipping into his seat, desperately swung the 7.62-mm gun toward the boarder. Lund calmly aimed and shot the German in the heart. Then he called back over his shoulder.

"We got all four of them. Are you guys wounded?"

"I got a scratch on my left arm, but it's not bleeding much."

Per actually sounded upbeat about it.

"What's your report on the engines?"

Ole picked up a flashlight and inspected them.

The Ford caught several bullets, it sure won't run again tonight. The Chrysler has a damaged distributor, but maybe we can coax it to haul us the rest of the way, slowly."

X

The Steensholt estate dated from the 16th century, when the Lutheran Reformation swept Papal influence from Northern Europe. It had belonged to the Holstein-Ratlows, nobility with roots in the Viking Age, but the advent of democracy and high taxation had spelled the end of hereditary privilege and caused the breakup and sale of the old estate. Steensholt had been bought by Claus Feldsted, a successful merchant, whose ownership of the estate allowed him to indulge his two passions: bird hunting and flying. The latter was facilitated by the level land, with a well groomed beech forest on the eastern edge of the property as the only obstacle on the horizon. The landing strip itself was a grass field with some 1,800 feet of E-W distance, more than enough to accommodate private fliers. At the eastern end was the hangar, built in the style of the local barns. With the forest as backdrop, it blended into the landscape as perfectly as the owner had intended.

Hansen had been cordially received by Feldsted and his wife, a hospitable couple in their sixties, who had invited him to stay with them at the estate while working on the plane. Late in the forenoon he had almost completed his initial checkup, when Claus Feldsted walked into the hangar.

"How is my beautiful plane after two years of storage?"

Feldsted's voice revealed his feelings about turning his most precious possession over to the Germans, and when they had talked about it the previous evening, he made no secret of his desire to thwart the project.

"You know," he continued, "I don't want to lose my hangar, but couldn't an "accidental" fire occur, when you test the engine outside during a run-up? By the way, my wife says it's time for lunch, and we have some smoked herring, just received from Bornholm."

Hansen smiled.

"Let me think about how we might keep your plane from ending up in German hands. There may be other and better ways to solve the problem than by burning it."

He had in fact been thinking hard about a scheme that would deny the plane to the Germans, while solving his own desire to work for the Brits. The extra tank he was about to install would extend the KZ-3's range to some eight hundred kilometers, enough to reach the English coast at about the latitude of Newcastle, <u>if</u> the winds *en route* would change from the prevailing westerly and calm down to light or moderate strength. With the plane's airspeed a mere eighty knots, wind strength and direction would spell the difference between reaching England or splashing into the North Sea well short of dry land.

Feldsted's voice brought him back to the here and now. "I see the mailman arriving; maybe he has word about the tank."

The rural mailman, Landpostbudet, came down the driveway on his bicycle, hailing them with a cheerful "Good morning."

He handed some letters to Feldsted, who after a quick scan passed one to Hansen. It was a notice that the tank had arrived and was ready to be picked up. The gasoline shortage precluded delivery of goods, so that people had to provide their own transport. Hansen nodded to Feldsted.

"After lunch, I'm going to the freight office in town. The tank is light; I think I can carry it on my bicycle."

x

In his RSHA headquarters office, SS-Reichsführer Heinrich Himmler leaned back in his chair, pondering the report in his hand. The Reichssicherheitshauptamt—understandably abbreviated to RSHA–was as always quiet, although activity in many of its parts never ceased. Situated in Berlin's Prinz Albrecht

Strasse, this was the nerve center from which the Nazi state monitored and directed all its official as well as secret police and security organs through the black-uniformed elite troops of the Schutzstaffel, the SS. The demeanor of the personnel, from the all-powerful Gestapo to the humblest city police, was subdued and uncommunicative, self-absorbed and mirthless. Quiet was a natural state on these premises, where laughter was never heard.

Himmler read the report a second time. Incredible. After Stalingrad the Führer had ordered the swift destruction of the Warsaw Ghetto, and here they were still fighting, more than a month later. Initially Himmler had put von Sammern, the police leader, in command and the Jews had routed, actually *routed*, his Panzer-Grenadiers. Furious, Himmler had sacked him on the spot and turned command over to SS-Brigadeführer Jürgen Stroop. Capable and ruthless, Stroop had used every means to subdue the Jews, had even brought in tanks and armored cars, but that Jewish scum had resisted like cornered rats. Evidently they had made crude weapons, supplementing them with German ones they managed to take. The whole affair had been embarrassing from beginning to end and had to be kept under wraps.

Himmler put the report away, polished his glasses, and picked up a memo from Albert Speer, whom Hitler last year had put in overall charge of armaments production in the Third Reich. Most interesting. Himmler was aware, of course, that the research of Werner Heisenberg and Otto Hahn had caused the formation of this new group in Hechingen, officially code-named the Z-Group. They were working on a recently formed scientific operation of notable military interest, some new explosive of greatly enhanced power. The Wehrmacht could well use something like that. To be sure, the swastika now flew over German troops from Norway's North Cape on the Arctic Sea to the deserts of North Africa, and from the Atlantic Ocean to the threshold of Central Asia, a comforting manifestation of German power. And on the sea lanes, the U-boats were taking a huge toll on the supply stream from America to Britain. America could hardly keep that up much longer, having no engineering talent to speak of, as the Führer had pointed out.

Still, he sensed that the Eastern Front was bothersome. The Führer spoke grandly of the Russians being finally beaten, and he was not stingy expending German lives to that end, but that Russian general, Zhukov, kept throwing in entire new armies, some of them equipped with American trucks and rations. Stalin's generals seemed able to draw on inexhaustible manpower and to spend it with abandon. Those Soviet sub-humans must be breeding like vermin.

Yes, a new explosive created by German ingenuity could well be a timely boost to fighting power. Since Speer was put in charge of armaments production, the output had soared, and he had spoken in favor of giving the Z-Group what Heisenberg asked for. It had to do with mathematical calculations of slowing down a chain reaction in Uranium 235, whatever that meant. Anyway, picking up a Dutch mathematical physicist and taking him to Hechingen was a small matter. Last year Heisenberg had visited Niels Bohr in Copenhagen to benefit from his calculations, so why didn't Heisenberg have them also collect Bohr back then? Now Bohr had flown the coop, absconded to Sweden, and Abwehr had reported that he had gone on to America.

As always, Himmler let his methodical mind go over the proposed transaction for possible difficulties, but he saw none. He had better use SD personnel for this. Heydrich had done a fine job of building the SD into a first class instrument to gather intelligence. When Heydrich was assassinated in Prague in May, Himmler had put SS-Brigadeführer Werner Best in control, while making frequent use of a few SD agents as his personal aides. He leaned forward and pushed the intercom button.

"Fräulein Hofer, send Lammers in, please."

Six seconds later there was a knock on the door, an aide entered without waiting and saluted. Heinz Lammers was above average height and powerfully built. His dialect revealed a Holstein background, and he was endowed with blond hair, the physical attribute most lauded by Nazi pseudo-scientists as showing Aryan ancestry. His face was coarse, with heavy lips and a weak chin, features that most reliably betray defects of character.

Himmler kept studying the memo in his hand for another two minutes. Lammers was from the SD and in civilian clothes. It was always good for underlings to stand at attention, waiting to be spoken to. At last he looked up.

"Lammers, take a note on this: there is a professor at the Van Der Waals-Zeeman Institute at the University of Amsterdam. His name is Aaldert Voigt. Bring me a complete report on him Tuesday at two o'clock."

"Yes, Herr Reichsführer."

Lammers saluted, turned on his heel, and left, closing the door quietly behind him. Himmler followed him with his eyes and let his gaze rest on the door, as he thought about Lammers. Choosing and bringing up underlings to responsible positions was demanding, very demanding, in fact. The Reichsführer was well aware that the reputation of the SS, including the respect accorded his own name, hinged on the people in the upper echelons of the organization. Heinz Lammers had done well so far. He had developed a certain interrogation technique and used it very successfully on parents with young children. It involved a dismemberment of small toes and fingers that left the suspect parent uninjured and well able to speak. The Reichsführer knew that Lammers at times had become so caught up in the process, that he had indulged in other, more personal interrogation techniques, but no matter, his results were impressive.

Chapter 5

It was three minutes past eight in the morning, when Jack Hawes ushered Colonel John Howard into McKinnon's office. After introductions and a few polite remarks, McKinnon came to the business at hand.

"I understand, Colonel, that you have some kind of problem we might be able to assist you with?"

Colonel Howard cleared his throat.

"We have under development a highly secret military-scientific research operation of the utmost importance, for which we have gathered a high level group of scientists from Britain and Europe to work jointly with our own people. They would like to add to the group a certain Dutch researcher, a mathematical physicist. His name is Voigt; so far as we know, he is still working in Amsterdam at the Van der Waals-Zeeman Institute. We would like to extract him, partly for our own benefit, and partly to make sure he is not grabbed by the other side, in case they should become aware of his potential value."

Howard stopped for a moment to let his listeners digest the information so far.

McKinnon said, "So, you would like to have us scoop him up and send him to you?"

Howard lit a cigarette. "That would be most appreciated."

Hawes had been taking notes; now he asked a pertinent question.

"Does the other side have a similar research operation in the works?"

Howard shrugged. "We cannot be sure, so we have to assume that they do. We had a traveling commission explore the matter; their findings were inconclusive, but a German chap by the name of Heisenberg was fishing for information last year

62

from Niels Bohr, a physicist in Denmark, prompting us to invite Bohr to the States, where he is now working with us."

"Do we know whether this Voigt chap is willing to come when we contact him?" McKinnon wanted to know.

Howard hesitated, choosing his words carefully.

"We don't know. It was Albert Einstein who called him to our attention, and he thinks Voigt would come. Voigt is believed to have no family."

"That simplifies the operation considerably," McKinnon allowed, "but if the Germans are aware of this man's potential value, it could still be a rather difficult undertaking. However, we will get to work on it and give it our best. And, the Minister called and would like to see you after this. I'll have Miss Curtis escort you to his office."

McKinnon reached for the intercom. In response to his call, Ann Curtis entered.

"Miss Curtis, please take Colonel Howard to see Minister Dalton in his office."

He shook hands with Howard, and when they had left, McKinnon turned to Hawes.

"Jack, it's not going to be easy to come up with Dutch-speaking agents suitable for this project."

"Well, sir, it so happens that there is one in the pipeline. Do you recall Elizabeth van Paassen?"

"Oh yes, the one from Kenya. We talked to her a few weeks back."

"Yes, sir. I got Mac's report on her; he thought she was the best shooter we have sent him for quite a while. She is now at Arisaig."

"So, that's one. Female. Better get her back down here right away. What else do we have?"

"Not much, sir, but let me comb through the files."

X

In the field outside the hangar, Claus Feldsted hefted a jerry can and passed it to Hansen, who was standing on a short step ladder, testing the newly installed, long-range tank for possible leaks.

"This should fill you up completely. It cost me a ten-pound smoked ham to the Feldwebel quartermaster, and I had to swear I'd bring back the can discreetly." He paused. "Amazing what a ham can accomplish these days. That one is probably already on its way to his family in Hamburg."

Hansen pried open the jerry can, which was painted in German camouflage colors, lifted it above the new tank and carefully directed the stream of gasoline into the funnel.

"Yes, this will top it off."

When Hansen had confided his plan to Feldsted, the latter had been immediately enthusiastic. Flying the plane to England would not only withhold it from Hitler's grasp, it would put it at the disposal of the Brits who might well be able to make use of it. As if the weather gods meant to bless their undertaking, the wind had backed southerly and moderated to a light breeze. Aiming for Sunderland on the English coast, the distance to be covered was about three hundred and thirty miles. With a headwind component of ten knots, that would require almost five hours of flying time. The extra tank would keep the KZ-3 flying for almost six hours, a modest but acceptable margin of safety, Hansen thought, if the weather holds. Feldsted was dubious, but Hansen persisted.

"As I see it, we're at war, and taking a chance like this is hardly to be considered risky at all."

While Hansen was tuning the engine to perfection, Feldsted had put a cork flotation belt onboard–"just in case"–and had painted Royal Air Force rondels on wings and rudder.

"If a German sees you," Feldsted mused, "he will shoot you down in any event, but these markings may keep the RAF from blowing you out of the sky before asking questions."

The little plane had minimal instrumentation: for the engine, a fuel gauge, tachometer and oil pressure warning light; the flight instruments consisted of an altimeter, an air speed indicator, and a small magnetic compass. Not exactly the kind of instrument panel that invites a pilot to strike out for distant shores; but such as it was, the plane was ready.

Hansen lay down to rest before takeoff but his mind kept working on the upcoming flight. Would the wind hold? Could he navigate at low enough altitude not to arouse the Germans before reaching the coast? He wasn't really a pilot, had flown just a couple of times when doing in-flight testing, sitting right seat, always with a certified pilot in the left seat, ready to take over. Was this a totally hare-brained scheme, doomed to failure?

Feldsted roused him at 10:30 p.m. Mrs. Feldsted had packed a basket of food and two bottles of beer—no point in going hungry. Then they all walked to the hangar, letting their eyes get used to the summer night's reduced light, and Hansen shook hands with his hosts. He swung the prop by hand, and the 100-hp Cirrus engine caught with a roar. While he did the runup, testing the magnetos, setting the altimeter, Feldsted went to the far end of the field and lit a tin can of gasoline, a primitive guiding beacon that also marked the end of the runway. Time to go.

Hansen lined up the plane and looked toward the end of the field, where the gasoline beacon showed as a cheerful point of light. Then he took a deep breath, shoved the throttle full forward, and was airborne before halfway to Feldsted's improvised marker. At two hundred feet of altitude he pushed the nose down to level flight, throttled back to cruising speed, 80 knots, and turned slightly left onto a course of 250 degrees. This was what he and Feldsted had decided on as the best guess: not too close to the German and Dutch coast, not so northerly as to make the distance to England too far. There was just enough light left in the sky to make the horizon visible, just as well, for he was neither trained nor equipped for instrument conditions. He trimmed the plane for level flight and tried to relax. Why hadn't he practiced more flying and gotten his license? Fortunately, the twenty-mile stretch between Steensholt and the North Sea was without obstructions of any kind. The sea was already visible, even from this low altitude.

Minutes later he passed over the dike that protected the low lying coastal farmland, when storms from time to time flung the sea in furious assaults against the west coast of the Danish peninsula. Below him lay the area outside the dike, Vadehavet, an inter-tidal realm where man and sea for centuries had contended for ownership, man by building dikes and groins and revetting with fascines, the sea occasionally in a single night of cataclysmic storm flood taking back what man with decades of patience had gained. On the right and left the view retreated into dim perspectives of groins and flats of sand and mud. From a thousand encounters during his boyhood on the coast he knew its color scheme in all its shadings. It varied from light fawn, where the highest levels of sand had dried in the wind, to brown where it was still wet, to slate grey where patches of mud soiled its clean bosom. Tonight, from his new vantage point, the color was a deep violet.

As the small plane churned into the great void ahead, he cast one last glance back at the receding land. Then he locked his attention onto the altimeter and the magnetic compass, the two small instruments on which his fate now depended.

X

Marek walked into the meeting room without limping. Dr. Panowicz and about a dozen others were seated around the large table; it was the assembly Panowicz referred to as his executive council. They had all gathered to hear Marek, once again, recount the story of the destruction of the Warsaw Ghetto and the desperate fight, as the SS slowly annihilated the defenders. He had told this story weeks ago at his arrival, but it had been brief then, as he had been weak from loss of blood. Fully recovered, he now recounted it in all the details he knew. As he spoke, Marek relived the last months of the ordeal, torn between the agony and the exaltation of being Jewish. When he had finished, the room remained silent. In the flickering candle light tears could be seen on the grim faces of some listeners, for many of them had family in the Warsaw Ghetto, all of whom must now be assumed dead. Dr. Panowicz finally broke the spell.

"We may all wonder why God has chosen this time to test us, as He once tested Job, but let us rejoice with pride in what our brothers and sisters in Warsaw have done. And now we shall help Marek to take the message about their struggle beyond the reach of our tormentors."

Among the sundry skills in the older part of the group were those of a former printer, who had become highly accomplished in forging passports, personal IDs, and the numerous permits needed by anyone traveling in German occupied territory. Dr. Panowics turned to Marek.

"I will ask Joshua Goldstein to invoke all his skill to help you safely on your way."

x

The clock in the hallway showed precisely 2:00 p.m. when Lammers walked into Himmler's office and saluted the SS-Reichsführer.

"Herr Reichsführer, I have here the report on the Dutch physicist Aaldert Voigt. My investigation has revealed that the name itself is fictitious; the person in question is actually a Jew, Abramek Blum, of Polish origin."

Himmler raised his eyebrows slightly, as he took the dossier Lammers proffered.

"*Ausgezeichnet*, Lammers," he nodded approvingly, "that will be all for now."

When the door closed behind Lammers, Himmler settled back in his chair to peruse the dossier. It contained copies of scientific papers published by Aaldert Voigt, a few pictures, and the report itself. Himmler skipped the publications, glanced at the photos, and read the report attentively. Most interesting, a dirty Jew posing as an Aryan. It could have been possible only with the connivance of someone in the University administration. They would soon discover who that was. First, he wanted to talk with Heisenberg in Hechingen. He pushed the intercom button and told Fräulein Hofer to place the call. Several minutes passed, then he heard Heisenberg's voice.

"Hallo, hallo? Heil Hitler, Herr Reichsführer."

Soft spoken as always, Himmler made a few preliminary comments. Then he came to the point.

"Are you aware that the Dutch researcher you wish to take into your Z-Group actually is a Polish Jew living in Amsterdam under a false name?"

The line was silent for some seconds before Heisenberg answered.

"No. I did not know."

"Do you still want him?"

"Yes."

"Are you saying that you actually want to work with a Jew?"

"Herr Reichsführer, had it not been for the work done by Jewish scientists, starting with Albert Einstein, there would have been no field of atomic research for our Z-Group to explore. Nor would the Americans be pushing ahead, as I suspect they are doing. And surely, you are aware that the Dane, Niels Bohr, also is Jewish."

"*Gewiss* – of course, I knew that. So why didn't you have us seize him, when you visited Copenhagen?"

"Herr Reichsführer, it is not that simple. Genuine cooperation comes about only when it is voluntary."

Himmler snorted derisively.

"Are you proposing to let Aaldert Voigt continue to exist in his false identity?"

Heisenberg thought quickly. It made no difference to him whether Voigt were to continue in his assumed identity, and it might simplify matters. He decided to treat Himmler's question as a proposal.

"Herr Reichsführer, that is a brilliant idea."

When Himmler hung up the phone ten minutes later, the details had been agreed upon, and he called for Lammers. When his aide appeared, he was ready with precise instructions.

"Lammers, I want you to go to Amsterdam by car, pick up Aaldert Voigt and take him to Dr. Heisenberg in Hechingen. But before you leave Amsterdam, take Voigt to our local office. There, find out who has provided him with cover and sheltered him under a false name, so that our local people can clean that up. And be careful, don't let him slip away. *Verstanden?*"

"*Jawohl*, Herr Reichsführer."

"But do not leave until Wednesday."

That was in three days. It was best to give the impression that the SS had other and more important things to do. And sending Lammers after Voigt would insure that no stone was left unturned in finding out who in Holland had helped in hiding this piece of Jewish filth.

x

Jeremy Polwheal was moving his sheep to the old fen on the eastern downslope. He had been farming this land on Flamborough Head for almost fifty years, chalky ground, not nearly as good as the soil just a couple of miles farther inland, but his forebears had farmed here since...he wasn't sure how long, maybe since they stood guard on the high point of the promontory on lookout for Viking longships materializing from the North Sea mist. He had never thought to question his lot, for he harbored an ever unspoken disdain for town living, but his son had taken a job in town when he got married, leaving farm life behind. With his eyes Jeremy caressed the meager ground, now clad in the rich green of the summer grass. Hard to understand how anyone could be content living in a town.

He became aware of the distant drone of a small plane, incoming from the sea. He shaded his eyes against the rising sun to catch sight of it, finally spotting it: very low, Royal Air Force markings. What could they be doing? Must be a sea search for downed fliers. The plane seemed to be aiming for his paddock, yes, sure enough, it was going to try to land there. Jeremy watched it skim low over the fence, touch down hard, bounce twice, and come to a stop barely before crashing into the fence at the far end. Jeremy clapped the sheep gate shut and started walking toward the paddock. The pilot got out, looked around, wiped his forehead and leaned against the plane. Surprisingly, he was in civilian clothes, seemed exhausted.

Jeremy wondered what this could be all about. Approaching the plane, he saw the pilot lift out a picnic basket and extract two bottles of beer, turning toward him and waving the bottles at him in a most enticing manner.

Now, this was something that didn't happen to town dwellers!

x

The RSHA office in downtown Amsterdam had the usual complement of Gestapo, Abwehr, Kripo, and SD. After the recent elimination of significant parts of the Dutch Underground, the SD personnel had been reduced by transfers to France and Scandinavia, leaving only two seasoned agents, Martin Hagen and Erich Wolff, plus a secretary and a file clerk. As the most senior, Hagen was in nominal charge, and this morning he was in an expansive mood, thinking about the report he had sent a few days ago to Berlin headquarters, revealing Voigt's double identity. It had been a stroke of luck, a tip from a low level informer, but Hagen had phrased his report carefully, implying that the discovery was attributable to diligence and competent security work. Over coffee this morning, he leaned back in his chair and addressed Wolff, whose desk was at the opposite wall.

"Erich, that report we sent to Berlin should impress Lammers. It's not every day you find a Jew posing as a prominent Aryan Dutchman. RSHA may have been tipped off about Voigt, but they did not give us any hint, and <u>we</u> were the ones who discovered his double identity."

Wolff chuckled, lighting a cigarette.

"You're absolutely right, Martin. It will look good in our files. The SD *Mitarbeiter,* colleagues in the Amsterdam office, have again proved themselves to be alert. You know, we could just go out and pick up Voigt, alias Abramek Blum, and put him in the Westerbork *Transitlager*. He will be going there anyway."

Hagen pondered the proposition. The *Transitlager* was a temporary holding camp for Jews destined for transport to the East. Headquarters usually frowned on local initiative in such matters, but this seemed a straight-forward step to take. Why not earn additional credit and attention by showing some initiative?

"I think you're right. Let's stuff him into Westerbork before he can slip away. It will be a good item to include in our weekly report to headquarters on Friday."

In a small seminar room at the University of Amsterdam, a handful of graduate students were busy taking notes, while Aaldert Voigt stood at the blackboard, finishing his lecture on topology, one of several preparatory steps toward coming to grips with an elusive phenomenon that was becoming known as the Uncertainty Principle. He had been raised in the Warsaw Ghetto and had from a very early age shown a remarkable aptitude for mathematics that had attracted the attention of a professor at Warsaw University. To protect this unusual scientific talent from the pervasive Polish anti-Semitism, his mentor had used a family connection to secure Abramek Blum a temporary appointment at Amsterdam's elite Waals-Zeeman Institute when war seemed imminent. The chairman at the Institute had with foresight suggested a change of identity to forestall any Nazi attempt to "Aryanize" the faculty in the

German pattern, and Abramek Blum had become Aaldert Voigt. Since he lost his wife to tuberculosis after only two years of marriage, he had devoted himself entirely to his work, and the temporary appointment had become permanent. Life in Holland had offered little in the way of human companionship to the transplanted Jew, who had concentrated all the more on his work. At the age of thirty he was still at the peak of his intellectual capacity.

While the students were still writing, Voigt gathered his notes from the lectern and left the seminar room. Outside his office, the two SD-men stepped in front of him. Hagen spoke, while Wolff kept his right hand in his pocket, clutched around a Dreyse semiautomatic pistol.

"You are Aaldert Voigt?"

"Yes."

"In that case, you are also a dirty Jew by the name of Abramek Blum, and you are under arrest."

While a small knot of students watched in alarm and disbelief, Hagen and Wolff clapped a set of handcuffs on Voigt, marched him quickly out of the building, and shoved him into a waiting Opel Kapitän that left without delay. The entire action took less than three minutes, a typical SD arrest. The car sped away in an eastward direction.

Chapter 6

Major Hawes picked up the phone, cradling it on his left shoulder. The specially adapted instrument allowed him free use of his one and only hand which he needed at the moment to light his first cigarette of the day, Players Navy Cut, the only brand he smoked. It was the screening office, and the voice of the young WAAF officer made him sit up with immediate attention, while the flame of his lighter flickered out.

"A Dane, you say, and he speaks Dutch? Do I understand he speaks Dutch in addition to Danish? Hmm...I see.... And how is his English?"

Hawes listened to the answer, grunting approval of the WAAF's detailed appraisal. Then he spoke to cut her off.

"Send him right over."

As he got up from his chair, his phone rang again, but he ignored it and walked down to McKinnon's office. McKinnon was on the phone but hung up when seeing Hawes walk in.

"Oh, Jack, I was just trying to call you. Look at this report from Turnbull in Stockholm. It arrived this morning from Signals. This man, Lund, speaks Danish, not Dutch, but otherwise he sounds made to order for our project. Sank a German patrol boat more or less single handed, is eager to join the RAF, but can no doubt be convinced that an SOE career promises more action."

Hawes read the page McKinnon handed him, then allowed himself a rare smile.

"Sir, I believe I have an applicant to match that, and perhaps then some. How would you like a Dane who does speak Dutch as well as his native Danish, and who flew here himself overnight in a two-seater private plane stolen from under the noses of the Germans, without being a licensed pilot, landing it in one piece at Flamborough Head?"

Their eyes met, and the two men both burst out laughing.

"The summary facts would seem to make it a difficult choice, Jack. Let's get them both here as quickly as possible and see how they qualify. Did Miss van Paassen get down here yet?"

"Yes, sir, she checked in last night."

"And I seem to recall that Mac rated her highly. If the team we send after Voigt should have to protect him, that could become a critical question, although I hope not."

This had been much on McKinnon's mind. The agents were told to rely on stealth and avoid violence at almost any cost, but if events gave them no choice, shoot to kill.

"Mac gave her high marks, not only as a marksman. He also said she shows promise of staying cool under stress."

McKinnon looked relieved. Then he brought up another problem.

"Jack, with the situation in Holland being fluid just now, it may be too risky to send them in by Lysander. Why don't you see if we can come up with an alternate method of insertion."

SOE's preferred method was to take their agents into enemy territory by plane, using the Westland Lysander, a high-wing monoplane with a powerful Bristol Mercury radial engine. Its 45 mph landing speed and excellent short-field performance made it ideal for covert work, but it required local support for security at the landing site and for transportation of personnel. That ruled out Holland at the moment.

"I am looking into the possibility of insertion by boat, sir. Some of our Commandos have reconnoitered the German fortifications on the Channel coast by this means. It just might be an option."

Thank God for an aide like Hawes, McKinnon thought. He had again anticipated impending difficulties. Britain's Commandos had begun forming in 1940, with the specific purpose of mounting raids and carrying out reconnaissance in

German-occupied Europe. SOE had on prior occasions relied on this elite force.

"Alright, Jack, that should be preferable to parachuting. See if the Commandos have anything to suggest."

x

On Tuesday Heinz Lammers was leisurely getting ready for his trip to Amsterdam. This was going to be as close to a pleasure trip as SD excursions came: picking up an unsuspecting Jew—almost certainly unarmed—and taking him to Hechingen, no rush, just an agreeable auto excursion in pleasant summer weather. He had selected Kurt Reinhart as his back-up man and Hans Ziegler as his driver, two of his favorite SD colleagues, to share the outing. They were long-time *Mitarbeiter*, and Ziegler spoke Dutch. Although German was widely spoken and understood in Holland, it was always good to have someone along who could eavesdrop on local conversation.

This morning he went personally to the SD motor pool to survey the current inventory. As expected, it consisted chiefly of Opel Kapitän models, a design influenced by General Motors' high power-to-weight ratio, the preference of American consumers. As the fastest standard model in widespread use, it was inconspicuous as well, and thereby suitable for SD work. The manager of the pool noticed Lammers's scrutiny and emerged from his cubicle to satisfy his curiosity.

"Nah, Heinz, you are admiring my cars, I see. Are you thinking of asking me for one?"

Lammers turned toward him, instantly taking on a mien of solemnity appropriate for confiding state secrets.

"Rudolf, your Opels are fine for ordinary city errands, but I have a top secret assignment coming up. It will involve long distances and the crossing of frontiers, so you can understand I would prefer a more substantial conveyance."

"Will you be traveling east or west?"

"West, but keep your mouth shut about it."

"So, you are going west, crossing a frontier, most likely into Holland. If you will bring me back a couple of bottles of genever, I could perhaps upgrade your transport accordingly."

"I might be able to do that. Show me what you have tucked away for a situation like this."

Rudolf led the way to the basement, where the vehicles of the upper echelons of SS and SD were kept. There was one Opel Admiral, the rest being Mercedes, Horch and Wanderer, all of them large, elegant models. Rudolf stopped at a Wanderer sedan.

"This Wanderer is a 1939 model. I doubt you have seen it before; very few were made before the outbreak of war halted the production. I could let you have this one, if you can remember the genever."

"*Prima*, Rudolf, I'll remember."

Lammers looked approvingly at the black sedan. In this vehicle he could travel in comfort and in a style commensurate with the importance of his mission.

X

Hansen was seated in the office of Major Hawes, smoking one of the Major's Players Navy Cut and contemplating with puzzlement how he had been expedited through what was clearly a screening process. At first he thought it was due to his donation of the KZ-3 to the British war effort. An RAF pilot had arrived within hours, driven by a woman in WAAF uniform. The pilot had taken the plane off from Polwheal's paddock, while the WAAF had taken Hansen in tow, directly to London. Unable to stay awake any longer, he had slept on the way and cleared his mind. Then came a painstaking interview about his background, training, family status, and dozens of detailed questions about his life up to now. A burst of official interest in his person seemed to have been suddenly triggered when he mentioned Sophie and his Dutch language proficiency. That did not make much sense, but he found himself quickly shepherded to SOE and an even closer grilling, this one by Major Hawes, focusing on his time in Holland: where he had worked, how much of the country he had seen, where Sofie lived, who her parents were, where their sympathies and allegiances were in the present world conflict. Hansen answered to the best of his ability but hedged that in some matters he was only guessing.

Major Hawes put down the phone after another of numerous calls. He turned to Hansen and slowly lit a cigarette before he spoke.

"Have you ever heard about SOE?"

Hansen shook his head.

"Well, then let me tell you about us. During the Blitz in the summer of 1940, Britain stood entirely alone. The United States was still at peace, and the Russians were even allied with Hitler. We decided to try to mobilize the German-occupied nations in Europe to play an active part in the struggle, and Prime Minister Churchill in a radio speech called on those people to 'set Europe ablaze' with resistance to the Nazis."

"That was reported in Holland, where I was working at the time," Hansen remembered, "but nobody was willing to tackle the problem."

"I'm not surprised," Hawes said, "very little happened at first, and we took the step to set up an agency to help people over there get organized into an Underground and to supply them with the means to interfere with Hitler's war machine. That was the reason SOE was set up, and we have been busy ever since."

He went into a brief description of SOE's work, ending with a straight question.

"Would you like to enlist and work with us?"

Hansen had felt the proposal coming. Up to now he had only thought of seeking work in his chosen field, if necessary in uniform helping to keep the RAF flying. This was a very different proposition, one for which he did not feel qualified at all. It struck him that flying the North Sea had also appeared as something beyond his realm of experience and qualifications, yet he had considered it to be imposed by circumstances that could not have been foreseen or imagined a few days earlier. When old Mr. Zeuten had suggested that he "use his judgment," did it not extend beyond keeping the KZ-3 out of the Germans' clutches?

Hawes watched him closely while leisurely smoking. He read and interpreted with certainty the hesitation in Hansen's demeanor. It perfectly reflected what millions of Europeans were going through under Nazi overlordship. Small wonder that ordinary law abiding citizens found it hard to go against the inclinations fostered by a civilized society and turn to Underground resistance for which there was no precedent. He cleared his throat.

"We in SOE are quite aware that none of us is prepared for what we are called upon to do, but in the larger scheme of things, neither is anyone prepared for war per se. We can train men to be soldiers, that is, to drill and shoot and take orders, but in a civilized society we cannot truly train anyone to kill. The situation forced upon all of us by Hitler goes against all our inclinations and instincts, yet we have to deal with it. Not doing so, letting the Nazis have their way, is really unthinkable."

Hansen took a deep breath.

"I would like to volunteer."

X

Lund descended the short ladder from the DC-2 and stepped onto the tarmac with a feeling of euphoria: finally, he was standing on British soil! This was what he had dreamed about ever since that April day three years ago when the Wehrmacht made his country into a satellite of Hitler's Third Reich.

After the shootout on The Sound, the sequence of events that brought him to this point had flowed smoothly, in an almost dream-like manner. He had managed to scuttle the patrol boat by wedging his second grenade between the diesel engine and the hull, pulling the pin with a piece of string. The two brothers, Per and Ole, had coaxed the severely wounded Chris-Craft to within a few hundred meters of the Råå harbor on the Swedish coast, where they punched a hole below the water line in the already weakened hull. The weight of the two engines pulled the craft down like a stone, while the three occupants swam to shore without difficulty. In a lengthy interrogation by the Swedish police they stuck to a simple story of having been discreetly let off a fishing boat whose owner did not wish to be known. Lund parted with the brothers, took a train to Stockholm, and at the British embassy volunteered for military service against the Germans. He was shunted on to a small office, where the occupant, Ronald Turnbull, had quizzed him about his activity since the outbreak of the war. Lund gave a truthful and detailed report, which the questioner jotted down on a pad, ending with the incident on The Sound. Turnbull listened in disbelief.

"You actually <u>sank</u> the patrol boat?"

"There wasn't any other solution."

"Ah...hmm...right, makes sense." He had scribbled a long note on his pad.

That was two days ago, and here he was, already in England.

"Are you Svend Lund?"

The question came from a woman in WAAF uniform, and Lund nodded confirmation.

"My name is Ann Curtis. Please come this way."

She walked briskly ahead of him through a hangar and an office building, both bearing the marks of bombing damage, to a Morris Minor parked outside, motioned him into the left front seat, and took the wheel on the right. Lund had already in Sweden overcome the awkwardness felt by drivers used to right hand traffic, when they first encounter left hand driving. As they pulled away from the curb, he gave in to simple curiosity.

"Where are we, and where are we going?"

"We are going to London, about seventeen miles from here, to the offices of SOE in Baker Street, where you will meet Brigadier McKinnon."

"Who is he?"

"He will tell you." She had obviously given as much information as she was willing or authorized to provide, and they proceeded in silence.

The Baker Street offices were unassuming except for the location near the nerve centers of the British Government's direction of the war. Lund followed Ann Curtis as she ascended a stairway to the second floor, where she knocked on an unmarked office door.

"Come in!"

They entered, and Lund saw that the voice, just loud enough to be heard, belonged to a middle-aged man working at a desk with his back to the windows. Ann closed the door and turned toward the desk.

"Good morning, sir. This is Mr. Svend Lund, who just arrived from Stockholm."

"Ah, yes, thank you, Ann. Be kind enough to bring us some tea and ask Major Hawes to join us." He waved her out with a friendly smile and extended his hand to Lund.

"So, you are the one sinking German patrol boats on The Sound. My name is McKinnon."

They shook hands, and McKinnon motioned him to a chair. Lund was taken aback by McKinnon's knowledge of the incident. News apparently traveled fast around here. A knock on the door brought Jack Hawes. McKinnon made introductions, then turned back to Lund.

"Tell us exactly what you did in the last twenty-four hours before setting foot in Sweden."

Lund retold his story, starting with the rupture of his suitcase, without dwelling on details. His listeners paid rapt attention, throwing in an occasional question. Ann brought them tea, and when Lund had finished, McKinnon leaned back in his chair, eyeing him pensively.

"Why didn't the machine gunner on the foredeck open fire when you were throwing the grenade into the German cockpit?"

The question came from Hawes, curious about a practical detail.

"I believe he was unable to depress his gun enough; we were very close, you know, and low compared with the patrol boat. Besides, the Danish grenade has a short fuse."

"Hmm...I see."

McKinnon liked the detached manner in which Lund discussed a matter involving split-second timing with life-or-death outcome. He turned his questions in a different direction.

"And you did a short stint in Finland during the Winter War. How did you find the Finnish soldiers?"

"They are tough, very different from other Scandinavians. In close combat they use their knives effectively—every Finn seems to carry one—slim and razor sharp. My instructor, Corporal Olavi Paloheimo, taught me how to use it to kill silently. Can't say I enjoyed that."

Lund gave a brief, vivid description of Finnish techniques in close combat that had the two SOE officers momentarily at a loss for words. McKinnon recovered his equilibrium first, clearing his throat.

"Indeed extraordinary. Now, the reason I had you brought here directly is this. We have a operation coming up that calls for a man of your particular abilities and qualifications, and we are somewhat short of time to carry it out. I would like Major Hawes to take you to his office and explain about the work of SOE and perhaps touch on the project."

x

It was a rare opportunity to be entrusted with an SD task <u>not</u> calling for speedy execution, and Heinz Lammers was determined to make the most of this one. To make sure the trip to Amsterdam would include an overnight stay along the way, he had scheduled departure for 11 a.m., by which time the

Wanderer was waiting with two of his colleagues, Hans Ziegler, at the wheel and Kurt Reinhart in the back. Lammers was senior to the others as well as in charge of the operation at hand, both important distinctions in a bureaucracy fiercely dedicated to internal competition. They were all aware of this, as he greeted them with jovial condescension, taking his seat in the back, and giving the signal to start.

"*Los*, Hans!"

Ziegler nosed the car into the Berlin traffic, a meager stream of mostly commercial vehicles, nothing like the prewar street picture. Gasoline shortages had pretty much eliminated private driving except for a few in the upper echelons of the party, or for security personnel whose transportation always enjoyed top priority. Fifteen minutes later they entered the Autobahn, the east-west artery of Hitler's vaunted superhighway system. Building these concrete ribbons through the placid German countryside had helped eliminate unemployment after the Nazi takeover. It had also added a new dimension to military strategic thinking, facilitating rapid east-west movement of troops. These days the Autobahn showed the telltale signs of heavy use and inadequate maintenance during three years of war. The traffic was also different from what had been foreseen by confident military planners. Gone were passenger cars except for a sprinkling of security transport, such as the SD party. The rest of the country's private vehicles sat perched on blocks in their respective garages, awaiting better times. In the place of these, commercial and military traffic dominated, with commercial trucks being light models, the heavier rolling stock having been requisitioned by the military at the outbreak of the war.

The three SD agents discussed the war news from the Eastern Front. The discussion had to be in guarded terms so as not to sound defeatist. The Stalingrad disaster was still on everyone's mind, and both Reinhart and Ziegler could speak from personal experience, having fought in Russia until declared unfit for military service. Reinhart had lost a foot to frostbite the first winter in the drive to Moscow; Ziegler had lost two fingers to shrapnel. In comparison with the Russian ordeal, SD work was an outright godsend. They looped around Braunschweig, as the Autobahn everywhere kept well away from towns and cities, a feature that took full advantage of the countryside's pastoral beauty, but the occupants of the Wanderer were too focused on their conversation to notice the landscape.

"The way the Soviet commanders use soldiers has no parallel in Europe," observed Reinhart. "They fight like Genghis Khan's Mongol hordes must have fought. I've read some about them, and Europeans at the time couldn't stand up to them."

"The Führer says they are subhumans. We are superior to them in every way and are surely bound to beat them eventually." Lammers found it wise to throw in a word of official ideology before anyone got carried away on statements that could possibly be construed as critical.

"Subhumans!" Ziegler sneered but refrained from further comment, leaving interpretation of his exclamation up to the listener. Lammers stepped in again.

"Yes, they really are subhuman, just look at the way they treat the lives of their own people." The staggering German losses were best dealt with by pointing a finger at the Russians.

"One thing is for certain: they cannot keep it up forever," Reinhart said, omitting that this truism applied both ways.

It was dinner time when they reached Hannover and checked into the Schweizerhof, arguably the city's best hotel. The manager needed only a quick glimpse at Lammers's ID to turn on his most ingratiating hospitality.

"Our restaurant is closed, but I would be glad to have the chef prepare anything you like."

His obsequiousness was not lost on Lammers, who reveled in such attention.

"No, that won't be necessary. We will be eating at Konrad's in Knochenhauerstrasse. But have your man polish our car when we return."

"*Gewiss*, Herr Lammers."

X

McKinnon was on the phone, when WAAF Lieutenant Ann Curtis entered his office carrying the morning tea. She quietly placed it before him on his desk and started to withdraw, but McKinnon motioned her to stay, reaching for the mug and continuing his conversation.

"Yes, Minister, we are about to insert a team to get him, it's a go for tomorrow night...no, we can't use a Lysander, Three Commando will take them in...yes...I hope so." He hung up the phone.

"Thank you, Ann, and would you ask Major Hawes to come in, with his file on *Dutch Treat*, and offer him some tea as well."

Conforming with standard practice, McKinnon had assigned a code name to the impending operation in Amsterdam. When Hawes appeared, they quickly got down to details.

"So, Jack, let us review what we have so far. I assume you have seen the van Paassen girl; how is she shaping up?"

"Very well, sir. I explained to her the risks involved, in particular the risk to females, if captured by the SD. We talked about the L-tablet, and I told her about some cases of our agents who have used it, but she never flinched. Signed up without any hesitation."

The L-tablet was a cyanide pill, instantly lethal, that SOE agents carried and were encouraged to use if captured.

McKinnon nodded.

"She is qualified, and we don't have much choice. What about Hansen?"

"He is quite a different case, contemplative, had never thought of taking up this kind of service but was prepared to work for the RAF, willing to put on a uniform and do his bit.

When I presented him with our alternative, he gagged at first but then came around and volunteered without my putting words in his mouth."

"And what does Mac say?" McKinnon wanted to know.

"Says he has a steady aim and an unruffled manner that results in above average marksmanship with handguns, and even better results with automatic weapons."

"You think he will keep his cool under fire?"

"Impossible to say, sir, few people do; but I would have been glad to have him in my command. I believe he proved his steadiness on that flight across the North Sea. And I was told that on arrival in the farmer's paddock, he produced two bottles of good beer, so that he and the farmer could toast to a happy landing."

"Really? Alright, he's in too. And now to Lund. Even without speaking Dutch, he seems in every other respect naturally suited for the task at hand. Wouldn't you say so?"

"Yes, sir. If anything, he might be too quick on the trigger, trying to shoot his way through before exhausting other methods."

"Hmm ...yes, good point. We had better warn him about that...not to blow his cover unless unavoidable. It's a rare pleasure, though, to find a volunteer who has methodically prepared himself for this kind of work."

"Yes, sir. He was not happy about missing out on the RAF, but we compromised by saying those plans would only be on hold for the time being."

"Indeed. He may decide to stay with us, when he gets a taste of it. Our operation needs his talent more than the RAF does. What have you found out about insertion?"

The highly pressing problem of getting the agents safely to Amsterdam was still uppermost in McKinnon's mind, and he had been monitoring the classified weather forecasts for the Dutch coast.

"I have discussed a couple of alternatives with Captain Davies of Three Commando. He suggests taking our team up the Ems River and dropping them by rubber boat on the Dutch shore, well inside the coastal defenses. The route is marked on this chart."

Hawes unrolled a nautical chart of the Ems estuary, and the two men studied it in silence, eventually broken by McKinnon.

"That's rather far from Amsterdam. Wouldn't Den Helder be more convenient all around? In the summer of '39 I was doing some yachting and found Den Helder to be easy to get in and out of."

"Perhaps for that reason they have gone to some length to secure it. Davies says Three Commando has probed and found it too tightly sewn up."

McKinnon stared at the chart. The proposed route would take the SOE team deep into enemy territory. Into the Lion's mouth. He looked at Hawes whose experience on another beach had left him without his left arm.

"What's your judgment, Jack?"

"Davies is capable, sir, and cautious, as Commandos go. I believe his proposal is our best bet."

"Which may not mean too much, I'm afraid. Did you discuss with Davies how we might retrieve the four of them, assuming our team gets hold of Voigt?"

"I did, sir, and he did not feel a second sortie would be advisable anywhere on the Dutch coast for some time afterward. I thought we might consider taking them out by Lysander, using that private field from which Hansen took off."

"Hmm...that would involve some travel and border crossings. Get Hansen's opinion about the field; if it's favorable, let us plan accordingly and get Henderson started on their IDs and travel documents."

McKinnon reflected for a moment, well aware that his decision would be crucial to the outcome. Then he continued.

"The weather is favorable right now. Tell Davies to set insertion up for tomorrow night. Assemble the team in your office this morning for mutual introduction. Then let Cranton from the Beaulieu school give them as much final training as he can cram into the hours we have between now and tomorrow night. Let me know how late Davies can take them off our hands here in my office. Get the team dressed and ready here half an hour before that. And when you have turned them over to Cranton, come back here and let us work out the details of their trip taking Voigt to Denmark."

Chapter 7

When Hawes walked back to his office after his meeting with McKinnon, he saw Liz and Lund seated in the small waiting area and signaled them both to follow him. Inside, he turned and introduced them with a slight hand gesture.

"Svend Lund...Elizabeth van Paassen. Take a good look at each other. You will be working together and will be depending on each other, with your lives."

They shook hands, very formally. To Liz the introduction held no surprise, as she had expected to work with male agents, but the look on Lund's face told her that he had not been even remotely prepared for a female co-worker. She suppressed a giggle but could not resist a comment.

"Svend Lund, you really must control your facial expressions; they do give away your private thoughts, you know."

She said it with a faint smile, but it made Lund blush. Seeing his embarrassment, she couldn't help laughing. Maintaining his reserve, Hawes pushed the intercom button and leaned toward the mike.

"Lieutenant Curtis, please send Mr. Hansen in as soon as he arrives."

"He is walking in right now, Major."

Hansen entered, everyone was introduced, and Hawes wasted no time.

"Do sit down and listen carefully. You have all been through some training, rather minimal, I'm sorry to say. Certainly far less than our normal practice. The reason is that we have been handed a operation of some urgency, and you three among you possess qualifications that render you collectively suited to carry it through."

He paused to light a Players and to let his words sink in. Liz was seated so that she could see both men, and she instinctively evaluated each as someone she might have to rely on in very trying conditions. Hansen appeared steady and solid, unperturbed by this novel situation. Lund was distinctly different and more complex. He moved with deft assurance, radiating self confidence, and Liz realized that her introduction throwing him off stride must be a rare occurrence. He exuded mental strength, and he was attractive, very attractive...Hawes' voice pulled her back to the here and now.

"Our work is inherently risky, even to the best trained agents. To someone like yourselves with very little training, the risk is considerable. Before I reveal to you the operation at hand, I want you to think clearly and dispassionately. You know yourselves better than anyone. If you wish to decline this assignment and go through our full training schedule before any assignment abroad, do say so now. SOE understands and respects your decision."

Liz said quietly, "I'm in, Major."

Hansen said, "Yes, certainly."

Lund added, "Of course," with a trace of impatience in his voice.

Hawes accepted their consent with a thoughtful nod.

"I thought that would be your decision. Now, the operation is code named *Dutch Treat*, and it involves the following. The Waals-Zeeman Institute of the Amsterdam University has on its staff a professor by the name of Voigt–Aaldert Voigt–who is working on research of possible military value. SOE has been tasked to send in a team to find Aaldert Voigt and bring him here to work for us. Our aim is a dual one: to make use of his work for our side, and to preclude that his work might be made to benefit the Nazis. It is possible that the other side has already grabbed him, but we have no information to make us think so. In any event, speed is of the essence in taking this action. You three are the team we are going to send to Amsterdam."

Hawes paused, carefully chose another Players and fumbled for his lighter, while studying the three serious faces across the desk.

"Do you have any questions so far?"

There was some headshaking. Lund said, "Go on."

Hawes stubbed out his cigarette, lit another and continued.

"We usually send our people in by plane, landing on a remote field or parachuting them. We won't use that method in your case. The Gestapo has made inroads on the Dutch Underground, and to minimize your risk, we will not count on local contacts. We will give you some local names we believe are still good, but that will be for emergency use only."

"So, how will we get there?" Lund wanted to know.

"We are handing that job to our Commandos. Captain Davies of Three Commando will tell you tomorrow night."

Liz said, "When do we leave?"

"Tomorrow night. Today and tomorrow will be used for training. You will not be trained on radio communication, but one of the local Dutch names you'll get has a radio and is still in touch. He may be used, with caution, in an emergency. And you will be given the name of a Danish operator to summon a plane for your return. Clothes are critical, English cloth and styles are easily noticed on the Continent. Lund and Hansen fortunately are wearing their clothes from Denmark. Miss van Paassen will need to change, and we have a fairly good selection on hand. This will be your schedule from now until departure." He handed each of them a typed sheet. "You have all done well on the firing range, so we won't take any more time for that. Besides, we hope and expect you won't need marksmanship. You will, however, each be issued a handgun, the Walther PKK for Lund and Hansen, the Belgian 6.35-mm for Miss van Paassen."

Liz said, "Please, Major, call me Liz."

"Alright. Lund has had the most Underground experience. He will be the leader of the team. It is necessary to designate one person as leader. His word will be final when it comes to tactical field decisions. The schedule I have given you takes over in twenty minutes. Are there any questions."

Three pair of eyes scanned the schedule. Hansen said, "You *do* have radio training on here."

"This is just to familiarize you with the equipment, not to make you into a proficient operator," Hawes replied.

"When do I get my new wardrobe?" Liz inquired.

"At the end of today's schedule we'll take you to Mrs. Hollingsworth, who is in charge of clothes. And you will from today on hold the rank of WAAF Lieutenant. It will make you a prisoner of war, in case you are caught, and should in theory protect you from Gestapo torture. I have to tell you, though, that the other side does not usually play by the rules."

"So, if we're caught, we're on our own?" Lund cut in.

"I'm afraid so."

Liz was studying Lund, when he asked the question. He had been designated leader of the team, which meant that his judgment and reactions under fire could spell the difference between success and failure. Or between life and death for the three of them. She listened, as he calmly posed a few practical questions, and she felt with a strange certainty that no one could be better suited for the operation they were embarking on. Was she sexually attracted to him? She thought so, but her life in Kenya had offered her no opportunities for intimacy with the opposite sex.

X

The train was bowling along in midsummer sunshine with the Weser River on the left. In the rolling landscape of the Wesergebirge stubble fields were being plowed everywhere to produce the grain to feed Germany's armies and population in this, the third year of Hitler's war. The work was being done by imported *Fremdarbeiter*, foreign workers, actually slave labor gathered at gun point in the Ostmark, the areas of the Soviet Union under German control. These field workers were the

91

lucky ones, for there was always enough food, however low grade, to keep farmers and their workers alive. The factory workers met a different fate, starvation rations that kept the death rate so high that an unending stream of replacements must be brought in from the East. That was understood and accepted by the Nazi administrators, who would explain that these workers were not real people, only subhumans without souls.

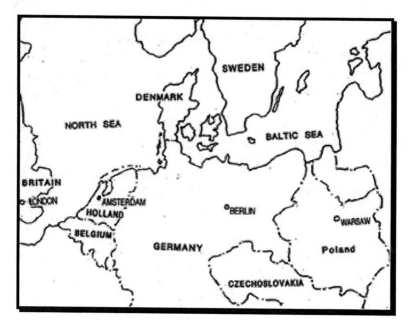

A two-man police patrol that had boarded the train in Braunschweig was methodically checking passenger IDs and travel papers. It was one of numerous such unscheduled checkups, randomly ordered by the Gestapo to see what might turn up. Horst Braun and his colleague of the Ordnungspolizei, the Braunschweig city police, both deeply resented this duty that took them out of their ordinary routine and away from home, sometimes overnight, but you didn't argue with any order issuing from Himmler's RSHA. So they were slowly working their way back from the head of the train, leapfrogging each other through the compartments and making sure that no enemy of the Reich was riding along among legitimate travelers.

Braun slid open the door to a second class compartment and ran his eyes over the occupants. In one window seat a young man was reading a day-old newspaper. The other people in the compartment were a fat old man sucking on an unlit pipe, three young women in BDM uniforms, and an elderly textile manufacturer on a business trip. Braun's professional attention immediately focused on the young man; he should be in uniform and at the front, where he was needed. The young man handed over the papers that told his story. He was Tadeusz Kalisiak, a Polish concrete worker and one of the Spezialarbeiter, a specialty worker, in Organisation Todt, the giant German construction firm that was still expanding the Channel Coast fortifications. His orders specified travel from Warsaw to Amsterdam to report to OT's office there. Polish father, mother's maiden name Slovakian, that would explain the broad, Slavic face. His clothes and rough hands further completed the picture. The policeman silently handed back the papers.

Marek relaxed. The passport and travel documents produced by Joshua Goldstein, the retired printer in the partisan camp, had so far passed the scrutiny of four inspections. Dr. Panowicz had also given him enough money for railroad tickets plus a little extra, for emergency. Ari had guided him to the outskirts of Konin, and when they parted had handed him a small caliber automatic pistol with a thoughtful comment.

"This came off a German officer; it's too small to be of use to us, but it might get you out of trouble some time. Besides, it's small enough to be easily hidden."

The pistol was of Belgian manufacture, 6.35-mm caliber, with six cartridges in the magazine. Marek now carried it in a pocket sewn inside the front of his pants.

X

Darkness had descended on the city of Braunschweig, when Ziegler parked the Wanderer outside the restaurant. A sign on the wall near the entrance bore a proclamation from the Reich Cultural Board: SWING DANCING PROHIBITED! A subdued piano could be heard from inside the establishment, with a soft female voice crooning "Drunt in der Lobau," the song vying with "Lili Marlene" as the most popular in a nation starved for romance. When they entered, the reception of the SD party was comparable to the one received at the Schweizerhof, with Konrad himself rushing to greet Lammers like a long lost friend and chatting nervously while seating them.

"Herr Lammers, I have a few bottles of your favorite Münchener Bräu. I have aged it to gain an extra bit of strength."

He brought the beer, including one for himself, and poured it with a mien like a conspirator revealing the ultimate secret of the treasure chamber.

"Prost!"

They drank, and Lammers leaned back in his chair, letting the alcohol begin its soothing influence.

"Konrad, we shall want your finest Schnitzel with Klöse, and a bottle of Rüdesheimer."

"Certainly, Herr Lammers, such a pleasure to serve you again." As he turned to leave for the kitchen, the air raid sirens began to wail outside, warning that Hannover was facing imminent attack. Ziegler put his beer down with an oath. "*Die Engländer* are coming." Lammers' reaction was a heartfelt "*Scheisse.*"

The restaurant was rapidly emptying, the patrons leaving for a nearby public air raid shelter, while two waiters hurriedly collected payment from the departing guests. Konrad leaned over the SD table.

"I have had a small shelter installed for my personnel, more convenient than the public one. If you will follow me."

He walked ahead through the kitchen and a short corridor to a reinforced entrance.

"As you will see, it is quite comfortable, and it has an exit to the back street as well."

He waved to the cook who was shutting down the stove, "Heinrich, quickly, let us have three schnitzel before you cut off the heat."

Heinrich obediently turned back to carry out the order, while the SD party sat down inside the shelter together with the waiters, older men whose age group was still beyond the draft. Lammers took in their surroundings with unfeigned pleasure.

"*Fabelhaft*, Konrad, this beats the public accommodation. Of course, we need not run for cover, if we elect to finish our meal." It was always pleasing to remind people that they felt, and were, above the law.

"But of course," Konrad hurried to assure him, "and we shall not let the *Engländer* spoil your dinner." He bustled off to the wine cellar to fetch a bottle of Rüdesheimer. While the SD party was finishing the beer, distant explosions could be heard from the direction of the railroad yards.

The RAF's Bomber Command had become well skilled in a new concept of destruction from the air: carpet bombing, in which the heavy bombers methodically saturated a pre-selected area, usually industrial sites or rail yards.

X

It was early afternoon when Hawes returned to McKinnon's office. He placed on the desk several maps, the RAF issue of 1:500,000 which had useful details of highways, railroad lines and significant terrain features. They had been marked and annotated to indicate such bombing destruction along the planned route as aerial reconnaissance had shown to be not yet repaired.

McKinnon lit his pipe and looked inquiringly at Hawes: "What was Hansen's reaction to our using the private field at...what was the name of that place...Steensholt?"

"It was positive, sir. He says it has perfect east-west approaches, oriented with a view to prevailing winds, and the length is more than adequate."

"What about the owner, will he be cooperative?"

"Hansen is totally confident on that point, says the owner of the estate was very helpful in sending him off in the first place."

"Hmm...this will be different, though. It may carry some risk of being suspect of helping our side. You know the Krauts react badly to that."

"I pointed that out to Hansen. He suggested maybe the owner could establish some sort of alibi, like being away from home when the pickup takes place."

"It sounds like Hansen is a quick thinker. Well, let's look at the probable route."

They bent over the maps on which the railroad route from Amsterdam to the Danish peninsula had been marked.

"The train takes them through Hamburg," McKinnon observed, "a fairly short and direct route. There will be inspections, of course, so we will need to make their IDs and reasons for travel convincing. What do you propose for their rôles?"

The creation of credible rôles for agents being sent abroad always presented the most severe test for the organizers in Baker Street, for the lives of the agents hung in the balance. Would someone on the other side–a guard, policeman, customs officer, train conductor–at the first glance consider the person being checked a routine case, or would something, some trifling detail, arouse suspicion? McKinnon did not doubt that Hawes had burned midnight oil to make the group as inconspicuous as possible. Hawes looked at his notes.

"We might make Lund into a Swedish business man, who has traveled to Amsterdam to marry his Dutch fiancée, Miss van Paassen, and take her back to Sweden. Lund can easily handle that rôle; his Swedish is not perfect but good enough for any impromptu test. And it would open the possibility of their traveling all the way to Sweden, if the Lysander pickup is problematic. Hansen can be his own self, simply repeating his recent trip from Amsterdam to Copenhagen. As it happens, he had with him his old travel papers, which are being updated. In regard to Voigt, he could travel as having been invited to the Copenhagen University to fill a one-year teaching post. As for his ID and travel papers, we can start them here, but they would need to be completed with his own picture in Holland."

McKinnon cut in, "You have one highly qualified man who survived the latest dustup. Am I correct?"

"Yes, he's still intact in Groningen."

McKinnon thought for a while, absentmindedly cleaning his pipe. Hawes lit a Players. McKinnon put his pipe cleaner down, reached into his desk drawer to extract a yellow pack of Cremo pipe tobacco and started filling his pipe before he spoke.

"I like the fact that the group will be very low-profile. We should let Lund and Liz go all the way to Sweden only in an emergency, for the Swedes would immediately see through the scheme. That would compromise them, and if they pull this off, we will certainly want to use them again. Frankly, Jack, I can't see any weak points. That should probably worry me." He lit his pipe. Then he added, "What time will we meet with them here for send-off?"

"At five-thirty, sir." Hawes had expected the question.

X

On the night of the SD party's dinner at Konrad's restaurant, Bomber Command had scheduled two small raids. One went after the Krupp factories in Essen; the other targeted the Hannover railroad yards. The Hannover raid was laid on by 44

Squadron out of Waddington, using Avro Lancasters, the most recent addition to RAF's inventory. After the big bombers had crossed into enemy airspace, a few desultory AA-guns opened up, but their altitude made ground fire ineffectual. Pilot Officer Gary Holroyd had his number three Lancaster trimmed to perfection and relaxed slightly, reaching for his thermos of hot tea as he peered ahead. Visibility in the summer night was good enough for a night fighter to find them with any kind of decent ground control. German radar wasn't much compared with the British screen on the Channel coast, but luck might favor some nightly hunter.

At a Luftwaffe base near Oldenburg, Leutnant Fritz Steiner had finished a routine take-off check in his Heinkel 219 and received clearance to taxi. The twin-engine HE 219 was the Luftwaffe's best night fighter. Its two 1,400 hp Daimler Benz engines gave it both speed and maneuverability, and two 30mm cannons in the rear fuselage were angled upward at sixty-five degrees to attack Allied bombers from below, their most vulnerable aspect. Among night fighter pilots, this oblique innovation was spoken of with great respect and had been nicknamed *Schräge Musik*. Steiner loved this plane and its armament and used both expertly. He already had two RAF bombers to his credit. As he was climbing to altitude, the radio crackled its first message.

"Enemy bombers bearing one hundred sixty degrees."

Steiner acknowledged, swung onto the indicated course and firewalled his throttle.

Six minutes later, Holroyd's tea time was interrupted by the impact of cannon shells ripping into the Lancaster's left wing, and he glimpsed the silhouette of the HE 219 darting past below, turning in a wide arc to return for another pass. The outboard Merlin engine coughed and died, as he barked out a series of orders on the intercom.

"Jack and Ozzy, that fucker is circling left, get him when he comes back. Les, report on the number one engine."

The intercom briefly became a babble of replies, while the rear gunner, Jack Bolton, and Ozzy Roberts in the nose turret depressed their quadruple .303 Browning machine guns in readiness for the circling German. Engineer Leslie Neal's instruments told him the number one was a goner; he feathered the prop and reported.

Before he had finished, the Heinkel had completed its circle and was coming in fast. Steiner carefully lined up on the slower bomber, his finger on the cannon trigger for a second and deadlier rake of the Lancaster, which was not equipped for downward defense. Only the rear gunner could hope to get him in his sights while he was still at a distance. Well aware of their disadvantage vis-à-vis the German's *Shräge Musik*, the crew was waiting with bated breath. The silence was broken by a long burst from the rear guns, followed by Bolton's scream, "I got him! I got him! The fucker is on fire!" greeted by a bedlam of cheers.

It took Holroyd only a moment to make his decision. The Lancaster was a sweet aircraft, a pilot's dream; it performed well on three engines, and they were near their secondary target.

"We are going to diverge to our alternate. Will, give me a course."

Navigator Wilfred Carroll replied almost immediately, "Osnabruck at 142 degrees."

Fourteen minutes later number three Lancaster dropped its bomb load on the city of Osnabrück. The telephone exchange, a key point of inter-city lines received a direct hit.

x

The Schnitzel fully justified Konrad's reputation as worthy of the highest respect. The SD party was eating with obvious relish, determined not to let the move from restaurant ambience to shelter austerity spoil their dinner, and Lammers ordered a second bottle of Rüdesheimer. The noise from rolling explosions as the rail yards were demolished reached into the shelter like distant thunder, and the vibrations intermittently shook concrete from the reinforced ceiling. After many previous times of being on the receiving end of Allied air power, the experience had long since ceased to generate much excitement in the shelter occupants, but certain danger signals had been imprinted on their subconscious perceptions. One of the bombers had strayed from the carpet pattern, or maybe the pilot had special instructions, for his bombing run drew a line toward Knochenhauerstrasse. In the shelter this was instantly detected by the occupants from a series of explosions increasing in strength, as each bomb impact–like heavy footsteps–came nearer and nearer. Reinhart's fork paused in midair with a morsel destined for his mouth; Lammers' glass likewise froze as he had just lifted it from the table; Ziegler was reaching for some Klöse on the serving platter, but suddenly lost interest. Each person in the shelter knew that this run would come close, very close, maybe trace its imaginary line right across Konrad's establishment. That would leave only one hope, that the bombs would straddle the shelter, rather than make a bull's eye hit.

An immense crash confirmed that Konrad's restaurant had come close to the bull's eye position. One wall of the main room had disappeared, the three upper floors hanging without any visible support on one side, spilling their contents of furniture into the night darkness. The shelter's entrance from the restaurant had collapsed and crushed the chef in his seat. His helper and one of the waiters were partly buried under debris, the helper unconscious, but the waiter screaming in agony with one leg pinned under the collapsed mantel. Lammers lunged for the street exit and found it still functioning. The three SD people exited without a word, Reinhart holding his right arm, which was spreading a blood stain on his jacket.

The street in which they found themselves ran parallel to Knochenhauerstrasse. They started running around the block to get to the car and almost stumbled into the bomb crater, a gaping hole in the middle of the street, several meters deep and quite close to the building. The Wanderer had suffered a few dents from falling debris but appeared essentially undamaged. Lammers ordered Reinhart into the back seat, jumped into the front himself, and started snapping directions at Ziegler.

"Go straight, turn left at the first intersection. There is a hospital just a few blocks from here."

They arrived at the emergency entrance just as two ambulances brought the first casualties from the rail yards. Lammers flashed his ID at the receiving nurse and pointed to Reinhart.

"Take care of this man first."

Reinhart's injury was not serious. A nail in a piece of falling debris had torn a gash in his arm; it required a few stitches and a temporary sling, with which he was discharged, allowing the duty intern to turn to more needy casualties. When the SD people emerged from the hospital, the all-clear signal was sounding. On their way to the Schweizerhof, they dodged another bomb crater that had blown away the street side of a four-story building. The upper floors were on fire, while from the ground floor women were carrying out household linen, a rocking chair, vases and a grandfather clock, adding to items already on the sidewalk: a coffee table with a pile of carefully folded towels on it. An old man sat in an armchair as if still in his living room, staring vacantly at two passers-by who hurried along the sidewalk, looking straight ahead. The scene reflected the simple fact that this was part of every-day life in a country devoted to total war.

Chapter 8

At four o'clock in the afternoon Hawes led the little group assigned to execute SOE's operation *Dutch Treat* into McKinnon's office. When they were all seated, McKinnon spoke. His voice was calm, matter of fact, with no hint of excitement or urgency.

"We are breaking with our normal procedure of thoroughly training our people before sending them into the field. We do so reluctantly but yield to the dictates of circumstances that justify risks in war which would not be acceptable under peace time conditions. We feel the three of you are capable of carrying out the plan, as I shall now describe.

"You will tonight be landed in enemy territory at or near the town of Delfzijl on the Dutch side of the Ems River. From there you will proceed by bus or other means to Amsterdam. There you will contact a physicist at the Waals-Zeeman Institute which is part of the Amsterdam University. You will invite him to go with you to England, where his services are wanted in the war effort. You may tell him that Albert Einstein has suggested to us that we extend this invitation. If he agrees, you will take him with you to a certain Johan Winkler in Groningen, a retired typographer who will complete this set of travel permits and his personal ID. Use the code word "Documents" to identify yourselves to Winkler. The four of you will then travel to the Steensholt estate in Denmark, where we shall pick you up by plane when we receive your radio signal. A certain Ole Lauesen in Copenhagen will transmit the signal on your request. Before you leave here, Major Hawes will give each of you a typed sheet with all the information I have just given you. Between now and the time you are landed near Delfzijl, you will memorize the information. Captain Davies of Three Commando will collect your sheets before you leave his boat. Are there any questions so far?"

While talking, McKinnon had kept his gaze on the group, speaking entirely from memory. He now leaned back in his chair and looked from one to another of his silent listeners. Lund had a question.

"What if we cannot persuade Voigt to go with us?"

McKinnon's voice was level, and he met Lund's eyes.

"In that case you should warn him not to work for the Nazis. If he does so after this warning, he would be liable to prosecution after the war."

"Would it be acceptable to kill him?" Lund persisted.

"Yes." McKinnon did not hesitate. "Please understand that the potential ramifications of this man's work could be crucial to the war effort. We therefore will back you unequivocally, if you choose that course of action, but we do not insist that you do so. Are there any other questions?"

When there was none, he continued.

"I have here your IDs and travel documents. Mr. Lund, you will be a Swedish engineer, Svend Lund, from the gun manufacturer A/B Bofors. You have obtained permission to go to Holland and marry your Dutch fiancée, Elizabeth van Paassen. Your papers include a marriage certificate, dated two days ago, and you are now taking her back to Sweden. Mr. Hansen will be repeating the trip from Amsterdam to Copenhagen which he undertook a few weeks ago. The travel permits have been updated. As you see, we have kept your original names to make matters simple. The Gestapo in Copenhagen will certainly have Lund's and Hansen's names on file, but they will not be known at any checkpoint or border crossing you will be passing. In the envelope with your IDs you will find a small map of Delfzijl and one of Amsterdam, as well as Dutch money sufficient for the trip, plus some German and Danish money. You will also find some ration coupons that you will need if you eat in restaurants; without them, you might attract attention. Major Hawes has your weapons, loaded with full magazines, but no spares. Come in!"

The last was in response to a knock on the office door. The officer who entered wore the uniform of a Commando with a captain's insignia and carried a rolled up chart under his left arm. He was young, looked to be 24 at the most, and he moved with the agility of a competition gymnast. Liz was struck by the similarity between him and Lund. They both looked to be moving in a state of constant alertness. He saluted McKinnon, who turned toward him.

"Good evening Captain Davies. These are your charges."

McKinnon gestured toward the team and made introductions.

"Please run through your itinerary for tonight."

"Yes, sir."

Davies unrolled the chart and pinned it to the wall, visible to everyone in the room.

"This is an Admiralty Chart of the Ems River estuary. After leaving this office, we will go by car to Yarmouth; there we will board a boat operated by Three Commando. It will take us across a slice of the North Sea, entering the estuary approximately here." He pointed to a mark on the chart from which a stippled line led into the river. "At this point you will change into two inflatable rubber boats that will take you to your destination. The river bank on the north side is German, the south shore is Dutch. There is enough wind blowing tonight to muffle our movements, and we expect to be able to land you at two in the morning near the town of Delfzijl without causing any alarm. Should we be detected, we will withdraw and vacate the area. After landing you, Three Commando will make a sortie over here, on the German side of the river," Davies' finger touched a point near Emden, "just to keep enemy attention focused elsewhere. You may hear us visiting them."

X

It was dinner time when the SOE team and Captain Davies arrived on the pier where MTB 223 was moored. The Royal

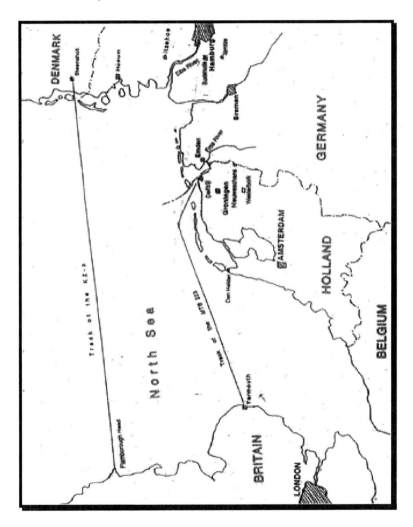

Navy did not bother to name these fighting craft but merely assigned a number to each, which did not diminish the passion with which the crews regarded their boats. Davies proudly led

his guests aboard and down the companionway into the cramped cabin below, on the way snapping out an order to cast off.

"You will have enough light for a while to study your papers, and we'll be eating shortly. This boat is powered by three 1,400 horsepower Packard engines; we'll be cruising at 30 knots, a bit noisy but otherwise quite a comfortable speed in the sea that's running tonight."

With that he left them and bolted back on deck. They heard the engines being started and felt the boat beginning to move. After a few minutes they cleared the harbor entrance, and the noise from the Packards changed from a murmur to a subdued roar, as the boat lifted and cut through the North Sea swell. For a while, the trio concentrated on memorizing the information on the handout sheet. Initially secure in the knowledge that she had conquered sea sickness early in her trip around Africa, Liz paid little attention to the motion of the boat, but she soon discovered that the motion this time was unpleasantly different. A crew member appeared with steaming hot soup, which she declined. She wedged herself in a bunk and found the motion easier to take when lying horizontal. Lund and Hansen also turned down the proffered soup and instead donned pea jackets and went on deck.

Liz tried to sleep, but the events since her first interview with McKinnon and Hawes crowded her consciousness, forcing themselves into repetitive review when she tried to relax. She had put her L tablet in a small locket she wore on a thin gold necklace. Would she have the courage to use it? Would she be able to shoot to kill if circumstances demanded? Scoring well on a cardboard cutout was one thing, facing a real opponent, a live human being, was something else. She liked her team mates. Lund and Hansen in their different ways were rock solid. With luck she might not be called upon to do any shooting. She fell into a half sleep, troubled by Nazi agents sneaking up to capture the team before it could carry out its mission.

She woke with a start, when the roar of the Packards suddenly diminished to a murmur, and the motion subsided to a gentle pitching. In the dim cabin light the clock showed one in the morning, as she tumbled out of the bunk and groped her way to the toilet. She splashed some tepid water in her face, climbed the companionway steps, and gratefully breathed the cold night air. A hand gripped her arm, and she heard Lund's voice saying, "Step over here and hold on to this." She put her hands on some kind of bracket and held on while her eyes adjusted to the gloom all around. No light was visible anywhere, as MTB 223 almost silently moved from the open sea into the mouth of the river, sheltered by sand banks on both sides. Lund and Hansen stood next to her, peering ahead, and she realized that someone on the bridge was stealthily conning the boat upriver. She shivered without a pea coat and decided there was nothing to be gained by getting cold.

"I'm going below again," she announced and went back down into the cabin. She reviewed her information sheet one last time, lay down and closed her eyes to get as much rest as possible before the landing made demands on her strength.

The cabin clock showed a little after two, when MTB 223 turned into the wind and held steady. Davies emerged from the bridge and called the team into the cabin.

"We are about here," he indicated on the chart a point just off Delfzijl, "and we will land you here, just west of town," he indicated a point on the beach. "You will be right near this road. We have not been detected, I am quite sure, and you should have enough time to get inland before daybreak without attracting attention."

He collected their papers, and they went on deck. He ordered the launch of the inflatable boat, which four ratings and a boatswain slid down into, three of them armed with Sten guns. Hansen and Lund followed, and Davies bent toward her, mumbling "Goodbye and good luck," as she grasped the rope fall, the last to slide down. The ratings started to row in a firm cadence, and the craft moved through the darkness that immediately obliterated the MTB. Liz looked at her wrist watch, trying to estimate the distance covered. The boat scraped onto the beach after eighteen minutes, so the MTB must be about three-fourth of a mile from shore, she thought. The team stepped onto a clayey beach, the boatswain called out a low "Goodbye, mateys," and the inflatable was gone.

The three walked to higher ground, passing some fish nets hung out to dry. They continued by a shack and found a narrow asphalt road less than a hundred yards inland, as shown on their map.

"I'll walk ahead," Lund said. Liz, keep about a hundred feet behind me, but keep me in sight. Hansen, you stay the same distance behind Liz."

He set off at a brisk walk, and twenty minutes later they passed through Delfzijl, proceeding toward Groningen. Just when they left the town behind, a flash from across the river lit up the sky, followed a few seconds later by the sound of a powerful explosion. MTB 223 had fired one of its torpedoes at a German target.

Three hours later a loaded milk truck on its way to a dairy in Groningen stopped and offered them a lift. Powered by a wood gas generator, it rumbled along at a thirty-mile per hour speed, while the driver tried to engage them in conversation. Liz kept him happy with a stream of small talk about their visiting family in Delfzijl. They parted at the dairy and got on a bus to Amsterdam, where they arrived in the afternoon.

x

In the morning after the bombing, the SD party got off to a late start from Hotel Schweizerhof. Reinhart was cursing his bandaged arm and needed his shirt and jacket cleaned. The damage to the Wanderer turned out to be more than first estimated. One rear window was broken and jammed. Ziegler rushed off to a workshop, one of a very few still operating. Bullying and threats moved a surly mechanic to immediate action but were useless in speeding the process of finding a replacement window.

"If this had been an Opel, there would be no problem," exclaimed the mechanic as he telephoned hither and yon, "but Wanderers are rare, you know. Fine automobiles, yes, but a problem when it comes to finding parts nowadays."

The elusive object was finally located, and a messenger on a bicycle brought it. Installation consumed another half hour, before Ziegler could return to Schweizerhof.

After departure their progress became slower as they drove westward, for they were getting into the regions of the Reich most exposed to RAF bombers. In a continuing effort to strengthen air defense and protect the infrastructure, the Wehrmacht was adding more and more anti-aircraft guns, so that nearly one-half of all German artillery was getting deployed on the home front, pointing skyward, being served by 1.1 million personnel, and consuming ammunition at a voracious rate. Despite these defenses, damage to the Autobahn and railway installations was everywhere in evidence, with bridges as favorite targets for the aerial attackers. Where the highway engineers had thrust the Autobahn's concrete spine in soaring arches across river valleys, the RAF had with deadly precision demolished the structures, so that the broken highway lanes ended in midair, with chunks of concrete dangling from torn rebars high above the valley floor. The necessitated detours were time-consuming, and it was after dark, when Lammers checked them into a hotel in Amsterdam. They had no taste for seeking out elegant restaurants or entertainment but ate sausages and baguettes in glum silence in a corner bar.

In the morning Lammers decreed that they go directly to the Waals-Zeeman Institute and collect Voigt.

"We will take him to our downtown office for interrogation and shake out of him the names of those responsible for creating and accepting his false identity. The little clipcock will sing, when I get my hands on him. Then we'll be off to

Hechingen with him, while our local boys chase down his helpers."

Lammers visualized with pleasure the report he would be able to submit to Himmler upon their return to Berlin.

When they arrived at the University, Lammers left Ziegler with the car and ordered a clerk in the reception to take them to the President's office. They were led through the administrative section on the mezzanine floor to an office set back in the oldest part of the building where floors covered with antique carpets pleased the eye and walls adorned with wood paneling from the Far East offered distinctive scents to the nostrils. President Andries Koenderink was in his late sixties, tall, spare, and possessed of a natural dignity. He received them with cool cordiality, as Lammers flashed his credentials with a curt, "Deutsche Sicherheitsdienst," and continued, "I wish you to take me immediately to Professor Aaldert Voigt."

President Koenderink was momentarily nonplussed before he replied with more than a trace of scorn in flawless high-German that contrasted with and clearly reproved the lower-class Plattdeutsch of Lammers.

"I am afraid I cannot oblige you, sir. Your people took Dr. Voigt away a couple of days ago."

Lammers' mouth opened involuntarily, no sound coming out, as the significance of the information and its implications registered. He sprang to the President's desk and began furiously to dial the Amsterdam SD office. After two unsuccessful tries, he bellowed at the clerk to get him connected, scratching the number on a pad on the desk and holding it under the man's nose with a hand shaking from furor. When the connection was made, he snatched back the receiver and screamed, "Give me Hagen." When Hagen came on the line, he continued, "Who in hell told you to pick up Aaldert Voigt and what did you do with the bastard?...You took him where?!...to Westerbork?!...Shit!...Get your ass out here on the double...no, at the University, meet me in Voigt's office."

He banged down the receiver and glowered at Koenderink.

"Now, take us to his office," and to the clerk, "My car is at the main entrance, tell the driver to stay there and wait for us."

x

Marek arrived at Amsterdam's Sloterdijk/Muiderpoort station at noon. Like the rest of Europe's railroad stations, Slot/Muider had been transformed from its normally sedate peace time routine to hectic wartime activity, as the movement of goods and people hitherto handled by highway transport now was shunted onto the railroads. Throngs of travelers mobbed the station day and night, waiting, eating, sleeping, watching baggage, caring for old people or children. Marek instinctively appreciated the safe anonymity any mob affords the individual, as he surveyed the scene. He had little experience with city life outside the Ghetto, but leisurely observation as he moved around the station area told him how to proceed. On a map of the city he found the university, and he memorized the way to get there. Then he made a brief reconnaissance of the station's immediate neighborhood and succeeded without ration stamps in buying a loaf of bread in a nearby bakery. By the time he was ready to start out, it was too late in the day, and he decided to sleep on the floor in one of the waiting rooms among several dozen other stranded travelers.

In the morning he started early on the route he had memorized to the university. He ate breakfast in a café, reluctantly spending two marks of the small hoard of German money Dr. Panowicz had given him. He explained to a sympathetic waitress his lack of ration coupons by claiming to be from Czechoslovakia and on his way to study at the Amsterdam University.

He arrived at the university and inconspicuously blended with a few students as he surveyed the layout of the part of the main building housing the Waals-Zeeman Institute. He found his uncle's name on the faculty guide and at length realized that the Voigt office number indicated its location as being on the second floor. He went to the wide stairway off the main entrance hall and started to ascend.

X

When she slid under the comforter in her bed at Hotel Albert, Liz did not think she would be able to sleep. The events of the last twenty-four hours kept running through her mind as if insisting on review and attention. The nauseating hours on the boat, the clandestine landing, and the subsequent hike and bus trip to Amsterdam had been amazingly easy and at the same time taxing. She was in enemy territory, where one incautious word or move would be fatal. It would probably be good procedure to review their moves up to this point. Before the thought had completely established itself, she was asleep.

In her dreams, the recent events took on a menacing aspect. From the moment they set foot on Dutch soil, they were pursued by non-descript but murderous Gestapo, getting into fire fights in which her small Browning misfired, or she saw the bullets leave the barrel only to drop lazily to the ground a few feet away. The enemies triumphantly closed in around the team and she was seized by a German soldier who flung her to the ground and bent over her.... She woke with a start, as Lund was shaking her awake.

"Rise and shine. We have a busy day coming up."

His steadiness felt like balm, totally removing night fears and agitation, and she suddenly felt without the slightest doubt that his demeanor would be the same under fire. She sat up and smiled. No matter how this venture would turn out, she was determined not to let the team or SOE down.

They had breakfast at the hotel and set out for the university on foot. Lund estimated it would be a 45-minute walk, which proved about right. While walking and out of earshot of other pedestrians, they discussed the best way to approach Voigt.

"Liz, you are the one looking most like a bona fide student," Lund said, "so you can find out the location of the Institute and of Voigt's office. When we get to his office, Hansen and I will go in and talk with him, while you hang around as our backup. I'll try to leave the door cracked."

They entered the main building, an 18th century edifice that had witnessed generations come and go while wars and other calamities haunted the continent. The student body had shrunk from its peace time size, but the team arrived at a break between classes and blended with the students milling around on their way to the next session. In the hallway of the faculty offices there were no students. Liz kept back some thirty feet from the others, as they went slowly down the hall, reading the name plates on the office doors. Liz saw her companions stopping at a door, knocking, opening and entering. Hansen was ahead but stopped just inside, forcing Lund to stop on the threshold. Hansen turned toward Koenderink, trying to assess the situation.

"You must be Dr. Voigt, and we'd like to have a word with you, but I see you have visitors. We can come back later, if that would be convenient."

Before Koenderink could answer, Lammers cut in.

"Shut up and step inside."

Hansen ignored him, still looking at Koenderink and pleasantly repeated, "We can come back later, if we may?" His right hand moving casually toward the Walther in his back pocket. In a flash of speed the two SD agents had their guns out and pointing at the SOE people. In a loud and frightened voice that sounded down the hall, Hansen cried out, "Hey, don't point guns at us, we haven't done anything."

Lund who was also in their gun sights, took up the cue, speaking German.

"Hey, we just have a greeting for Dr. Voigt."

"Shut up and get in here." Lammers moved a step forward and waved his gun menacingly.

They both stepped into the room, while Koenderink watched uncertainly, backing up against the far wall. Lund walked a few steps to the right, nudging Hansen who followed him, leaving clear lines of fire for Liz.

Down the hall Liz kept her eyes glued to the bulletin board, staring at but not registering class schedules. Her two team mates had suddenly been neutralized. Worse, they were caught and destined for torture and death unless she took action. Quick action. *The quicker, the better the chance of success.* She stuck her hand into her shoulder bag and closed it around the little Browning. God, it felt small and insignificant. How many opponents was she up against? There might be more than one, and she would have to deal with all of them. The hall was empty, as she pulled out the gun and pulled the slide to slip a cartridge into the chamber. She walked down the hall, breathing deeply. She could hear voices through the half-open door and she stopped two steps short to listen. Lund was speaking in German.

"We are from Denmark and have a greeting from Dr. Voigt's cousin, Professor Hans Voigt, at the University of Copenhagen. Here you see my ID. I am leaving Amsterdam today."

He was speaking in an unnaturally loud voice, as someone frightened, and she realized it was for her benefit. Could they convince the ones holding them up?

"You must be German police, maybe Gestapo? Well, as you will see from our papers, we are harmless."

Lammers sneered. "Voigt could not have a cousin in Denmark using the same false name. Turn around and put your hands on the wall. Kurt, check them for weapons."

Liz heard motion inside. This would be the best moment. Holding the small gun in a two-handed stance, she pushed the door open with her foot and took in the scene. Reinhart had just stuck his gun in his belt and was reaching to check Hansen. Lammers had his gun aimed at her companions but turned his aim toward her as the door swung open. He was a fraction of a second too late. Her bullet struck him in the heart, tumbling him backward to the floor. Before he crashed, her second shot hit Reinhart, also in the heart, as he frantically grasped to pull the pistol from his belt. Before Reinhart was down, Lund's gun was out. He put it back in his pocket.

"Thank you, Liz." Lund and Hansen spoke almost in unison, but she looked at them without comprehending and took an uncertain step toward the nearest chair. She needed to sit down.

Chapter 9

Marek mounted the stairs to the second floor and arrived at the end of the hallway, still some forty feet from the Voigt office door, when Hagen and Wolff from the Amsterdam SD office walked briskly past him. Ahead he saw a young woman with a gun push a door open and fire two shots in rapid succession into the office, which must be his uncle's. In a fraction of a second Hagen and Wolff had their guns out, covering the last few feet in a dead run. Hagen rushed through the door and struck Liz from behind, sending her to the floor while her Browning bounced off the desk harmlessly and landed in a corner. Both SD men had their guns trained at Lund and Hansen before either could reach for theirs.

Marek slowed to a stop a few feet from the door and started digging for his well-concealed gun, while listening to the people inside. All the action from the time Liz pushed the door open had taken but seconds until Lund and Hansen again were at gunpoint.

"Hände hoch!" yelled Hagen, seeing both of them reaching for their guns. "Turn and put your hands on the wall. Erich, get their weapons!"

Wolff stuck his Walther in his belt and then expertly checked Hansen, extracting a Walther.

"Verdamt!" shouted Hagen at the sight of the weapon, *"Englische Agenten!"*

The words electrified Marek. If these were British agents, he would have to act *now*. He pulled back the slide on his Browning and slipped a round into the chamber. Then he gripped the small gun with both hands to steady his aim, stepped to the open door, and took in the scene in a quick glance. Hagen was covering Wolff who was starting to search Lund. He saw Marek out of the corner of his eye and started to swing toward him, but too late. Marek shot him through the temple. Wolff spun around and grasped the gun in his belt. When his hand closed around it, Marek fired twice, both shots aimed at the heart. Wolff staggered, lost his grip on the pistol and crashed to the floor.

Without lowering his gun, Marek looked at Lund and Hansen and asked in halting English, "Are you British agents?"

They hesitated. Liz in the meantime was getting up from the floor. She looked at Marek and smiled sweetly.

"We sure are."

x

At RSHA headquarters in Berlin SS-Brigadeführer Werner Best knocked on the door to Himmler's office. When his knock was acknowledged with a curt *"Herein,"* he entered, clicked his heels and saluted the Reichsführer with a *"Heil Hitler."* Himmler looked up from the document he was reading.

"What brings you here, Werner?"

"Herr Reichsführer, you may recall sending Lammers to Amsterdam to pick up a certain Aaldert Voigt, a Jew whose real name is Blum, and take him to Hechingen. I have just received a weekly report from our SD at the SS Zentrale in Amsterdam. It mentions that Voigt, alias Blum, has been taken to Transitlager Westerbork by our local *Mitarbeiter* on their own initiative."

Himmler frowned.

"Since when do we use local initiative in such important matters?"

"It is most unfortunate, Herr Reichsführer. I shall find out who is responsible and have Blum brought back. Maybe Lammers has already taken this step."

Himmler did not comment on this speculation. It just occurred to him that Blum might have been expedited from

Westerbork onto Auschwitz, that Blum even might be gassed right now and beyond any retrieval. Not that he gave a damn about that rotten Jew, but it could make the SS look as if one hand didn't know what the other was doing.

"Listen, Werner, get in touch with Westerbork and tell them to have Aaldert Voigt alias Abramek Blum ready to be picked up and taken out for interrogation. If by any chance he has been put on a transport to Auschwitz, stop the train and dig him out."

"Jawohl, Herr Reichsführer."

"Keep on top of this matter, Werner, until it is resolved, and keep me informed. And make sure your people don't exercise that kind of initiative again."

Himmler laid a slight emphasis on "your people," just enough to remind Best who would be considered responsible, should the affair take a bad course.

"Certainly, Herr Reichsführer. I shall take immediate action."

He saluted and rushed back to his office suite, where his secretary looked up with surprise at his hurried arrival.

"Fräulein Thöne, get me the Westerbork Transitlager in Holland on the phone. Very urgent!"

He waited impatiently, his fingers drumming on the polished surface of his desk, while Giselinde Thöne was speaking to the supervisor, trying to get the call through. After some discussion, she knocked on his door and reported.

"The connections to Holland are down, and they cannot estimate how long it will take."

"Then never mind the telephone, send the message by telegram."

She scurried out and came back, steno pad in hand. Best gathered his thoughts and dictated.

"Sturmbannführer Erich Deppner Transitlager Westerbork Stop Priority Stop Prisoner Aaldert Voigt alias Abramek Blum will be picked up for interrogation Stop Have the prisoner ready for departure immediately Stop Confirm that the prisoner is ready Stop Brigadeführer Werner Best Stop"

He was pleased that the wording gave no hint of any mistake having been made. This should put things in order. As soon as the confirmation arrived, he would inform Himmler.

"Fräulein Thöne, take one more telegram." Best leaned back in his chair, again phrasing his words with care.

"Agent Hagen Amsterdam SD Stop Report immediately on the unauthorized arrest and transfer of Voigt alias Blum to Westerbork Stop Brigadeführer Werner Best Stop"

X

Marek smiled back at Liz and lowered his gun.

"Then I go with you. My name is Marek."

Avoiding a pool of blood, Lund stepped over two bodies, closed the door, turned and smiled at Marek.

"You have certainly earned our gratitude. Very impressive marksmanship."

He turned toward Koenderink, who was standing behind the desk, "Are you Aaldert Voigt?"

Koenderink sat down heavily in the desk chair and took a deep breath. The action of the last two minutes had been too fast and furious to allow him time to think or guess at the identity of the people he was now facing. Marek's question and the reply from Liz tended to raise more questions rather than clarify the situation. He looked at Lund and shook his head.

"No. Dr. Voigt was taken away by German police three days ago. I am Dr. Koenderink I am president of the university, and I gathered from this man's telephone conversation in my office," he pointed to the dead Lammers on the floor, "that Dr. Voigt was taken to Westerbork, which is a transit camp for Jews being transported east for resettlement."

Lund thought for a moment. If the other side had decided to make use of Voigt in their research, they would have taken him to Germany. It made no sense to put him in a transit camp. He looked straight at Koenderink, trying to assess whether he could trust him.

"Why would they send him to Westerbork?"

Koenderink met his gaze calmly.

"Who are you and why are you looking for Voigt?"

Lund weighed his words for only a few seconds before answering. There was no time for equivocation.

"As you heard, we are in fact British agents, and we have come to offer Voigt passage to England, if he wishes to go with us. Now, tell me why they would take him to Westerbork."

Koenderink did not hesitate.

"I cannot be sure, of course, but I suspect that they have discovered Aaldert Voigt's true identity. He is actually Jewish, and his real name is Blum."

"Abramek Blum, and he is my uncle."

The voice came from Marek, and they all turned toward him, but before the conversation could go further, Lund broke it off.

"Listen, this is not the time or place for discussion; we have to get out of here quickly. Hansen, take the IDs and other papers off these four," he swept with a gesture the bodies on the floor, "Liz, put their weapons in your handbag. Marek, you'd better take one of the Walthers, the Browning is too small to rely on."

He turned back to Koenderink.

"Is there anything else you can tell us that might be of help in getting to Voigt, I mean Blum?"

Koenderink shook his head.

"I cannot think of anything, but before you rush off, be aware that the car these two men came in is parked in front of the main entrance, and the driver is waiting there for them."

Lund said, "And the car these guys came in is probably there as well, maybe also with a driver waiting."

"I don't think so," Hansen cut in, jangling two keys on a key ring, "for these are car keys that one of them had in his pocket."

"Let's hope you're right," Lund said. "Now, Dr. Koenderink, it would help us greatly, if you can delay reporting to the authorities what has taken place here. Perhaps you can pretend confusion about our identities and say you believed us to be German SD and the dead bodies to be English agents. I'll leave it to your judgment, but we can use any delay you can provide before the SD spreads the alarm."

He held out his hand and Koenderink took it with a quiet "Good luck."

When they emerged from the office, half a dozen students had gathered down the hall by the stairway, attracted by the sound of the gunfire. As they approached, Lund waved a Walther at the crowd and hissed at them in German.

"German police, get out of this hallway."

The students scattered and fled.

The main entrance was separated from the street by an esplanade a hundred feet wide where students were coming and going. Lund stopped at the open doors in the entrance and looked toward the street curb where the Wanderer was parked with Ziegler in the Driver's seat. Parked just behind it was an Opel Kapitän without a driver in sight.

"Hansen and I will handle the driver and go in the black sedan. Liz, take the keys and check whether they are for the Opel. If so, you and Marek take that and follow us. If the keys don't fit, we all go together in the sedan. Hansen, you walk around to the driver's side and make sure he doesn't try to bolt and make a run for it. I'll get in next to the driver and talk with him. Let's go."

He walked with Hansen across the esplanade at an oblique angle, not aiming directly for the Wanderer. Ziegler was sitting relaxed, looking ahead through the windshield. When they were close enough, Hansen diverged, cut behind the Wanderer and opened the left front door. Ziegler turned in surprise and looked into the barrel of Hansen's gun. Simultaneously, Lund opened the right front door and slid into the seat next to Ziegler.

"Just put your hands on the steering wheel and sit still," Lund admonished, removing Ziegler's gun from its shoulder holster. Still speaking German, he continued, "Hop in the back, Hansen, and keep your gun trained on his neck. At the first sign of trouble, blow his brains out, as we did to his *Mitarbeiter.*"

As Hansen got into the back seat, Liz said through the open door, "The keys fit."

Lund acknowledged with a grin and addressed Ziegler again.

"Show me your ID."

Ziegler fished it out of his pocket and handed it over.

"Your name is Ziegler. Hm...Now listen, Ziegler, your two *Mitarbeiter* are dead, because they didn't follow my orders." He poked Ziegler in the ribs with the gun barrel. "Do you understand?"

Ziegler grunted. Lund went on.

"You will now drive us to Westerbork Transitlager, where I have some business to transact. Drive at normal speed. At the first hint of trouble, you die. *Verstanden?*"

He poked Ziegler again, this time receiving an actual answer.

"*Ja.*"

"Alright, then. *Los!*"

His hand shaking, Ziegler started the engine and put the Wanderer in gear. As they moved away from the curb, the Opel followed.

X

Back in his office, President Koenderink slumped into the armchair at his desk. He sat motionless for several minutes, breathing deeply, trying to get his thoughts into an orderly pattern. The events of the last fifteen minutes were beyond anything in his experience. Actually beyond anybody's experience, he told himself. His next move would be critical: it could mean life or death for these young people–one of them an attractive young woman, looking like she could have been one of his students. And she had killed the two SD agents, swiftly and expertly. He reached for the telephone and dialed an Amsterdam number.

"May I speak with Commissioner Brugh, please...Filip, this is Andries Koenderink. I need to talk with you. It is urgent. Can you come to my office?...No, it cannot wait, it is very urgent...Thank you..."

He went to a mahogany cabinet in the corner of the room and returned to his desk with a bottle of vintage port and two glasses. He sat down and poured himself a glass, emptied it in two gulps and leaned back in his chair with his eyes closed. He was still sitting like that when Police Commissioner Filip Brugh walked into his office more than a quarter of an hour later. Brugh and Koenderink had been close friends since their school days, and both were near retirement after long careers in their chosen fields. Brugh had risen to head the police department's Office for Internal Security, a counterpart to the Nazi SD but clean and respectable as befits any police agency in a democracy. Like Koenderink, he was tall and well proportioned, and he moved with the ease of a natural athlete. He walked across the office and sat down across from Koenderink, as the two shook hands.

"Andries, what has happened? This is a fine port, and you look like you need a glass."

"Truthfully, Filip, I already had one, and now we'll have one together."

He poured two glasses and for a moment they savored the fragrance and taste of the sweet wine. Koenderink leaned back in his chair, cleared his throat and slowly and carefully told his friend the events of the morning from the time Lammers had arrived in his office until his telephone call to Brugh.

"So you see, Filip, I want to give these young people the best chance to carry out their mission. It sounded like they might try to get Aaldert Voigt alias Abramek Blum out of Westerbork. Do you think that is possible? And what course of action should I take now?"

"First let me ask you a couple of questions. Can you think of any reason why the British want to get hold of Blum?"

"No. I have been trying to think of a reason, but I can't come up with anything."

"What is Blum's field of expertise?"

"He is a physicist, deals with physics on a mathematical basis, same as Albert Einstein."

"Hmm...doesn't tell me much. I remember Einstein went to America. And you say this Lammers from SD flew off the handle when he learned that Blum had been taken to Westerbork. It sounds to me as though the Germans have some plans of their own for Blum. Could it have something to do with military research?"

"If it does, I can't imagine what or how."

"Alright, now to your question about what to do. Andries, when Himmler's henchmen find out that four SD agents have been killed and that you have witnessed the shootout, they will move heaven and earth to take revenge. The British agent's suggestion that you delay reporting by pretending to be confused won't fly. Not for two minutes. Particularly not if you delay enough for the killers to get away. They will get the true story out of you by torture, every word of it, just as you told it to me. You are going to have to go underground, you and Eva both. That will save your life and, in the bargain, it will give the British agents the maximum time, as you wanted."

Brugh did not add that his own life now was on the line together with Koenderinks. Under torture, Koenderink would divulge their meeting and discussion over vintage port. Koenderink was not a fool, and he suddenly realized the danger in which he had placed his friend.

"Filip, forgive me, I now see that I have put you in danger as well by rashly calling you."

"That cannot be helped. Normal people cannot be expected to take the kind of precautions needed in the world Hitler is trying to create. Listen carefully, for we don't want to make any mistakes. Is Blum's office locked?"

"No, we lock the building at night, but we don't usually lock faculty offices."

"Do you have a custodian or such with keys to those offices?"

"Yes."

"Call him and tell him to go immediately and lock Blum's office, but under no circumstances to open the door."

Koenderink made the call and looked at Brugh who was scratching notes to himself on a pad.

"What next?"

"I think we have one small piece of luck: it's years since I have visited you here, and the clerk and your secretary don't know me–I think."

"No, they are both relatively new, have been here less than four years."

"Good. Your secretary was not in the outer office, and I didn't give my name to the clerk, just marched right in. Isn't there another entrance to your suite?"

"Yes, it's behind that drapery, very old fashioned, a narrow passage I never use."

"Good, I'll leave that way. Now, what you have to do is walk out of here and not come back. Is there anything in your papers the SD should not get their hands on?"

"Nothing I can think of, but I'm not sure where to take Eva."

Koenderink was voicing the insistent problem faced by ordinary citizens forced to drop out of sight in countries under German occupation. In reality, the Underground was only a concept, not an actual place standing ready with succor for people pursued.

"I have a small beach cottage near Leiden. Here is the address; the key is on top of the window frame to the right of the front door. I will come down to see you there on Sunday. Now let's take a last sip and be on our way."

The two old friends emptied their glasses, got up and walked out, Koenderink through the front office, Brugh by the back exit.

x

Magda Gruber, secretary in SD's Amsterdam office, read the telegram a second time. Hagen and Wolff's hasty departure this morning had given plenty of cause to worry. Magda had been Hagen's mistress for more than a year and took a proprietary interest in everything concerning him. There had been no word from Hagen or Wolff since their departure–in itself contrary to regulations–and now it was close to quitting time. She went down the hall and knocked on the door of Albrecht Meyer. He was with the Gestapo and a friend of Hagen's.

Meyer listened to Magda, read the telegram, and got up from his chair. "You say they went to the university, to the office of Voigt? You were right in telling me, Magda. I'd better look into it." He buzzed his partner on the intercom. "Hans, we're off to the university."

Only an hour later, a courier handed a telegram to Best's secretary, Giselinde Thöne. She read it, made a note in her log, and took it to Brigadeführer Best.

"This just arrived from Westerbork in reply to your telegram earlier today."

Best read it with satisfaction. Deppner had the prisoner ready to be picked up. Everything was in order. A small slipup by Hagen, just over-eager to perform. Still, a reprimand would be proper, to remind him always to communicate without delay.

Now he could tell Himmler that things were well in hand, had been so all along, in fact. He got up from his desk.

"Very good, Fräulein Thöne. I am now going in to see the Reichsführer."

x

Hansen said, "What it hangs on is our ability to play the rôles of SD personnel to perfection, and I just don't think we can pull that off." He was summarizing a lengthy discussion he and Lund had carried on about how to extract Blum from the

Westerbork camp. They were speaking their native Danish which conveniently kept Ziegler from understanding or even guessing about the subject of their deliberations. While they talked, the Wanderer, followed by the Opel, had covered most of the distance to Westerbork with Ziegler at the wheel, keenly aware of the gun in Hansen's hand pointed at his neck.

They rode in silence for a while, both turning over in their minds the formidable problem which no one had anticipated. Lund said, "Do you suppose we could scare this character into cooperating and help us getting Blum out?"

Hansen pondered the question. "It might be worth a try. He certainly knows their procedures. He would know whether SD can just walk in without further authorization and fetch one of the people. He'd know what to say."

Lund said, "We'll stop close to the camp and I'll tell him what to do. Watch him carefully then, and observe his reaction."

Half an hour later Lund ordered a stop about a mile from the camp entrance, the Opel pulling up close behind. Lund turned toward Ziegler, who was staring ahead with a glazed look.

"Alright, Ziegler, you have obeyed my orders so far. If you keep doing that, you will come out of this little affair alive. As I told you, your two *Mitarbeiter* disobeyed my instructions, so they died. Would you like to cooperate and save your life?"

Ziegler turned and for the first time looked into Lund's blue eyes that never wavered. "What do you want me to do?"

"Nothing very complicated." Lund said over his shoulder, "Hansen, call the others."

When Liz and Marek had crowded into the back seat with Hansen, Lund spoke slowly in German.

"Now, we will pick up Blum from the Westerbork camp down the road. Hansen will drive the Wanderer and I will sit in front with him. Ziegler will sit in the back next to Marek and will pretend to be in charge. Marek who is our finest marksman will be with him. I will use Lammers ID, Hansen will use Reinhart's ID, and Marek will use Wolff's ID. So, I am Lammers, you two are Reinhart and Wolff." He paused briefly. "When we get to the camp, Ziegler will order the guard on duty to find Blum, so that we can take him with us to Amsterdam. Ziegler, repeat my instructions."

Ziegler fumbled for words. "Uh...I will tell them to release Blum to us."

"Very good, Ziegler. Marek and I will be ready to kill you the instant we think you are forgetting your rôle. Is that clear?"

Ziegler nodded. Lund poked him in the ribs with his gun. "Speak up, I can't hear you." Ziegler said, "Yes, I understand."

They left Liz with the Opel and drove the last distance to the camp entrance. Westerbork comprised several rows of barracks, wooden huts surrounded by a single barbed-wire fence. It was guarded less elaborately than the concentration camps, and the SS personnel was largely over-age draftees, men in their late fifties and older. The gate was opened by a sentry with a rifle slung over his shoulder. When Ziegler flashed his ID with the words, *"Deutsche Sicherheitspolizei,"* he waved them on to the guard hut, a slightly larger building with a drive-around in front, a short distance from the gate.

As they got out, Lund mumbled in Danish to Hansen, "Keep the engine running."

Lund and Marek walked a step behind Ziegler, as they entered the front room, a large office with two doors in the back wall and the corporal of the duty watch, an SS Unterscharführer, seated at a desk in the center. He carried a P-38 pistol in a belt holster, and Lund judged him to be close to sixty. When Ziegler mentioned Blum, he came to attention.

"Oh yes, he is in there," he pointed to one of the doors, "we have had him ready for you since the telegram came. I will inform the Sturmbannführer." He picked up the telephone.

Ziegler stood perplexed for a moment, then walked over and opened the indicated door with Lund and Marek at his heels. The room was bare except for a small table with two chairs, hinting at its use for interrogation. On one of the chairs sat Abramek Blum. Before he could speak, Marek said in a low voice in Yiddish, "Be still, uncle."

"Come with us," Ziegler said hoarsely, turning around and addressing the Unterscharführer, "we will take him with us."

"Certainly, as your telegram informed us, but please wait a moment for the Sturmbannführer, he is on his way."

Ziegler was not a quick thinker. Sweat was running down his forehead as he looked inquiringly at Lund, who calmly said, "Of course. And we want to pay our respects to the Sturmbannführer." He turned to Marek, "Put the prisoner in the car and come back here."

Marek took his uncle by the arm and walked him outside to the Wanderer. He opened the back door and almost pushed his uncle inside with another admonition to be quiet. Just then, Sturmbannführer Dr. Erich Deppner arrived at a half jog, puffing heavily.

An alcoholic physician, Deppner had been employed in the extensive euthanasia program. The Nazis had designed the program to "purify" the national body by selecting for killing and disposal certain categories of "useless" people with whom the new German superstate did not wish to be encumbered. With the assistance of the medical profession, the SS collected thousands of citizens from hospitals and other institutions, taking them to be murdered and cremated. Deppner had recently been installed as camp commander at Westerbork and was eager to impress his superiors in Berlin.

They all gathered in the guard office, where Deppner shook hands with the visitors.

"As soon as I received the wire from Dr. Best, I had the prisoner prepared and ready for you. Will you be taking him to Berlin? He seems a rather ordinary specimen, hardly worth much attention. But of course, headquarters knows best. I have already informed Dr. Best of my actions."

At this moment, the other door in the back wall opened and two more SS guards appeared from what looked like a bunk room for off-duty guards. They both carried P-38s, and this encouraged Ziegler to desperate action. He jumped on Marek and screamed, *"Englische Agenten,"* at the top of his lungs.

Marek easily twisted out of his grasp and in one continuous motion drew his Walther and fired, hitting Ziegler in the chest. It took the guard corporal and the two recent entrants a couple of seconds to react, more than enough for Lund to draw his gun and shoot the guard corporal while Marek took down the other two SS arrivals. Deppner, unarmed, dashed for the door, but Lund's bullet hit him, as he opened it, tumbling him across the threshold.

Marek ran to the bunk room door and checked inside.

"Nobody in there."

Lund said, "Let's get out of here."

Outside, they jumped in the car, and Hansen sped toward the entrance. The guard at the gate had heard the shots popping like distant firecrackers and was unslinging his rifle. Lund rolled the car window down and fired two shots in his direction, which made him jump out of the way as the Wanderer crashed through the gate and tore up the road with wire and debris trailing from the front bumper and the smashed headlights.

Hansen at the wheel grinned happily and said, "It's a good thing we brought two cars."

Chapter 10

Hansen braked to a stop a few feet from the Opel, and Lund said, "We'll leave the Wanderer here."

They all got into the Opel, Hansen and Marek in the back with Blum between them. Lund got in next to Liz and pulled out one of the small maps McKinnon had provided. Turning toward Liz and Hansen, who was seated behind her, he spoke unhurriedly to his team mates. "Liz, you drive, and not too fast. I'll be your navigator. Our next step must be to get Blum fixed up with ID and travel papers from the forger in Groningen, but I don't like to drive there in full daylight. What do you two think?" He twisted toward Marek and added over his shoulder, "Marek, explain to your uncle that Albert Einstein would like him to come to England, and we are here to help him get there."

Marek launched into a torrent of Yiddish, his uncle listening with an expression of bewilderment.

Hansen said, "I agree with you that we had better be discreet. Maybe we can find a place out of sight and lie low till after dark."

"How long do you think it will be before they find the bodies in Blum's office?" Liz wanted to know. "I am sure the Germans will mount a major search, and before that starts, we must dump this car somewhere and become inconspicuous travelers." She was driving at moderate speed, restraining a natural urge to hurry away from Westerbork. The road they were on wound through farmland with scattered villages; it was almost devoid of traffic, like roads everywhere these days.

Hansen started to laugh. "Liz, it doesn't matter if they have discovered the bodies at the university. We just left five more dead Germans behind at Westerbork, and all hell must be breaking loose at this very moment."

Liz slowed down and pointed across a field to an empty cattle shed, open on one side. "How is that for a place to wait for dark?"

"Sure." The others agreed, and she turned onto a track leading there from the main road and nimbly maneuvered the car into the shed. The Opel was not completely hidden, but a passer-by would likely miss it.

"It will be dark in about three hours," Hansen said. Referring to the retired typographer whose name McKinnon had made them memorize, he continued, "We need something to eat; do you suppose Johan Winkler will be able to feed us?"

Lund chuckled. "Right now, just some dry bread would taste good. But we have to finish planning. Look at this map of Groningen. Winkler's house is marked here; we will drive to this intersection and walk the rest of the way." He indicated the two points on the map. "Hansen can drive the car to the bus station, over here," he pointed again to the map, "and leave it there. Maybe pursuers will start looking at bus schedules, while we will be getting on the train. Let's hope so. Are you comfortable with this plan?"

He looked at his team mates, keenly aware that the experiences of the day had not had time to register fully. A panicky state of mind would not be surprising, but as a team they could not afford any such reaction. He thought of a comment by Paloheimo during combat in Finland: "Never allow yourself to be afraid. Fear is too dangerous."

Outside, rain was beginning to fall, and inside the car it was almost too dark to recognize faces.

X

Jack Hawes looked through a handful of messages brought by courier from Bletchley. It was his last task of the day, usually an interesting one, but his lower left arm was painful tonight. It made little sense, for it was no longer there, but the doctor had told him to expect these "ghost pains" from time to time.

Distractedly he leafed through the intercepted German signals, decoded and translated. Ever since they had broken the German Enigma code, Bletchley had been a British trump card in the Empire's struggle with the Nazis. It was like intermittent peeks through a keyhole into the inner workings of the other side.

Absentmindedly Hawes rubbed the stump of his arm while scanning a wire from RSHA to SD in Amsterdam. Hmm...the telephone lines must be down. What was this, "Voigt alias Blum"? Voigt was the object of operation *Dutch Treat*. Hawes suddenly became alert, quickly pawed through the rest of the wires and extracted one from RSHA to Westerbork that mentioned Blum. He read both messages several times before calling McKinnon.

Five minutes later, having read the messages several times, McKinnon put the messages on his desk and looked at Hawes seated on the other side.

"Alright, Jack, what's your interpretation?"

"Well, sir, Blum is a common Jewish name. Perhaps that is Voigt's real name, and he assumed the Voigt alias to elude the Nazis."

"Yes, that seems pretty clear, but why does Best try to get him out of Westerbork before sending the wire to SD in Amsterdam? Who or what alerted him to Voigt's existence in the first place? But those questions are of academic interest compared with this one: How will Voigt's disappearance from the university affect our team?"

Hawes made a gesture of exasperation with his right hand.

"They may be walking into a trap–may already have done so. And there is absolutely nothing we can do about it from here."

McKinnon was recalling their faces. He'd had very serious reservations about sending a team with so little preparation. He shook his head.

"Let us hope they have sense enough to keep their heads down and get on the next train to Denmark."

"Will you be reporting the situation to the Minister," Hawes asked.

"Jack, what can we report? At this point we don't actually know what the situation is, where our people are, whether they have made contact or are involved," McKinnon replied wearily. "We can only wait and see what the morrow will bring us, if anything."

X

The house was located on the outskirts of Groningen, surrounded by a small garden given over entirely to potatoes and vegetables. A tarnished brass plate on the front door bore the name Johan Winkler. With Liz standing silent beside him, Lund knocked and was answered by muffled barks of a dog and slow footsteps approaching inside. They heard a key unlocking, and the door opened half way. The man peering out at them was holding the door handle with one hand, a large dog of indeterminate breed with the other. He was a wizened old fellow, beetle-browed, with a bush of grizzled moustache and a tuft of beard on his chin. Liz thought he looked like someone in a Bruegel painting.

Speaking Dutch, she said, "Documents."

Winkler froze, looked around furtively, and finally motioned them inside, quieting the dog with a stern "Hush, Saskia". The house smelled musty and was dimly lit with a 25-watt bulb, the usual means of keeping within the electricity ration. When he closed the door behind them, Liz continued, "There are three more coming; we thought it best not to come all together."

"There are five of you?" Winkler exclaimed, "why so many? Who sent you?"

Having difficulty following the exchange in Dutch, Lund broke in, "Do you speak English?"

Winkler shook his head but apparently understood the question and seemed relieved. A knock on the door brought Marek and his uncle, and Winkler led them down a narrow stairway into a basement workroom and turned on the light. Liz explained that the Germans were after Voigt, and as members of the Underground they were helping him to escape to Sweden. Lund handed him the partly finished ID and travel papers SOE had prepared for Voigt, and as the topic of their conversation settled on Winkler's expertise, the old man began to relax. After a while Hansen arrived and reported that the Opel was parked at the bus station, which was closed for the night.

It was after midnight when Winkler put the last touches on his handiwork. Marek's uncle had a set of papers no police or custom agent would challenge, and Marek's own travel orders had been changed, so that they now directed him from Amsterdam to Copenhagen, and all their travel papers now specified going via Groningen.

"This way," Winkler explained, "you can get on the train here in Groningen. If someone asks you why you are not going directly Amsterdam-Hamburg and so forth, you will have to give a plausible reason for stopping here."

By then he had become talkative, and even Saskia, his large mongrel, had accepted the visitors. His wife had died six years ago. The couple had been childless, and his reclusive existence with only Saskia for daily companionship suited him eminently for the Underground. When he learned that they had not eaten since breakfast, he had emptied his meager pantry to feed the visitors. They perused his train schedule and on his recommendation decided on a slow local train as having fewer police checks than the express across the border. Then they bedded down on the floor in the small living room.

x

The early summer morning was exquisite, so much so that Brigadeführer Best walked part of the way from his flat to RSHA headquarters in Prinz Albrecht Strasse. With Hitler holed up at Wolfschanze, his East Prussia headquarters, Berlin seemed relaxed, comfortably on the margin of Allied bombing range, and the nation had recovered some of its equilibrium after the Stalingrad debacle. A pleasant bustle of Berliners taking up their daily chores filled the air, as Best left the outdoors behind and strode into his office. He acknowledged his secretary's greeting almost cheerfully and quickly scanned the status report and his agenda for the day.

Five minutes later, pleasure drained from Best's existence as he stared in utter disbelief at the telegram Giselinde Thöne had just handed him. A prisoner–*their* important prisoner–spirited away by armed criminals, three guards and the *Lagerleiter* himself, an SS Sturmbannführer, murdered in the process. This was outrageous, and totally unprecedented. The immediate task at hand was to avoid blame and responsibility and mobilize the appropriate people. He would need to be able to report that vigorous action was unfolding before he could take the bad news to Himmler.

"Fräulein Thöne, call Schmied from Department IV-B4 in here, immediately." Westerbork was in Schmied's jurisdiction, better start with him.

Obersturmbannführer Jürgen Schmied marched into Best's office two minutes later and clicked his heels with a cheerful "Heil Hitler."

"Schmied, what is going on in your camps? Can't we pick up a Jew for interrogation without running into this sort of mayhem? What kind of guards do you have, to let such things happen?" He threw the telegram at the hapless underling standing at attention before him.

Schmied was young for his rank, having worked his way up in record time from Hitlerjugend into the SS, helped along by a family relationship with the Gauleiter of Westphalia. He caught the telegram, read it, and with a look of incredulity read it a second time. Best was beginning to see how this problem could be handled with minimal blame falling on himself.

"Now, Schmied I want you to get to the bottom of this, and I mean immediately, if not sooner! Find out the details and take all appropriate steps to recapture this Jew, Blum, before he can slip away." Best felt better already. Every word he spoke placed the burden of responsibility on other people.

"*Jawohl*, Herr Brigadeführer!"

With a heel click Schmied turned and fled from the office, almost colliding with Giselinde Thöne, who was entering carrying another telegram. Her hand shook slightly, as she passed it to her boss and stepped back, waiting. Best read the message, carefully reread it, and let go an obscenity that shook Gigi Thöne more than the message.

"Well said, Werner." The voice came from Heinrich Erhardt, who was walking through the door Giselinde Thöne had left open. "What's with your people, can't they take better care of themselves?" He threw a telegram on the desk and dropped into a chair. Erhardt was in charge of the Gestapo section and of equal rank with Best. They were at frequent loggerheads from the endemic friction and turf fights in the Nazi bureaucracies.

While forming a suitable answer, Best mentally calculated how many departments of the RSHA potentially had jurisdiction and responsibility. Fortunately there were several.

"I thought your people had the Dutch situation well in hand after we enabled you to break up the main Underground apparatus in the country," Best answered smoothly. "Why do you allow armed ruffians to run wild doing mischief?"

Their verbal sparring went on for a while, ending as usual in a standoff, before they settled down to agree on a plan of action. That they were dealing with SOE agents was beyond doubt. No local saboteurs would display such nerve and tenacity. Albrecht Meyer had already sent a perfect description of Voigt, derived from university files, but all they knew about the perpetrators was that one was a young female. Where would the SOE agents take Voigt? Best and Erhardt agreed that France was the most likely for transit to Britain, but Best postulated Sweden as well, though less likely. They decided to cover the southern exits from Holland with Gestapo and SD personnel, while calling in Kripo, the Criminal Police, from

Bremen to watch the northern border crossings from Holland into Germany.

Erhardt picked up a sheet of notes and got up from his chair. "Alright, Werner, with luck we should get Voigt back, or whatever his name is. I will talk to Nebe of Amt V, to get his Kripo people moving."

"We'd better," Best replied gloomily. "You're lucky, you don't have to report this mess to the Reichsführer."

X

In their heavily strengthened underground headquarters Air Marshal Sir Arthur Harris and his staff bent over aerial photographs and maps of Hamburg and the city's outlying districts. Dedicated to the proposition that his force could win the war independently, "Bomber" Harris had chalked up a record that went some way toward justifying such a claim and steeling the resolve of his nation. An early test of air power as a war winner had come three years before in the Battle of Britain, when the Royal Air Force had stood off the Luftwaffe and prevented *Seelöwe*, Hitler's plan to invade Britain, from materializing. At a time when only the Soviets could challenge Hitler on the ground, destruction from the sky became the one way by which Britain could strike at Germany effectively, meeting the demands of Churchill and of the Soviet ally who was bearing the brunt of ground fighting.

Harris took over Bomber Command in February of 1942, and the decision was made to level the cities of Germany, incapacitate her industry, and oblige her Luftwaffe to defend its home. Heavy bombers began to reach the Command in strength, and in the winter 1942-43, sixteen major night raids on Berlin caused a temporary exodus from the city and the closing of all schools. In May, Harris unleashed a thousand-bomber raid on Cologne that stunned the city's inhabitants. Precision bombing was still in its infancy but was being offset by "carpet bombing," the saturation of an entire city section,

138

and by a corps of specially equipped and trained pathfinders which preceded the bombers to locate and mark the targets.

Tonight Bomber Command had the city of Hamburg in its sights. Drawing on hard-won experience to date, the attackers would use the pathfinders, following with the first wave using fragmentation bombs. The second wave would dump incendiaries to overwhelm any firefighting that the city could mobilize. To make sure on this point, the attack would continue over a period of nine nights, a series of sledgehammer blows as yet not seen in this war. And tonight the attackers would employ a new technology intended to protect the bombers. Codenamed *Window* it would disburse clouds of tinfoil strips, hoping to confuse enemy radar.

Harris straightened up from his crouch over the map table, stretched and lit his pipe. This was the most elaborately planned bombing operation they had ever undertaken. Appropriately given the biblical code name *Gomorrah*, it was intended to destroy Hamburg as a functioning city, literally to wipe it off the map. He thought of Hitler's boast not so long ago, that he would "erase the city of London."

His eyes still on the map, Harris blew out the match and drew a cloud of blue smoke from his pipe.

"Now, let us see who will erase whom," he thought.

X

In Kripo's Bremen office, August Huber carefully studied the summary message from Berlin. Huber was a veteran of thirty years of dedicated effort to rid his society of criminals, big and small. He was methodical, patient and thorough. A Jew forcibly extracted from the Westerbork camp by a group of killers believed to be foreign agents, assumed to be on the run, possibly for Sweden. All border crossings were being alerted, but Bremen Kripo should check all train connections. There followed an excellent description of the escapee.

The Kripo worked as plainclothes detectives, and this was a welcome departure from a dull routine of catching small-time black market operators. First, a look at the map would provide an overall view of the situation. If in fact the Voigt fugitive were moving fast for Sweden, he could be on one of the trains that arrived today from Groningen. The connection from Bremen would be the evening express train to Hamburg, leaving at 1712 hours. Huber looked at his watch. There was just enough time to get on that train, but he also had to deploy his force, which consisted of three men. One would have to watch the Neuschans border crossing; one was needed to prowl the Bremen railroad station; and Huber would take the third with him for backup, obviously not too great a precaution if Voigt was traveling with these foreign killers for protection.

He started to bark orders while putting on his jacket. His men responded with disciplined speed, as he turned to his second-in-command. "Cetti, you come with me. Take your PPK and an extra clip."

They boarded the last car in the train with only moments to spare and sat down in the compartment reserved for the conductor. Huber told him only that they would be looking through the train for a fugitive, an almost routine occurrence, and Huber gave no details. When the conductor left the compartment to begin his checking of tickets, the two experienced policemen agreed on how best to proceed without prematurely alerting the fugitive or his protectors, if any. Starting at the back of the last car, Huber would scan each compartment through the glass panels in the doors. If a compartment contained an occupant approximating Voigt's description, Huber would signal Cetti for a second opinion. The method was fast, efficient and attracted no attention, as Huber resembled just another passenger looking for a seat.

The last car yielded only one suspect, and Cetti thought him to be too old. The two policemen checked the next car and cleared it: no suspects.

They continued their progress.

Chapter 11

WAAF Lieutenant Ann Curtis knocked on the office door, entered without waiting, and placed the usual mug of Bangalore tea on McKinnon's desk. He was on the telephone, and what she heard from his end of the conversation told her both the caller and the topic. "Yes, Minister...but we cannot tell at present...of course, Minister, but it is unlikely..." It was another call, one of several, about the ill-fated *Dutch Treat* project. The Minister didn't want to inform the Americans that SOE had been unable to extract Voigt. At least not until all hope was lost.

The Bletchley messenger was waiting in her office with some intercepts, lingering beside the tea pot. She smiled as usual. "Sergeant Donovan, help yourself; stop looking like an ownerless dog." She looked at the intercepts, stopped half way through, and gasped. This would stir things up. She actually <u>ran</u> back to McKinnon's office, her heels clicking against the floor, and walked back in without knocking. Her chief had finished the conversation, was in the middle of sipping the pungent brew that would start his day properly. Without speaking, she placed the intercepts before him on the desk and stood back, waiting. His glance at the first one made McKinnon put his mug down with a jerk that spilled hot tea on his knee. He swore, as he got up, trying to brush off his trouser leg and snapped at Ann to fetch Hawes. Moments later, they were poring over the intercepted messages, seven in all, flying back and forth between RSHA headquarters and Westerbork and Amsterdam. Hawes was the first to speak.

"I *thought* Lund might be rather too quick to shoot his way out of a tight spot."

McKinnon said, "Apparently they shot their way both in and out of this Westerbork camp, and they seem to have Voigt with them, wherever they are now."

"Yes, sir, but both the Gestapo and the SD are in an uproar, pulling out all stops in their pursuit. Can our people hope to get away, with every available enemy agent on their trail?"

"I don't know." McKinnon reached for his mug, regaining his composure. "But trying to catch up with them may prove fatal to more Germans yet."

Hawes read the intercepts a third time and brought up a question that also puzzled McKinnon. "Apparently three *men* broke into Westerbork. Could they have mistaken Miss van Paassen for a man?"

"Doesn't seem possible, Jack, even in the heat of battle, but who else could it be? A local Underground fighter?"

"I don't think there has been time for them to make contacts, and we did not supply them with the name of anybody suitable for such an assignment."

They continued their discussion over tea without arriving at any satisfactory answers. McKinnon was about to call the Minister but thought better of it. Time just might answer some of the questions first.

x

The mainline express out of Bremen picked up speed through the suburbs. In a second class compartment Liz leaned against Lund, her make-believe husband, and closed her eyes. The trip had gone smoothly so far, actually amazingly so. Winkler's train advice had been good, for they had encountered no police patrols of the kind Marek had experienced. The border crossing itself had been uneventful. The German customs officers already looked at Holland as part of the Reich, as virtually all of Europe was destined to become, when Hitler's Neuordnung, the vaunted New Order, was fully implemented. They had bought second-class tickets and in order not to attract attention had split into two groups: Lund and Liz as a couple in one car, while Hansen, Marek and Blum rode as individual travelers in the next car forward.

The subdued beating of the iron wheels over the rail joints and the rhythmic motion of the carriage began to lull Liz into a state of almost hypnotic relaxation. Yesterday's violent encounters, her own swift killing of two German agents...had she really killed two people, without a moment's hesitation? And why did she not feel any regret or horror at the memory? It bothered her no more than the shooting of spurfowl near the Kikuyu shambas. Was she a natural, cold-blooded murderer? Sinking into sleep, she only heard Lund and Hansen in unison repeating, over and over, "Thank you, Liz...Thank you, Liz..."

With her head drooping only inches from his face, the fragrance of her hair had an unsettling effect on Lund. Like most Danes his age, he had enjoyed several affairs but had kept from permanent entanglement with the opposite sex. Liz was different, he realized, very unlike any other woman in his experience. He was not sure how or why, but she was different, and she attracted him. After the initial shock at working with a female agent, he was secretly pleased that SOE had cast them in their rôles of husband and wife, and he found himself toying with the idea of converting it into reality. Then he pulled himself mentally back to the present and looked around at their fellow travelers.

They were sharing the compartment with another couple, a Marine officer and his wife on their way to her parents in Hamburg, and in the far corner sat a middle-aged physician from the Rheinland on his way to the military hospital in Lübeck. Outside in the corridor a man stopped and looked through the glass panels in the door. For a fraction of a second his eyes met Lund's, before they continued to sweep the compartment, stopping at the physician in the far corner. The outside observer studied the Rheinländer for maybe half a minute before moving on, and Lund suddenly realized that his careful scrutiny was not that of a casual passer-by looking for a seat. Before he could react, another man stopped and peered in, immediately fixing his glance on the physician and subjecting him to the same careful study before moving on.

Lund inclined his head over the sleeping Liz, so that his lips touched her ear, whispering her name. She responded, drowsily at first, then snapped fully awake. She tried to straighten up, but Lund tightened his arm around her and whispered into her ear, "Relax and listen. There are a couple of characters snooping around in the corridor. They may be looking for us. I'm going out to check on them."

She nodded, and he got up, stepped out, and closed the door behind him. A few travelers were standing in the corridor, smoking or viewing the scenery. At the forward end, Huber and Cetti were engrossed in quiet discussion that quickly ended, with Huber walking into the next car to continue checking. Lund lit a cigarette and strolled up the corridor, squeezing past Cetti and noticing the slight bulge under his jacket on the left side. So, he was carrying a holstered gun. Lund proceeded leisurely, passing first Huber and then Marek's compartment. At the forward end of the corridor, he stopped and opened a window slightly to draw out the smoke from his cigarette while he looked out. When Huber reached Marek's compartment and gave it his long scrutiny, Lund became certain, that he was seeing two police agents searching for a man of Voigt's description. Of course, they would have a perfect description of Voigt, but none of the SOE team. Obviously, the physician in his own compartment had been briefly considered suspect, mostly because of his age.

Huber signaled Cetti and moved on, stopping next to Lund, who lit another cigarette and studied the countryside. After a quick check of his own, Cetti arrived and nodded. They were standing so close to Lund that he could hear their mumbled conversation without being able to make out the words, but it was not necessary. They showed every sign of being satisfied that they had found their man. Would they arrest him here? If they tried, he would have to intervene, although this would be an awkward place for a shootout. He felt the gun in his back pocket. No, one of them was heading back through the train, while the other stayed to keep an eye on the compartment. Apparently they were going to wait, perhaps making their move at the arrival in Hamburg.

x

The air attack on Hamburg was reaching a crescendo. With cool concentration and dead on schedule, the first line of pathfinders had released yellow illuminators, followed by lines of red 250-pound target indicators for the 746 bombers coming in behind. The leading Lancasters and Stirlings unloaded huge numbers of incendiaries that lit fires over a large area and sent the city's firefighting teams racing to tackle the blazes. Then came waves of Wellingtons carrying 2,000-pound parachute mines fused to explode fifty feet above ground, knocking down large buildings in order to block streets with rubble. The final waves comprised Halifaxes and more Lancasters with a mix of 8,000-pound blockbusters and delayed action 1,000-pound bombs to destroy water and gas mains and trap fire services in blocked streets.

The resulting enormous devastation was what Bomber Command had planned on. What had not been anticipated was a hitherto unknown phenomenon: the firestorm. Only half an hour into the raid, the congested dock area, eight square miles of narrow streets and clustered warehouses, was transformed into a lake of fire which superheated the air to 1,800 degrees, a monster conflagration creating fierce currents of flame rushing through the streets at speeds up to 150 mph, incinerating debris, trees and people until the asphalt street pavement started to burn and spread the fire yet further, making it a hurricane of fire such as had never been witnessed before and against which human resistance was powerless.

When day dawned, more than forty thousand people were dead. Of the remaining inhabitants, one million started an exodus in all directions from the stricken city, families and single individuals fleeing by the nearest passable road. A dozen main arteries provided escape to the surrounding farm land, with more than twice that many secondary roads adding to the total, all of which quickly became filled with traffic. The fleeing populace made use of all manner of wheeled conveyances, but most simply departed on foot. Trains inbound to the city were halted as far away as possible and rerouted or returned to their point of departure. Germany was used to being a bombing target, but the scale and effects of the Hamburg attack were unprecedented.

x

SS-Reichsführer Himmler glowered at Brigadeführer Best, as the latter finished his brief verbal report.

"Are you telling me, Werner, that this Blum, this piece of Jewish dog meat, has slipped away? And that in the process we have lost five of our Sicherheitsdienst and four of our SS, including a Sturmbannführer?"

Himmler's voice never rose nor otherwise betrayed agitation. It merely grew ice cold, which always unsettled his underlings more than any bluster or visible anger could have done. His demeanor matched his position, which in practical terms was that of possessing unlimited power. Best's voice, on the other hand, had noticeably changed. It was subdued with a note of pleading in it, that betrayed a state of mind near desperation.

"Herr Reichsführer, it appears that the British have sent a large group of well trained agents just to steal away this one scientist. We had not been provided with any advance intelligence about this."

"You understand, Werner, that I expect you to recover this fugitive Jew. What are you doing to accomplish that?"

"Herr Reichsführer, we are using SD, Gestapo and Kripo to watch all Dutch border crossings. We are having Kripo search the places where the shootings took place and do scientific analysis of all evidence. We are sending Blum's description and photograph to all our field personnel, including the Feldpolizei, which has also been alerted."

Himmler's face did not change its expression of cold displeasure and disapproval.

"You understand, Werner, that events such as this one sooner or later come to the notice of the Führer. Before that happens, it would be well if you had recovered the fugitive."

Himmler waved Best away with a slight hand gesture, and the flustered Brigadeführer quickly saluted and fled the office.

X

Half of the car's compartments were marked Nichtraucher for non-smokers, which made a few passengers use the corridor to indulge their smoking habit. Lund slowly strolled through the corridor, briefly lingering at each window to observe the landscape. At the end of the corridor Cetti kept a sharp eye on the compartment occupied by Marek, Blum and Hansen. Passing their door Lund caught Hansen's eye and with an imperceptible head motion signaled him to come. At the time Lund reached the end of the corridor and went into the next car, Hansen emerged, stretched, yawned, lit a cigarette, and went in a pretended search of a toilet. In the next car he caught up with Lund, who quickly, quietly, and in Danish explained the situation. Hansen was not surprised.

"At home our criminal police would have caught up with us before this," he said. "So, you think they won't make a move until we arrive in Hamburg?"

"That's my guess. Remember, we must have a reputation by now, so they will want reinforcements. Two men on a moving train against an unknown number of armed agents of unknown description, not an attractive proposition. Let's be prepared to kill them, if we have to, but it would attract less attention to knock them on the head or handcuff them to the baggage rack or something like that. They must be carrying handcuffs in their pockets."

As they were talking, the train had slowed and was pulling in to a small provincial town. As it came to a halt, they saw a sign on the station building proclaiming the name Sprotze, and to their surprise the platforms were crowded with people.

Lund said, "This is an unscheduled stop; obviously, something's going on. You'd better get back and put Marek in the picture. I'll get Liz, and we'll hang around and keep an eye on you three."

Lund had barely time to get Liz before the conductor came through the corridor, calling out the announcement that the train would not go any farther toward Hamburg but would return to Bremen shortly. In the general hubbub caused by that information Lund put his arms around Liz and whispered in English, "Two plainclothes police have recognized Blum and may try to arrest him. Stay close enough to back me up."

He walked rapidly to Marek's car, where the corridor was filling up with new passengers, prompting Cetti to take up position at the door to the compartment. Hansen emerged and, seeing Lund in the corridor, turned in the other direction, putting Cetti between them. At this moment Huber arrived. Hurrying past Liz and Lund, he whispered a few words to Cetti, and the two opened the door to enter the compartment. Hansen stepped up right behind Cetti and poked the barrel of his gun into his back, while Lund did the same to Huber, urging them inside.

Lund said quietly, "Don't try to pull your guns, we've got far more firepower."

There were two uninvolved passengers in the compartment, who hurriedly fled when Marek ordered them out. When they squeezed past Lund, he whispered just one word to them: "Sicherheitspolizei". They disappeared, asking no questions of the feared security police.

Marek relieved the two Kripo of their weapons, IDs, and two sets of handcuffs, which he used to lock each of them to a cast iron seat leg. From their bent-over position they could see neither through the window nor the door. Then Lund gave them an earnest admonition.

"I will be standing outside the door. If I hear any sound from you, I will open the door and kill you both."

The corridor had filled with people who kept back respectfully at the sight of the guns. Lund addressed them quietly: "We are Deutsche Sicherheitspolizei. Do not go near to this compartment before we return."

Without undue haste, they left the train and blended into the refugee stream outside the station. Choosing the road leading north and west toward Cuxhaven, Lund told Marek and his uncle to walk ahead with Liz some fifty feet behind them, while he and Hansen followed another fifty feet back, and the density of traffic allowed them to keep visual contact without being noticed as a group.

As soon as they were deployed and walking, Lund said, "We've got to get around Hamburg, and this road will get close to the Elbe River west of the city. If we can get across the river and maybe to Itzehoe, we should be able to get a train and continue north. What do you think?" He was speaking in Danish, which came naturally when he and Hansen were alone, and it prevented others from eavesdropping.

"That sounds reasonable," Hansen said, "and I'll welcome being on ancient Danish ground again. But I wish I had better hiking shoes. Never thought the spy business involved so much walking."

x

Johan Winkler returned to his house in an elated state of mind. He had just seen off his SOE visitors on the train to Bremen, and although he did not know anything about their mission, he sensed that it was an important one. He bent down to open the lower left drawer of his desk and reached for his last pack of Schimmelpenninck, precious javai cigarillos. They were now irreplaceable reminders of peacetime smoking pleasure, long since gone from the shelves of his tobacconist, where tasteless European tobacco had taken their place. He had saved these to be smoked only on occasions when celebration was in order, and the activities last night and this morning were certainly worth celebrating. He lit one of the little cigars, leaned back in his chair, and savored the utter pleasure of the moment. What fine young people, these SOE agents, relentless foes of Hitler's legions, pitting their intelligence against mindless force. He wished he had been young enough to take a more active part in fighting the Nazi forces of evil. All he could now contribute was his skill in making forgeries to confound the evil ones.

He was roused from his daydreaming by the sound of the doorbell, followed immediately by simultaneous crashes as both the front and the back door were kicked in, furious barking by Saskia, and a pistol shot and yelp from Saskia. Three civilians rushed in from the front hall, two grabbed Johan, clapped handcuffs on him, and did a quick body search. The third, evidently the one in charge, asked in German, "What's your name?"

"Johan Winkler."

The leader nodded, satisfied. From the back two more civilians entered the room, one of them wrapping a handkerchief around his left hand to stop the bleeding of a deep gash from Saskia's teeth. His partner swept the pack of Schimmelpenninck into his pocket and searched the desk drawers. After looking through the rest of the house, they hurried Winkler into a car waiting outside and departed before attracting attention.

Chapter 12

In the Amsterdam RSHA office, Gestapo agent Hans Bauer walked into Albrecht Meyer's office and sat down.

"Listen to this, Albrecht. We picked up an old printer in Groningen today who has been making false IDs for the Underground. I just got through squeezing him, and he told us that this morning he put an SOE group on the train to Bremen and on to Denmark. They must be the same ones who killed our SD people at the university and then snatched the Jew Voigt out of Westerbork. Voigt was actually with them. I have only my notes here, no time to write up a report yet, but I thought, better tell you right away."

Galvanized, Meyer pulled his feet off the desk and snatched the notes from Bauer's hand.

"*Mein Gott*, Hans, this is what Berlin is screaming about...I see...descriptions of the Engländer and everything. Prima! Can you get anything more out of this man Winkler?"

"Nah, he croaked on us, while he was hanging by his arms. Looked like a heart attack. But we got most of what he had, I think."

"Very, very good, Hans. I'll send a wire to Berlin and alert the Gestapo in Hamburg."

"Albrecht, our Hamburg offices are shut down. There has been some unusually severe bombing, and it's still going on."

"Hmm...then I'd better talk with Schwesing of GFP. We need some of his *Kopfjäger* to get on this search." Meyer spoke with a sneer, proud of the Gestapo's brainwork in contrast to the Wehrmacht's "head-hunting" and crude reliance on force. "If our fugitives have not passed through Hamburg, a patrol should be able to catch them in the train or elsewhere along the way."

Sonderführer Anton Schwesing of Geheime Feldpolizei Gruppe 131 looked up in surprise from the report he was reading, when Meyer from the Gestapo burst into his office. Five minutes later, he started telephoning. The lines to Bremen had been restored.

X

The road the SOE team had chosen had traffic moving in both directions, a common pattern whenever refugees spilled out of a metropolis in search of family or friends with whom to seek shelter. As night fell, the Royal Air Force bombers returned to continue to lay waste to Hamburg. Pathfinders were no longer required, as the city's fires had congealed into one mighty beacon clearly visible to the pilots from more than fifty miles away, and the moving mass of people could see the reflection of the fires light up the sky and could hear the bomb detonations as an intermittent, dull rumble.

In the darkness, Lund and Hansen had shortened their distance from Marek, and Liz had likewise closed up in order to keep them in sight. It was after midnight, and they had walked in silence for a long time, when Lund looked at his watch and asked, "What's your estimate of our average speed since Sprotze?"

Hansen thought for a while before answering.

"I'd say between four and five kilometers an hour. Blum is slow and keeps us from going any faster than that."

"That's also my estimate," Lund agreed. "I think we're far enough west to head directly for the river. I sure wish we had a good map. Let's take the next crossroad to the right."

He moved faster, caught up with Marek and explained his plan. Returning to Hansen, he said, "You were right about Blum. He is worn out and won't be able to keep up even this pace much longer."

There were no crossroads coming up, and the group shortly filed into a town which announced itself on a sign, barely legible at the city limit, as Buxtehude. At the city center a three-man army patrol had parked its Kübelwagen in the middle of the street and was scrutinizing the traffic, apparently checking certain of the passing refugees in the traffic stream incoming from Sprotze. The patrol wore Wehrmacht uniforms, but they were Geheime Feldpolizei, Secret Field Police, with the stamped white metal title bearing the monogram "GFP" on their shoulder straps. They had taken up positions with one man on each sidewalk and the third in the center by the Kübelwagen. As people walked or slowly rode by on bicycles, the patrol checked the passing faces with flashlights, only rarely going further by checking an ID.

Marek realized the danger too late and distanced himself from his uncle. The flashlight briefly illuminated his face before moving on to a refugee couple, searching out only the man's face. Then the beam swept to his uncle's face, and remained fixed.

"Stop! Your ID!" The voice permitted neither excuse nor delay.

Blum stopped, fumbled in his pocket, and handed over his ID and travel permit. The Feldwebel only glanced at it; he now had his P-38 unholstered and made a menacing gesture with it. "Go to the Kübelwagen." Blum started walking toward the middle of the intersection, and as they approached, his captor grabbed him and triumphantly called out, *"Hermann, ich hab' ihn!"*

Marek had stopped in a doorway, and in a matter of seconds the SOE team had caught up. Lund had observed what happened and said, "We have no choice but to take them out, now. Marek, you take the one on the other side of the street. Hansen, you take the one who stopped Blum. I'll take the one in the center. Liz, you're backup. Go."

Inconspicuous in the darkness, Marek doubled back thirty feet, crossed to the north side of the street and walked toward his target behind a group of three refugees. Hansen and Lund made a similar but shorter circuit to approach the center, while

Liz trailed behind them. The two patrol soldiers on the sidewalks were armed with 9-mm P-38 pistols, but the one by the car had an MP 38/40 submachine gun hanging across his chest. He was studying Blum's papers when Hansen and Lund both fired, almost simultaneously. The two Germans went down, while nearby people in a confused melee struggled to get away from the shooting.

The third soldier came bounding toward the Kübelwagen, the sound of his jack boots audible even over the traffic noise, pulling out his weapon as he ran. Marek was racing after him, still twenty feet behind and unable to get a clear shot because dark human shapes kept getting between them. As if in a nightmarish dream, Marek saw his quarry bearing down on Lund, who had bent down to detach the submachine gun from the body of the German. When he saw the soldier he was pursuing aim at Lund, Marek raised his gun to attempt a shot while running. Before he could fire, two shots rang out on Marek's left, and the soldier fell, the momentum of his motion carrying him another few feet, while the gun slipped from his hand and clattered to the pavement at Lund's feet. Looking to his left, Marek saw Liz holding her PPK with both hands. As he watched, she dropped to her knees and began to shake, still clutching the gun.

From the Kübelwagen Hansen yelled, "I got it started, get in, everyone!"

Almost automatically, they piled into the vehicle. Hansen gunned the engine and took off, horn blaring, on the road to the northwest. Wielding the submachine gun in the front seat, Lund let off a couple of short bursts in the air to help clear the road ahead of them.

X

Brigadier McKinnon took a sip of the morning tea WAAF Lieutenant Ann Curtis had just placed before him. He restrained himself from asking for the Bletchley messages;

3

after all, he knew Ann would have brought them with her if the morning messenger had been there.

Ann Curtis knew her boss and with a woman's intuition could read his mind through the surface imperturbability he routinely assumed. She started to leave but stopped momentarily with her hand on the door knob.

"The Minister called fifteen minutes ago and asked if we had any further update on our operation *Dutch Treat*."

"Oh? About our *Dutch Treat* team?" McKinnon sounded as if he himself could barely remember the project. "Yes, of course, he is quite interested in that one."

Ann smiled inwardly. "I told the Minister that the Bletchley intercepts had not come in to us yet this morning."

"Oh, yes, very good, Ann. If anything should arrive, better bring it in directly, so I can inform the Minister."

At that moment, Major Hawes walked through the half-open door holding in his one hand several intercepts.

"Good morning, sir. I just relieved the Bletchley messenger of these and thought you might like to be informed right away."

McKinnon put his mug down and scanned the four messages, pursing his lips as if to whistle, but no sound came. Ann had closed the door but remained in the room.

"If this hadn't come from the Germans themselves, I'd have found it hard to believe." He picked up the phone and dialed. "Good morning, Minister. McKinnon here. I thought I'd just let you know that our team is still operative and progressing through the enemy territory...yes, they had a brush with the Kripo...yes, that's the German criminal police...no, minister, no killings, but they left two police agents handcuffed in their railroad car...yes, Hamburg is being hit very hard, they may not be able to get through...yes, Minister, right away."

McKinnon hung up and looked at Hawes. "Jack, how long can they stay ahead of the bloodhounds?"

x

155

"There, there is a road to the right!" Lund was pointing, and Hansen careened onto the narrow road and slowed the Kübelwagen. There was no traffic here, but deep ditches on both sides of the road showed this to be a marshy borderland along the nearby river. The hooded headlights showed only the closest features ahead, as they passed through a hamlet of half a dozen farm houses, all dark and silent. After another mile, the SOE team spotted a track to the right, and Hansen turned onto it. They crept along barely fast enough to resister on the speedometer, wary of more and more drainage ditches, until the river itself became visible ahead.

Squeezed between Marek and his uncle, Liz rode with her eyes closed, taking in the scents of the marsh grasses and the watery world ahead. To blot out the memory of the soldier tumbling to the pavement when her bullets struck him, she forced herself to think about the surrounding landscape, comparing it with the familiar African hills she had left behind.

The track ended at a large shack and a small pier where a fishing net was suspended on a simple frame of branches.

"Check out the shack," Lund said to Hansen, "and I'll take a look at the pier."

Hansen forced the door, walked into the shack, and struck a match. Most of the floor space was occupied by a partly built boat that rested upturned on two saw horses. The match flickered out, and he struck another. Along the wall oars, rope and tools indicated that this was a fisherman's workshop, perhaps an enterprising farmer augmenting the yield of his soil with some fruits of the river Elbe gliding near by. He went back out and jogged down to the pier, where Lund was testing the water depth.   "If there is enough water here, we could ditch the car and continue in that, if we can find oars," Lund pointed to a rowboat, moored to the pier.

"They're in the shack," Hansen said, "How much water is there?"

"About two-and-a half meters."

"That should be enough to hide the Kübelwagen, at least for a short while."

"Alright," Lund said. "You get the oars and I'll get the car ready."

Lund drove the car to within a dozen feet of the drop-off side of the pier, while Liz and Blum got into the rowboat. After Hansen had made the boat ready with oars and row locks, he joined Marek and Lund at the car.

"I got this to weigh down the accelerator" he said, brandishing a heavy sledge hammer and adding with a grin, "let's see if we can make this baby jump."

They started the engine, and Hansen leaned into the car, holding down the clutch pedal with his hand, while Lund put it in low gear and placed the sledge on the accelerator. The engine roared, Hansen let go the clutch and was swept aside when the car surged ahead, sped off the edge of the pier, hit the water several yards out, and was swallowed by the river.

Carefully, they all got in the boat and cast off. Lund took the oars and began a slow cadence that moved them to midstream. They began to relax, soothed by the gentle motion of the small craft and the serenity of the stream, as they floated in utter silence. The change of pace helped purge from their memory the encounter with the patrol and their frantic dash from the scene. They were not alone on the river. In the summer night's semi-darkness they could make out other boats heading downstream, no doubt carrying people fleeing the burning city that still lit up the sky behind them.

X

Sonderführer Anton Schwesing burst into Albrecht Meyer's Gestapo office, put his hands on Meyer's desk, leaned over it menacingly, and snarled, "Why in the hell didn't you brief me on what to expect? You gave me the impression we just had to pick up a stinking Jew, not to fight a minor war on German soil.

I just lost an entire patrol!! Who the hell are these crazy killers?!"

Meyer frowned.

"Anton, calm yourself. I thought your people were prepared for all possible eventualities. Now sit down and tell me what happened."

"What happened was that a whole fucking GFP patrol was wiped out in Buxtehude, all three dead, and the killers took off in the patrol's own Kübelwagen. I have ordered all available GFP to cordon off and comb the area, and of course to block all exit roads, but with hordes of Hamburg citizens fleeing the goddam bombers, those arrangements are not exactly airtight. And I've warned my people that we're dealing with British Commandos. Which is something you should have emphasized to me yesterday."

Meyer leaned back, pursed his lips and stared at the ceiling, trying to convey the impression of deep thought, Gestapo at its brainy best. In fact, he couldn't think of anything further to say.

"What you have done is all to the good, Anton. I will now get in touch with Berlin and discuss with headquarters what supplementary steps to take."

x

"Herr Reichsführer, this incident with the GFP in Buxtehude clearly shows that we are catching up with them." Best had just reported the GFP patrol's demise in Buxtehude to the SS-Reichsführer. His voice was closer to pleading than to his usual confident tone, as he tried to present the unacceptable facts about the Buxtehude shooting in something like a positive light.

The presentation failed to impress Himmler, who looked colder and more serpentine than ever, his eyes narrow slits. The thought flitted through Best's mind that he was staring into evil itself.

"Werner, so far these Commandos have foiled all your attempts at catching them, they have killed our personnel wholesale, they have slipped away, and they are still on the loose *inside the Reich*, together with the Jew. Do you expect me to take this tale to the Führer?"

"Yes, Herr Reichsführer, I mean no, Herr Reichsführer. It is most unfortunate that so many people are evacuating Hamburg just now, it presents a great hindrance and has delayed our capture of the Commandos, but we are sending fresh GFP patrols into the area. All roads are being monitored—there is no way they can escape."

"Make sure about that, Werner. Make very sure."

Chapter 13

Agent Albrecht Meyer of the Amsterdam Gestapo arrived in his office at eight o'clock. He was punctual as always, but he was tired this morning after an active night with Magda, Hagen's mistress who had lost her lover and needed consolation. He scanned the night's radio traffic from Berlin, three whole messages. Didn't they sleep at night for God's sake? Brigadeführer Best wanted another update on the hunt for the British Commando team: what steps had they taken in Amsterdam; what results had they turned up. Shit! What did Best expect? In all probability, the birds had flown and were out of reach by now. But the Reichsführer himself was for some reason taking an interest in this one lousy Jew. Meyer decided he'd better make his answer sound good. Thank God the telephone connection was still down. That gave him time to weigh his words carefully.

Meyer started to jot down the beginnings of a telegram to Berlin but Sonderführer Schwesing shortly interrupted his train of thought by wandering through the open office door. Schwesing had received an almost identical request for an update from GFP's headquarters, and the two quickly found common ground in padding their respective replies with details about steps taken that they would mutually support, if queried. Meyer got the bright idea of hypothesizing that the SOE team had succeeded, despite the dedicated efforts of Gestapo in Amsterdam, in getting Blum into Denmark, and that Gestapo in Copenhagen therefore should be enlisted in the search. Accordingly he requested that Berlin direct the Copenhagen office to take all appropriate steps. Schwesing wrote an almost identical report, placing the emphasis on GFP instead of Gestapo, and he added a similar request through GFP channels. When the telegrams had been sent, they both relaxed. That should divert Berlin's attention away from Amsterdam.

X

Hansen was sitting in the stern facing Lund who held the oars. Behind Lund, Marek and Blum sat side by side, while Liz was in the bow. The river was carrying them swiftly downstream, as they watched dark silhouettes of other traffic and the features of the north shore glide by. Hansen leaned toward Lund and spoke quietly in Danish.

"The current must be four or five knots. How far do you think we should go?"

"I think we should aim for Itzehoe," Lund answered. "There's a railroad station, and the line runs north from there, right up the Jutland west coast. Besides, between us and Itzehoe, lots of people from Hamburg must be moving on the roads, and I like the idea of joining them."

"If we are careful, we should be relatively safe on the roads," Hansen agreed. "Remember how easily they picked us out on the train? We were actually sitting ducks with no way to escape. It was just our luck that they were only two. Had it been a patrol like the one in Buxtehude, it would have come to a shootout with a questionable outcome."

Lund thought about it and laughed.

"You're right; whoever is after us cannot screen them all, and this time we'll know to spot a checkpoint in time to make a detour. But has it struck you, that the Krauts probably are searching for us only on roads and railroads. I'll bet they haven't thought to check on river traffic."

Hansen smiled. "Yes, it's too bad there isn't a convenient river running north to Denmark."

In the bow Liz had been trying in vain to get the gist of their conversation. On paper, Dutch bore some resemblance to Danish, but the spoken words did not, and the cadence and music of the two languages were different. She finally lost patience.

"What are you two plotting?"

Lund said over his shoulder, "Just trying to decide how far downstream to go to be the nearest to Itzehoe, and I think we should be just about there. Let's land at the first pier that looks inviting."

Liz said, "There are piers all along, and there is a town coming up; that might be a good place to land."

With a few hard strokes, Lund brought the small craft closer to the north shore and out of the strongest part of the current. The pier he was aiming for was built to accommodate more sizable craft, probably long shore coasters. When they were close enough, Hansen caught a ring set into the masonry and held the boat stationary, while they debarked in the darkness. Then he got off himself, sending the boat with a strong kick back into the current.

x

Major Jack Hawes was in the downstairs office when the Bletchley messenger walked in. It was raining, and the messenger had shaken off his oilskins outside; standing inside the door, he was still dripping and reluctant to track mud and water to Ann's office. When the sun shines, a motorcycle is great; it gives the rider an exhilarating feeling of being in touch with nature, of taking in the scents and sounds of the countryside. Riding a cycle in the rain is something else. Seeing the familiar figure of Major Hawes, the messenger—all of eighteen years old—brought out a folder with intercepts from his waterproof haversack and with relief handed them over. Hawes signed the receipt, walked back upstairs and skimmed the intercepts with an eagerness he would never allow himself to display in front of the downstairs staff. He carefully extracted three, skimmed them briefly in his office, and called Ann Curtis.

"Miss Curtis, I just received the Bletchley intercepts. They are on my desk, please record them. I am taking three to the Brigadier right now."

McKinnon read the three documents twice, slowly, and looked across the desk at Hawes.

"Jack, this is unbelievable. They actually took down a fully armed GFP patrol! Those are picked troops; it's simply beyond belief!"

Hawes nodded.

"If the Germans catch up with them...I can't even imagine what they will do."

McKinnon picked up the phone and dialed Minister Dalton.

"McKinnon here, Minister. You wanted me to keep you up on our current operation *Dutch Treat*, and we just received some intercepts...yes Minister, our team is very much alive, in fact they have taken down a patrol of GFP, the German secret field gendarmerie...yes Minister, the Germans have cast the biggest dragnet in my experience...indeed, the SD, the Gestapo, the Kripo, and the GFP, that I just mentioned, are all taking part, plus God knows who else...yes, they have had to shoot their way through once again, and apparently got away with it...hard to tell, Minister...of course, Minister, we select our people with great care...yes, Minister, right away."

He turned to Hawes and their eyes met, but neither of them smiled. It didn't seem possible that three agents and a refugee scientist could prevail against the forces now arrayed against them.

X

The Itzehoe train dispatcher looked down from his elevated control room which was situated some fifteen feet above the tracks in a small brick tower. In the afternoon light he was attempting to estimate the number of people overflowing the station's three platforms, a task made easier by the fact that almost all were sleeping, or at least sitting down. He had never seen his station so inundated by humanity before, not even when it had been one of the marshaling yards for the invasion of Denmark and Norway three years ago. Below him people were camping on benches and on the ground, families with children and grandparents, with whatever goods they had salvaged from the flames at their hurried departure from their homes. Outside the station the road was choked with traffic, most of it plodding by at barely walking speed.

Three soldiers were moving through the yard, gray shadows taking hard looks at the refugees. He had seen them before, GFP personnel hunting some human miscreant. He resented their intrusion, resented the menace they projected, and he wondered idly who could be their prey on this summer day. Well, in Hitler's Reich, manhunts were a recurring activity.

The railroad terrain was bordered to the east by a five-foot fence, four strands of smooth wire, to keep animals from straying onto the tracks. The side of the fence facing away from the tracks was dotted with several small groves of volunteer elderberry bushes that had burst into bloom. Concealed in one of these, Lund and Hansen were surveying the station area and watching the soldiers combing through the refugees, no doubt looking for Blum. Marek's uncle was no athlete, and the walk from the river had sapped his strength completely. He was lying in the next elderberry grove with Marek and Liz standing watch over him, while they were discussing the next move. Lund and Hansen had been trying to estimate how much information the searchers might possess. They probably had no more than Blum's description, for a list of five people would be too confusing to work with. Besides, Blum was by far the easiest to check for. At the end of their discussion, Hansen proposed that he and Lund pose as two SD agents and simply ask one of the soldiers. Lund agreed.

"Let's use the SD agents' IDs: I have Hagen's and you have Wolff's. Information with their names could not possibly have been disseminated at this level."

Hansen concurred. "Even if they have our descriptions, they would not broadcast the names of the SD and the Kripo we put out of commission. It must be classified information, definitely bad for morale. Let's try."

They walked to the station building and onto the first platform. Lund accosted the nearest soldier and flashed his ID.

"Deutsche Sicherheitspolizei. Who's in charge of your search?"

"The Feldwebel over there," the soldier pointed to the other platform, and Lund and Hansen noticed his GFP cuff title.

The Feldwebel responded politely when Lund again identified himself. An aura surrounded SD personnel that even the feared GFP reluctantly recognized, and Lund spoke with an assurance befitting his rôle.

"I presume you are looking for the escaped Jew?"

"Jawohl, his name is Blum, but he may have papers with the name of Voigt."

"Right. Now, when the next train from Hamburg comes through, my colleague and I will board the train, as we are going to Husum. On the way we will screen everyone on the train. You will then be responsible only for screening the passengers getting off the train here."

The Feldwebel nodded with a grunt of assent. He harbored no love for the SD, and strictly speaking, they had no authority to give him orders. But it was best to go along, and it made his job easier. He turned on his heel and walked away to instruct his men. Just then, the sound of an incoming train reached them. Hansen hurried off to get the others, while Lund kept an eye on the three GFP. As he had hoped, they spread out well away from the station building, while the people on the platforms got on their feet. The somnolent scene abruptly became one of bustling activity.

Lund made sure that the three GFP were taking up positions along the platform in anticipation of checking the new arrivals, well back from the head of the train, where he planned to get Blum aboard. The train came to a halt, disgorged a motley crowd of several hundred passengers, only to be crammed with a comparable number, people who had made it to Itzehoe by road and who were headed for friends or relations farther north in the hope of finding temporary living space to replace what they had lost to the fire in Hamburg.

The little group jostled their way through the mob to the first carriage behind the wheezing locomotive, Hansen and Marek almost carrying Blum between them. Lund caught hold of the conductor and flashed his ID.

"Deutsche Sicherheitspolizei. Clear the compartment next to yours. We are traveling with an important prisoner."

The conductor obliged without argument. They put Blum inside with Liz and Marek, while Lund and Hansen took up positions in the corridor outside.

From his vantage point above the tracks the Itzehoe dispatcher observed the bedlam below with a mixture of distaste and detachment. The regular schedule had been suspended days ago; trains were released as soon as the section ahead was cleared, moving people at maximum capacity. The habitual German discipline asserted itself to overcome a human inclination to panic under severe stress. As the train chugged out of the station under a cloud of coal dust, he followed it with his eyes, wondering how long Hamburg would keep disgorging its endless refugees, mumbling to himself. *"Wie viele noch?"* How many more?

x

The two Kripo agents the SOE team left behind at the Sprotze railroad station, ignominiously locked in the train compartment with their own handcuffs, stayed put for more than an hour before they succeeded in freeing themselves. They remained on the train and returned to Bremen, where they collected Metzger, the colleague Huber had left to prowl the railroad station. They were back at the office after hours, discussing all along how best to waylay and take revenge on the Engländer.

Huber guessed correctly that the SOE people would attempt to cross the river and head north, probably by train, and he realized that speed was essential if he and his men hoped to catch up with the fugitives, before they crossed the border into Denmark. The frontier crossing would be the logical point at which to apprehend them. That far north there would be no Hamburg refugees to confuse the situation. Huber decided to go by car, detour eastward around Hamburg and take up a position at the western railroad crossing on the Danish border.

Before leaving, he telephoned the Gestapo in Amsterdam and notified the clerk on night duty about their sighting of the SOE team at Sprotze, without going into the embarrassing details. Then the Kripo set out in their car, another Opel Kapitän. The roads within thirty miles of Hamburg were by now filled beyond capacity, as the exodus had peaked under the repeated onslaughts of the bombers. Those of the refugees—a large number—who had seen their homes totally destroyed by the fire and who consequently headed for friends or relations with whom to seek shelter, had been forced by the fire storm to depart the city by the nearest exit road, not necessarily the one in the direction they wanted to go. Thousands were therefore circling around the city to the east like the Kripo was, adding to the congestion.

Huber and his men patiently threaded their way through the mob, taking turns driving and sleeping. By sunrise they arrived at the Danish border crossing and alerted the German border gendarmes and customs officers who were responsible for monitoring both road traffic and railroad travelers. Huber placed Metzger at the highway gate and together with Cetti took over part of the railroad station master's office. Huber had a conference with the captain in charge of the gendarmerie, convinced him to double his guards and alert his people at the smaller, most westerly border crossing at Rudbøl. When hearing Huber's description of the SOE team they were expecting, the Captain agreed with his suggestion to arm the guards with Schmeisser MP-40 machine pistols.

After these initial preparations had been completed, Huber ordered breakfast brought from the nearby hotel. When it arrived, he settled down at the desk he had taken over in the station office and looked with satisfaction at Cetti across the breakfast table.

"Well, Leo, my instinct tells me they will be coming through here. Then we shall see who has the most firepower."

x

Standing steadily outside the SOE compartment, Lund and Hansen were debating their next move. They had taken turns snatching a couple of hours sleep inside the compartment, where Liz and Blum at the moment lay sleeping on the seats, with Marek stretched out on the floor. The train had been overloaded at the departure from Itzeho, but most of the refugees had trickled off as the cars rattled north through Holstein and Schleswig. The two Danes were both familiar with the frontier area, and they agreed that the highway and railroad crossings by now would be crawling with police of every variety, all looking for Blum and his cohorts.

"I liked the way we exited Westerbork," Hansen said, grinning as he recalled crashing the gate in the Wanderer, "but I don't think it would work here, if they are lying in wait for us."

Lund shook his head. "We could try to cross at Rudbøl, but I suspect they will be waiting for us even out there. If they weren't alerted, we could go cross country, for I doubt they bother to do much patrolling, since Denmark is occupied. As it is now, they are probably watching every foot of the border all the way to the coast...saaay...how do you suppose the frontier ends out there? I mean, is there a post right on the beach...or out in the tidal flats?"

Hansen looked thoughtful.

"Funny, but I have never thought about that before, although as a boy I often spent time exploring the tidal area just a little farther north. I know the frontier is very close to the road to

168

Sylt." He was referring to the northernmost of the North Frisian Islands, a twenty-mile, narrow sand spit frequented by summer vacationers and connected to the mainland by a road carried on a five-mile embankment through the tidal area.

"So did I," Lund said, "and the fact that we both know this stretch of coast so well seems almost like fate pointing the way."

"Let's get off in Niebüll," Hansen suggested, "for they are bound to be waiting for us at the frontier station."

It was dusk when they arrived at Niebüll, a small town and the third stop before the Danish frontier. Divided in two groups, Lund and Liz went ahead, with Hansen, Marek and Blum following within eyesight. The night was clear and the road to the coast lay deserted, as they hurried along as fast as Blum could manage. It was midnight when they reached the coast and proceeded half a mile out on the road, before they dropped in the grass on the side of the embankment. The tide was out, exposing the mud flats, but Lund and Hansen were keenly aware that there was no way to tell without a tide table whether the return of the flood was hours away or about to start.

Lund and Hansen had been discussing their prospects in Danish; now Lund changed to English.

"Listen people, we are going to walk north, parallel to the shoreline, about half a mile out. We hope that's far enough to get around the frontier, so to speak, which is less than two miles north of here. So, we will walk in the mud for two hours, hoping that will see us past any frontier guards and into Denmark. We can see it is ebb tide right now, but we don't know when the flood tide comes, and we don't know how high it will be. When it comes, it comes fast. The coast farmers always say it moves faster than a horse can run. Hansen will lead, then Blum, Marek and Liz. I'll bring up the rear. We'll stick together, but in case we are separated, walk toward the North Star. Do you all know where that is?"

There was a quick "No" from Liz and Marek. Having lived all her life in Africa, south of the equator, Liz found the northern sky unfamiliar, and Marek was a city dweller who had never given the night sky any scrutiny. Lund pointed out the Big Dipper in the summer sky and located the star for them. Then Hansen led them down the embankment, stepped onto the clayey surface of the tidal flat, and started at a brisk pace. Blum stumbled at his first step in the slippery goo, fell on his hands and knees, was pulled up by Marek, and set off after Hansen. Liz and Lund followed, and the little column melted into the dark void.

Walking in the mud was far more strenuous than on the road. They soon found themselves wishing for a good hard surface underfoot, as they strove to keep up a good pace. After half an hour Lund called a halt, and they rested, standing, for five minutes before proceeding. The shore was not visible to the right, nor was the island, far out on their left. All they could see was a circular area of tidal flats, some hundred feet in diameter, moving north with themselves in the center. At the second rest stop, Hansen asked, "How fast to you think we are moving?"

"A little less than two miles an hour," Lund estimated. "I would say we are just about abreast of the frontier right now."

"I hope so," Hansen said, "for I have the feeling that the flood is beginning."

They continued, and ten minutes later they could all see that he was right. The North Sea was starting the flood with a two-inch-high wave. From the rear Lund said, "Veer toward shore at a forty-five degree angle," and Hansen complied.

The flood came fast. Within minutes the water was ankle deep, slowing them considerably. Hansen doggedly kept on course, as the water rose to their knees. Lund knew the tide could vary as much as eight meters, depending on the position of the moon, but he had no idea how high they could expect it to rise tonight. If this was to be anything like a spring tide, they might be swimming in another few minutes. He wondered whether Blum and Marek could swim, but here was no point in asking.

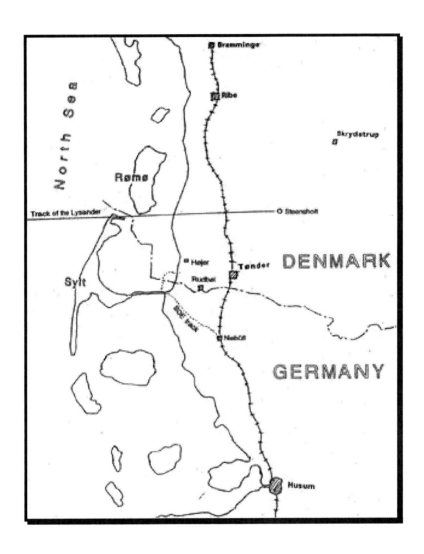

Ten minutes later the water had risen to their hips, slowing their progress still further, while they pushed on in silence. Fifteen minutes later Liz said, "The water is not getting deeper." They all realized she was right. The ground under them was rising slightly, and they could soon discern the grass covered shore area that only flooded at extreme high tides or in onshore storms. Hansen turned straight north again, and they walked for another half hour until Lund called a halt. They dropped to the ground in a tight cluster, shivering in their wet clothes. Hansen said cheerfully, "We're in Denmark! I can feel it in my bones."

Lund concurred.

"Somehow the ground we're sitting on feels friendly. For good measure, let us continue north for another half hour, then we'll cross the dike and find the road to the village of Højer."

They didn't know it, but they were actually sitting on the western upslope of the dike he was referring to. It ran for many miles north and south along the coast to protect the low-lying meadows and farmland from flooding, and it was becoming dimly visible in the predawn light.

"I don't think I've ever been so dirty in my life," Liz said, "but somehow it doesn't matter. If what you say is true, even the dirt feels friendly."

They got up and plodded on for another half hour before crossing the dike and descending on the landward east side. A sandy track separated the dike from the meadows, and in the early morning stillness they could scent the fragrance of hay. Most of the meadows had been cut, and in one the hay had been raked and stacked, ready to be hauled to the barn. They stepped over the fence, buried themselves in the nearest haystack, and fell asleep.

Chapter 14

From the SD office on the third floor of the Dagmarhus building, Agent Jan Randschau looked down on Copenhagen's city hall square. Despite the absence of gasoline powered vehicles, afternoon traffic was still substantial. Under wartime pressure Danes had turned to the bicycle, their traditional and favorite means of transport. The cyclists now dominated the street scene, girls in summer dress, office workers, staid elderly commuters, *Svajere* (delivery men on bikes with load-carrying shelves), and dotted in the stream some few motor vehicles with built-on wood-burning gas generators for propulsion.

Randschau observed the cheerful street picture with disdain and a touch of contempt. He was from the Jutland border region, one of the German minority that clung to their German roots and professed loyalty to the Reich, come what may. Such minorities existed all around the German perimeter, most of them by now incorporated on Hitler's order with the blood and soil of the Fatherland. Agent Randschau felt that the Danes had been allowed far more independence than they deserved, but as soon as the war was won, the Neuordnung–the New Order–would take care of that. Then Denmark would simply become one of the German *Länder*, like the Rhineland or Bavaria.

Randschau had volunteered for the Waffen-SS when the war started and had served on the Eastern Front. It had been great, mostly a matter of rounding up Jews and other undesirables. In the beginning he had kept a personal tally of the ones he had killed, but the numbers had grown beyond counting, particularly when the SS with automatic weapons liquidated the filth in huge groups. His service at the front had been cut short when a piece of Russian shrapnel destroyed the optic nerve in his right eye. He was transferred to the SD, where his fluency in both German and Danish had placed him in the Copenhagen branch office.

Minsa, the secretary from the records office, came in with two dispatches from RSHA in Berlin. Minsa was the one with the big tits, but she was the property of Major Halbach of the embassy staff. Too bad. He read the dispatches and became instantly interested. British Commandos liberating a Jew and cutting a bloody swath through German territory, now coming his way! He read the messages once again and consulted the large scale map on the office wall. He was from Tønder, a provincial border town on the western highway, and he knew that area intimately. They would in all probability be crossing the border in the west, but not by railroad or highway. Presumably, they were not idiots. They would go through the countryside and cross the line in some farmer's hayfield, not difficult, and then get to Copenhagen. Here, they would disappear among the capital's one million inhabitants. Logic dictated that he would have to catch them on the west coast. Where? Probably in Ribe or Bramminge. There would be only one daily train, two at the most. Easy to check. Ribe was also one of the towns where he had a local informer, this one a member of the small Danish Nazi party.

He called his *Mitarbeiter*, Dieter Braumüller, a Holsteiner who also knew his way around in the border region.

"Dieter, get the Opel ready with Jensen as a driver. We're going to Ribe!"

x

It was noon when Lund woke up. He was resting in the haystack with his head exposed on the north side, giving shade from the sun that stood high in a clear summer sky. Next to him Liz was still sleeping soundly, her breasts moving with the regular rhythm of her breathing. The bronze of her hair was flecked with masses of hayseed, and there was a smudge on her left cheek, a reminder of their hike through the flood tide in Vadehavet, southern Jutland's battleground with the North Sea. He lay utterly still watching her, resting on his elbow, thinking this was the most beautiful and desirable woman he had ever met, extraordinary in every way. What was she really like? So far, their acquaintance had only shown her to have unflinching courage to which they all owed their lives, but he wanted to know more about her, her personality, dreams, unspoken desires. Did she have a boyfriend? The thought had not occurred to him before and suddenly alarmed him. He'd had a number of liaisons, in fact quite a number, even for a Dane, but they had been short-lived affairs, quickly forgotten. Liz attracted him differently. With an effort he wrenched himself into the here and now. He tried carefully to slide away, but the motion woke her. She opened her eyes, looked straight into his, and smiled, still groggy with sleep. Drawn by an irresistible impulse, he bent toward her and kissed her gently. Dreamily she kissed him back, and in a flash she came fully awake, her smile widening.

"Svend Lund, your face still gives away your private thoughts, but I find it reassuring to read your mind."

As in Hawes' office he again blushed and silently cursed himself for it. Besides, this kind of dalliance did not befit the leader of the SOE team.

"Uh...I'd better get going and get us out of here."

He slid free of the hay, got up, started brushing himself and looked at their surroundings in the noonday light. There were no farms nearby, but to the northeast he could see the village of Højer on the horizon. He went around the stack and found Marek and his uncle still asleep, but Hansen was sitting a short distance away by a drainage ditch that separated the field from the wagon track along the dike. He was washing the mud off his shoes and socks to erase the marks of their nightly trek. Lund sat down beside him, and in a short discussion they planned their next moves. Lund and Hansen had to go to Steensholt to prepare for the Lysander's pickup, and they also had to visit the radio operator in Copenhagen to transmit their signal for the pickup to SOE. In their absence, the rest of the group needed a safe place to stay, and Lund suggested that they be placed with the Ribe group. Hansen agreed, and they moved on to the immediate problem of getting from the haystack to Ribe without being detected. Going by bus or train was far too risky at the moment, as German patrols certainly would be screening all traffic.

"Do you think they have descriptions of all of us?" Hansen sounded doubtful.

Lund laughed. "You can bet that they have a better description of you than your own mother would be able to come up with. And that goes for all of us. I would even imagine that Liz's red hair figures prominently in dozens of Gestapo dispatches right now."

After considering and discarding several ideas, Lund suggested that he telephone an acquaintance with a taxi service to pick them up after dark. They would stay put at the haystack until then. Once in Ribe they would place Liz, Marek and Blum with three of Lund's Ribe group while Lund and Hansen were away. The plan had the appeal of being simple.

"I'll walk to Højer and telephone the guy I know in Ribe to pick us up here tonight," Lund said. "I'll be back in a couple of hours. Let's keep everybody out of sight while it's daylight."

"And for God's sake," Hansen implored him, "find a grocery store in Højer and buy us some food before we all starve to death."

It took Lund less than an hour to reach Højer. From the village inn he phoned his acquaintance in Ribe, Henning Varming, who ran a small hauling business and cab service, and asked him to come to the Højer inn with his taxi at ten in the evening. In the village Brugsforening, the farmers' coop store, he bought food: sliced dark rye bread, two loaves of white French bread, butter, cheese, salami, sardines, liver paté, honey, tomatoes, soft drinks and beer, plus an empty flour sack to hold the hefty load.

He made the return trip with the sack slung over his shoulder and found the others sitting or lying on the shady side of the haystack, somewhat the worse for wear. Lack of food had drained them of the energy and desire to talk, and without the spur of imminent danger, they had slumped into a state of morose lethargy. Lund emptied the contents of the sack onto the grass, instantly changing the gloom to an almost festive air.

Liz cried, "This is the first real meal since Johan Winkler emptied his pantry to feed us."

They gathered in a circle, using the flour sack as a table cloth. Hansen was slicing French bread and cheese and salami with his pocket knife, exclaiming to no one in particular, "I always knew I wasn't cut out for starvation!"

x

Jack Hawes gathered the six Bletchley intercepts and arranged them on his desk in a sequence that produced a coherent picture of the mammoth effort Himmler's minions were exerting to apprehend the most potent SOE team yet to be dispatched from Baker Street. Reading between the lines told him clearly enough that operation *Dutch Treat* was still very much in progress, somewhere in enemy territory. It was also obvious that RSHA in Berlin was sparing no effort, none whatsoever, in covering every possible route the team might take. The descriptions of Blum and the three agents had been refined with meticulous details, including numerous comments about "the red haired female agent."

Every allusion to Liz reminded Hawes of his late wife, Jennifer. Her hair had been exactly that color, and she had set it in a classic Cameo until her WAAF service, when she too gave in to expediency and had it cropped short. Jennifer had perished in the Blitz, while he was in a military hospital being fitted with an artificial arm.

Having sorted the intercepts into the time sequence of the actual events, he gathered them carefully and walked down the hall to McKinnon's office.

"Sir, please look at today's material from Bletchley, all of it pertaining to *Dutch Treat*."

He placed the documents on McKinnon's desk in the sequence he preferred and waited for the other's reaction.

"Hmm...they are still ahead of their pursuers," McKinnon mused. "Actually, the other side has not one clue to their whereabouts since the clash in Buxtehude. Quite a lucky coincidence that the RAF laid on that Gomorrah attack just when our team needed to make a fast exit."

Hawes nodded.

"I still cannot come up with any explanation for the additional person who seems to have joined them. At first it sounded like a mistaken observation by the Germans, but these descriptions rule that out. *Dutch Treat* now comprises a group of five."

McKinnon chuckled. "We have a small army fighting its way through enemy territory. That causes a problem, if they succeed in getting to Denmark and we have to evacuate all of them. The Lysander can handle only two at a time."

"Yes, sir, and if some of them must go to Sweden, it will involve clandestine transport. The papers we supplied Lund and van Paassen with are now compromised and useless. Every border crossing in Denmark and northern Germany will be on the lookout for them."

x

Henning Varming's taxi was powered by wood gas. A gas generator, the size of a large water heater, had been mounted on the rear of the old Chevrolet. It was fueled with finger-sized pieces of beech wood, which was carried in fifty-pound sacks. The gas, largely carbon-monoxide was fed through the carburetor to the engine. Although it produced far less power than gasoline, it did suffice to move the vehicle, and German engineering ingenuity had thereby solved the problem of keeping buses, ambulances, fire trucks and a few other essential conveyances moving in occupied Europe, while reserving gasoline for the military. In Varming's case, his taxi service operated on a restricted license, allowing his small enterprise to survive wartime exigency.

Varming met Lund at the Højer inn. There were only a few customers at the bar as Lund and Varming sat down at a table out of earshot. Varming said, "I didn't realize that you were around. Rumor has it that you left the country."

"The rumor was not entirely wrong," Lund said. "At the moment I am helping somebody from Germany to dodge the Krauts and find a safe place in Denmark to sit out the war. Tonight we will take them to Ribe, and I can handle their further travel from there."

The appearance of people in the border region who were on the run from Hitler's Reich was not an uncommon phenomenon, and Lund counted on that fact to make his operation appear relatively harmless. Varming chuckled.

"You know, last week we had two Canadian fliers come through. Some local people were helping them to get to Copenhagen and on to Sweden."

"Really? And they made it?" Lund feigned interest. "Well, tonight all I need is to transport four people to Ribe, and I can handle it from there. How much do you need for that bit of transportation?"

Varming took a swig of his beer, assessing how much he could get out of the transaction. Such special wartime commissions made the hauling business prosper in a most agreeable manner.

"Oh, say, two hundred kroner should about cover my expenses."

Lund lifted his glass. "That's a deal. *Skål!*" He counted out the money without comment.

Just before midnight Varming unloaded the group at the house of Valdemar Nielsen, the leader of the Ribe group, and returned to his home on the outskirts of town.

Lund and Hansen explained their situation to Valdemar. The Ribe group would have to keep Liz, Marek and Blum safely out of sight, and the group must prepare and get ready to provide security at the Steensholt pickup. Both Lund and Hansen were uneasy about keeping three of their group hidden in a small town, where everyone knew everyone else. Wanting to hurry things along as much as possible, they informed the others and departed within an hour on two borrowed bicycles for Steensholt.

As Varming was putting the taxi in his garage, his neighbor, Lukas Frey was sitting on his doorstep, invisible in the darkness, smoking his pipe. Frey was a member of the small Danish Nazi Party and served as SD's eyes and ears on the local scene. He made a mental note of Varming's nighttime trip in his taxi. Maybe it was of no consequence, but it might still be worth mentioning in his next report to Copenhagen. He was constantly searching for material to pad his weekly reports.

X

It was late in the evening when the two SD agents and their driver arrived in Ribe. They checked into the Dagmar, the town's best hotel, located in the center of town. In the morning Randschau summoned Lukas Frey to his hotel room. The three SD people were all seated, looking at Frey expectantly. There was no chair for him.

"So, Lukas, what have you to report?" Randschau sounded all businesslike.

Lukas had sent in his weekly report only three days ago. It had contained nothing of note, just minor gossip. He cleared his throat, trying to sound important, but he was as always ill at ease when speaking in person with the SD.

"Well, uh, I have kept a sharp eye out for anything suspicious, but I can't say there is much to add to the weekly report that I sent on Saturday."

"That's not satisfactory, Lukas. We are paying you a generous retainer, and we expect solid information. Incidents have occurred here in the past, theft of Wehrmacht weapons that you could never account for or retrieve...." Randschau managed to make it sound as if Lukas was personally responsible.

Frey fumbled for words, tried to think of an answer to deflect the accusatory questions.

"Are there any new faces in town?"

Randschau's question suddenly struck a responsive chord.

"Well, now, what I observed last night could perhaps lead to an answer to that question." Frey made the statement with the air of a man broaching state secrets.

"What are you talking about?"

Frey was not a fast thinker, but he described as elaborately as his spur-of-the-moment inspiration allowed how he had observed a lengthy taxi cab trip in the dead of night, ending his story by neatly turning the table on the SD.

"If I was you, I'd sure go and ask Varming some questions."

Randschau considered the information.

"Did you see anybody being transported in the cab?"

"Why, no, but he was gone a couple of hours, and I'm sure he wasn't just joy riding." Frey suddenly sounded confident. In the light of day, the affair actually sounded plenty suspicious.

"Where does this Varming live?"

Frey told them.

"It isn't much to go on. I'll look into it, but first we have a train and some busses to check. Come back here at four this afternoon." Randschau signaled him to leave, and Frey made a hasty exit.

Checking the northbound train at 10:50 required that the two agents ride along to Bramminge on the main east-west line. No passenger came close to matching any of the descriptions

Berlin had sent. Sigurd Jensen met them with the car in Bramminge, and they returned to spend two hours patrolling the bus station's busy midday traffic. It was mid-afternoon when they finally started on the lead Randschau had deemed least important.

Varming's house was on the edge of town and Randschau routinely sent his driver around to the back door. Like Frey, Jensen was a member of the Danish Nazi party. He was employed by the SD only as a driver but carried a pistol, which gave Randschau extra manpower in situations of this kind. The front door was not locked—people rarely bothered to lock their doors during the day. Randschau opened the door and stepped inside together with Braumüller. Varming's wife, Rita, was cleaning the nursery, where their year-old son was sleeping in his crib. She gave a startled cry at the sight of the two strangers. Randschau made no apologies. His voice was low and menacing.

"Shut up. Where is your husband?"

Rita looked at him in disbelief but gathered her wits. Her voice was calm when she answered.

"In the garage."

"Right here." Jensen was hustling Varming through the back door with his pistol.

Randschau kept his voice low. "We are German Security Police. I have a few questions to ask. Both of you, sit down on the sofa." He pointed, and they sat down.

Randschau sat down slowly on a chair on the other side of the room and observed them placidly.

"Now, Varming, tell me where you went with your taxi last night."

Varming hesitated a moment. "I went to Bramminge and picked up some wood fuel."

Randschau snorted. "You are lying, and I don't have time to fool around. Dieter, lock them down."

Braumüller pulled out a pair of handcuffs and expertly clapped them on Varming, cuffing his right hand to his left ankle. Jensen produced another pair and locked Rita Varming down the same way.

Randschau went into the nursery and came back dragging the crib. He motioned to Braumüller. "Get me a meat cleaver or a big knife."

Braumüller went to the kitchen and returned with a large bread knife. Rita gave a piercing shriek, but Jensen clamped his hand over her mouth. Henning Varming tried to get up, but Braumüller pulled him back on the sofa.

Randschau kept his voice low. "Listen, both of you. In the Ukraine we had no trouble getting people to talk, and tell the truth. We just did a little chopping. Small hands and feet come off easily, just one whack with a knife like this." He weighed the bread knife in his hand. "Now, I am going to ask you just once more, and if you give me any chickenshit lies, your baby will have to learn to write left handed."

The SS had perpetrated countless atrocities on the Russian Front, but in Denmark strong-arm tactics had been confined to Gestapo headquarters and to people already destined for execution. The bluff worked, however. Varming yelled, "Alright, alright! Put the goddam knife away! I'll tell you. I just picked up some refugees in Højer and took them to Ribe. No big deal. Now take these goddam handcuffs off."

Randschau studied the knife thoughtfully.

"Refugees? How many were there?"

"Four." Varming did not think of Lund as one of the refugees.

Randschau pondered the answer. He was looking for a group of five. Berlin had been quite explicit on that point. This was probably just some Jews fleeing to avoid "Resettlement" in the east. Still, their arrest would make the trip worthwhile, even if he missed the Commandos.

"Hmm...and where did you take them?"

Varming told him.

X

183

In Berlin another beautiful summer's day was drawing to an end. On days like this, the war seemed so remote as to be unreal, and in geographic terms it was. For all that the citizens of the capital cared, the fighting in faraway Russia and North Africa might as well have been on another planet. Only the occasional air raid provided an unwelcome reminder that every German was involved and might at some point be held responsible.

At RSHA Headquarters in Prinz Albrecht Strasse the day workers were leaving, while the much smaller night crews were trickling in to take up their duties. In his office Reichsführer Himmler was still perusing reports from far flung parts of his huge apparatus to monitor and control the inhabitants of the Reich and the occupied countries. He closed his eyes for a moment and leaned back in his comfortable armchair. So much work for one man. The Vaterland owed him more than it could ever repay. He was secure in his knowledge that the Führer trusted him—to the extent that Hitler ever trusted anyone—but the workload was getting out of hand. Exterminating the Jews was putting a real strain on the SS. One would think that modern technology could reduce the time and resources that the task demanded, but so far, private industry had been disappointingly unhelpful. As usual, the SS would have to come up with its own creative ideas.

The telephone on his desk rang; he picked it up, reluctantly, and heard Heisenberg's voice.

"Heil Hitler, Herr Reichsführer! I am calling to inquire about the Dutch scientist Aaldert Voigt. When may we expect him here in our Z-Group?"

Himmler temporized for a few seconds, deciding how much to tell Heisenberg at this point.

"Voigt? Oh, actually the Jew Blum...yes, I recall. It turned out that he was not at the Institute, when my men went there. We are trying to locate him just now."

"He wasn't there?" Heisenberg sounded surprised. When Himmler didn't comment, he continued, "I was told by President

Koenderink at the University that Voigt was there, doing both research and teaching."

"President Koenderink is also missing at this time. It seems that academicians are somewhat unreliable, but perhaps you would know more about that."

"Hmm..." Heisenberg was temporizing now. "That's news to me, and quite surprising news, I must say."

Himmler was pleased to dispose of Heisenberg's inquiry without revealing anything embarrassing to the SS.

"Yes, well, we shall see if we can clear this up for you. I shall let you know when we find the Jew."

X

Claus Feldsted was a light sleeper, easily roused by a few pebbles on the bedroom window. He cracked the front door and shone a flashlight in Hansen's face. It took a couple of seconds for recognition to register.

"What...didn't you...didn't you get to England? Or what happened?"

Hansen burst out laughing.

"May we come in?"

"Yes...yes, of course."

He ushered them into the living room and turned on the light. It was three o'clock in the morning. Hansen introduced Lund, and Mrs. Feldsted joined them, dressed in a pink negligée.

"Mrs. Feldsted," Hansen said, "the food basket you gave me was wonderful. I ate the sandwiches in an English field and shared the beer with the farmer."

Feldsted brought out a bottle of port and four glasses. "This calls for celebration," he proclaimed. "Go ahead and tell us your whole story."

Hansen gave them a brief summary, skipping lightly over their experiences after being landed by Three Commando. He ended his report with the proposition of using the Steensholt

185

airstrip for the Lysander. Feldsted grinned with delight at the proposition.

"Of course the Royal Air Force can use my field. And I wouldn't miss seeing the pickup for anything. I have friends in Copenhagen who'll be willing to stick their necks out to provide an alibi for us, if we should need one."

Lund asked about the German reaction to the disappearance of the plane from under their noses. Feldsted told them that both the local Danish police as well as Gestapo from Copenhagen had visited Steensholt and asked a great many questions, which he had spent hours answering, while denying any complicity. Feldsted was laughing when he related that he had started a claim against the German authorities for the loss of his plane. His attorney in Copenhagen was looking into the possibility of restitution.

They got down to more immediate and practical matters, as Feldsted asked about marking the field for the British Lysander pilot. Hansen had suggested to SOE the kind of marker Feldsted had used at the end of the airstrip at his departure in the KZ-3, a simple gasoline flare, and word had come back from the RAF that two such flares, one at each end, would be sufficient.

Mrs. Feldsted had been observing Lund and Hansen carefully; at length she interrupted her husband's questioning.

"Claus, can't you see the boys are exhausted? They need sleep above all."

Chapter 15

Valdemar was the only married member of the Ribe group. As a stone cutter he had worked up a thriving business producing head stones and other decorative stone work of a permanent nature. He had located his small workshop on the tree-shaded walk on the east side of the cemetery, where he worked with one helper. Hard work, a good location, and absence of competition had made his enterprise an economic success and had enabled him to purchase a small, red brick house near his shop. To the delight of his wife, Valborg, Liz had in the dark of night been moved into their guest room, and the two young women had taken a mutual liking to each other. In the morning, Valborg had made a brief shopping trip to buy Liz a pair of shoes and a dress, as the items furnished by SOE could not be resurrected after the ordeal in the tidal mud.

The two women were having coffee and animated small talk in the living room, Valborg practicing her school English, when Randschau and Braumüller walked in unannounced. Liz instinctively dove for her handbag, but Randschau's reflexes had been honed at the Russian Front. He jumped on Liz with a snarl, "Oh no, you don't!" swiping the bag out of her reach and pinning her in the chair. Braumüller had handcuffs on her in a matter of seconds.

Valborg cried out, "Who are you?"

"Shut up and stay where you are," Randschau hissed, sensing that she presented no immediate threat. Jensen walked in from the kitchen, having entered through the back door. He looked at Liz struggling in Braumüller's grip, let out a low wolf whistle, and mumbled to Braumüller, "That's the best looking broad I've seen you put your hands on."

Randschau took a step back and looked at Liz in her silent struggle with Braumüller. He suddenly remembered the "red haired female" referred to in the dispatches from Berlin, and there was no doubt in his mind of her identity. That also meant that a team of well-trained killers, maybe Commandos, would be poised nearby at this moment, no doubt outnumbering and outgunning his force. Could they be in the house? Probably not, he decided, but surely nearby. At heart a coward, he had reveled in rounding up and massacring unarmed civilians, but he had no taste for real opposition. This town suddenly looked very unhealthy.

"Get her in the car. We're off to Copenhagen." He instantly regretted having said this in front of Valborg and turned toward her. "You will keep your mouth shut about our visit, or you and your family will disappear."

He picked up Liz's handbag, and the SD party hurried to their car, Randschau taking the front seat next to Jensen, while Braumüller pulled Liz with him into the back. Randschau had his gun out, his head swiveling right and left until they were out of town. Then he put the gun away and relaxed somewhat. There had been no time for a body search, a standard procedure of checking out all suspects. He examined her handbag and triumphantly held up her gun for the others to see. He turned around, looked critically at Liz, and reached across the backrest to take hold of her necklace. With a jerk he broke the gold chain, opened the locket and showed the others the L-pill.

"Listen, we've caught us a British agent, and she's part of a group of killers. Aren't you, bitch?" He was speaking Danish and repeated it in German, but Liz did not reply or react to either. Jensen spoke a very few words of English, but Liz ignored his attempts to communicate.

"Well, well," Randschau exclaimed expansively, "we have a silent bird here, but she'll sing in Copenhagen. We'll start our interrogation there with a group fuck, that never fails to loosen things up. I'll go first, but by the time we get the interested parties all together in my office, there'll be about a dozen of us, all wanting a piece of the action."

The three men laughed uproariously.

X

Ole Lauesen was testing a radio that had been brought in yesterday by an old lady in the neighborhood. This one, a B&O, a popular Danish-made set that could receive most European stations, had suffered from a burned-out vacuum tube, which Lauesen had replaced. He had been a marine operator and had spent twenty years on the high seas in the merchant service, six of them with the Cunard Line on passenger ships. Those had been his best years at sea: regular hours, excellent food, a fine cabin. He had retired and set up his shop in Valby, an industrial suburb of Copenhagen, just before the war.

A few months ago an SOE agent had contacted him with a request to fix a radio transmitter that had been damaged when parachuted into Jutland on a stormy night. Initially, Lauesen had tried to rebuild the transmitter but had ended up redesigning and vastly improving the set. That had led to an SOE request to do the actual sending of messages, and he had gained a reputation among the radio people at Bletchley of being SOE's best field operator.

He polished the old lady's B&O set, nice maple cabinetry. The bell on his shop door to the street rang as two men entered. One of them said in Danish, "Kalundborg is my favorite station." He looked at them sharply before answering in a casual tone, "It has good programs." The other completed the coded exchange: "And it is not far away."

He led them into the back room, where they all sat down, and Lund said, "We need to send a message."

Lauesen nodded. "What is the message?"

"The message is, 'Dutch invitation accepted', that's all." Lund said. "Do you want me to write it down?"

"You want me to send, 'Dutch invitation accepted.' No need to write it down. It will go out in two hours."

They shook hands with him and left, jumping on a street car to Hovedbanegaarden, Copenhagen's Central Railway Station. Hansen ordered a cup of coffee at the station café, while Lund went to the station's telephone office and placed a call to Valdemar's home. The operator directed him to an empty cubicle, and when Valborg answered, he spoke slowly and clearly.

"We have finished our visit in Copenhagen."

As many long-distance calls were monitored, they had agreed on this message to indicate that Steensholt was ready and the radio message had been sent. Valborg barely let him finish, before she blurted out a carefully memorized speech, having decided to throw caution to the winds: "The Gestapo arrested Liz here this afternoon, and they're on their way to Copenhagen with her. Valdemar is trying to find out the identity of our visitors. We are moving out now. Valdemar says for you to call your namesake in the group tonight."

Lund had a momentary feeling that his blood would freeze.

"When exactly did they leave?"

"Uh, about an hour ago, around three-thirty."

"What kind of car did they drive?"

"It was an Opel, the large model."

"How many were they?"

"There were three of them."

"Alright. Be sure to give Valdemar my message. I'll call back tonight, as he says."

Lund paid for the call and walked slowly to the café, where Hansen was sipping coffee and reading Berlingske Tidende, the city's leading daily. When seeing Lund, he put the paper down in disgust.

"It looks like the Germans have taken Kiev again; that's bad news, if it's true."

"I've got worse news."

Hansen looked at him sharply.

"What happened?"

"The Gestapo have Liz." Lund quickly related what Valborg had just told him, adding, "I'm going to try to get her out."

"Do you mean out of Dagmarhus?" Hansen sounded like he was hoping for a different proposal.

"Yes."

They sat without talking, each considering the proposition from different angles. Hansen took another sip of the ersatz coffee, leaned back in his chair and laughed.

"I will go with you, and if we pull it off, I dare say, this will impress Brigadier McKinnon."

"No, you are needed to organize the pickup and see Blum and Marek off."

Hansen shook his head.

"I heard you instructing Valdemar, and he's perfectly capable of taking charge. Besides, I think you have forgotten something."

"What?"

"I, too, owe Liz my life."

X

When Liz received her L-tablet from Major Hawes, her contemplation of using it—of actually ending her own life—had seemed an utterly remote proposition, somehow not a *real* possibility. Not that she thought she could stoically endure torture, but because she had reasoned that she would not let herself be taken alive. Better die from a bullet than from poison. It had seemed a simple choice. As she sat in the back seat of the Opel, her right wrist locked to Braumüller's left, she realized her reasoning had been naïve. She tried to imagine what Valborg would be doing right now. Calling Valdemar, of course. Was there any hope of rescue? To be realistic, not the remotest chance. She was a prisoner of the Gestapo, already beyond the reach of her team mates. How would Lund take the news of her capture? She was certain he would be devastated.

Maybe furious. Then he would concentrate on completing their mission, getting Blum to England. He had the self-discipline this situation called for.... Didn't he? She felt sure he did. Was he in love with her? Thinking about him suddenly made her realize that she loved him, and now he would never know. She would never have the opportunity to tell him. The thought almost made her cry. Why hadn't she told him, when he kissed her yesterday? Convention had kept her from doing so. And now he'd never know. Convention be damned. Right now she wished, more than anything else, that she could tell him just this one thing, this one simple thing. She closed her eyes and spoke with her inner voice.

"Listen to me, Svend Lund: I love you!"

On the Belt ferry, they stayed in the car, but Randschau sent Jensen to buy them beer and sandwiches in the ferry's restaurant. The men ate the elegant, open-face sandwiches greedily, washing them down with gulps of beer, and Braumüller offered her a swig from his bottle. She turned away in disgust, and the men laughed again.

Late in the evening they arrived in Copenhagen and drove directly to Vestre, a large prison taken over by the Germans. She was handed over to a matron in Wehrmacht uniform and registered in the prison log. After the SD agents left, two matrons took her to a W.C. and stood by, glowering at her while she was sitting there. Afterward they took her to a small concrete cell and made her lie down fully clothed on a steel cot hinged to the wall. With a thin steel chain they locked her hands to the cot's steel frame, left without a word, and turned out the light.

The tension from the closeness and hostility of her captors gradually ebbed away, and she was overcome with immense weariness. Unable to move she could only lie like a piece of dead meat. She felt hot tears running down her cheeks, tears not of self-pity but of impotent fury. She forced herself to think of Lund. Now she believed that he loved her.

In the blackness of the small cell she recalled his face, his voice, his walk, and she whispered into the darkness, "Listen to me, Svend Lund: I love you."

X

It was time to leave the office. WAAF Lieutenant Ann Curtis was well aware of this fact, and her day had been busy, filled with minor problems. Actually, she had long since concluded that SOE had no minor problems. When she considered all potential ramifications, virtually every simple problem had a nasty edge that could have fatal consequences for some hapless operative in the field.

McKinnon and Hawes were still at their desks, and for the same reason that she still lingered. The Bletchley messenger had not brought the latest radio intercepts, his last delivery of the day. Of course, there just might not be any this evening. Her two superiors were well aware of that possibility, but they were still waiting, the three of them pretending to be occupied, but all thinking about the fate of the *Dutch Treat* team.

There had been no direct trace of the team since their shootout with the GFP in Buxtehude, but dispatches and instructions flying from RSHA in Berlin to local offices of SD, GFP, Gestapo, Kripo, and some embassy staffs, all indirectly had confirmed that the team was still on the loose, somewhere. A heads-up dispatch to SD in Copenhagen showed that Berlin thought it at least possible that the team could have gotten that far. Somehow.

Ann locked her desk, gathered some personal effects into her handbag, and knocked on Hawes' office door.

"I'll be leaving, sir."

"Oh, yes, of course. Time to go home." But he didn't get up himself.

Outside, the evening traffic was lighter than usual, maybe a side effect of the heavy attacks Bomber Command was carrying out on Hamburg. The Luftwaffe had its hands full at home. Just as she began walking, the Bletchley messenger's Royal Enfield braked to a halt and Sergeant Donovan saluted her cheerfully.

"Shall I bring this one back in the morning, Miss?" He held up a single message.

"No, no I'll take it now."

She signed the receipt and walked back into the building, breaking the seal and reading the contents. Only three words.

"Dutch invitation accepted." Their code requesting the Lysander pickup.

She ran into Hawes' office, forgetting to knock, and put the message on the desk in front of him.

"They made it, Major!"

Hawes stared at the paper in disbelief. He got up with a jerk that threatened to knock over his office chair, regained his equilibrium, and cleared his throat.

"Quite so. Hmm...is the Brigadier still here?"

"Yes, Major. Shall I take it to him?"

"Uh...no, I'll take it myself."

He walked down the hall, knocked on McKinnon's door and entered, followed by Ann Curtis.

"Sir, we have a message from the *Dutch Treat* team. I thought you might like to read it before going home."

"Indeed, Major?" McKinnon was fully up to the situation, picked up a box of matches and started to light his pipe. "And what does it say?"

"It says, 'Dutch invitation accepted'. Just the code, sir."

McKinnon looked into the flame for a moment before blowing out the match.

"Hmm...rather extraordinary, Major, wouldn't you say? I think we can assume that they are finally out of imminent danger." He looked at Ann. "Oh, Miss Curtis, glad you're still here. Please notify Tempsford about the Lysander for tomorrow night. And tell Ralston at BBC to include 'Elizabeth' in tomorrow night's broadcast."

194

With an inward smile, Ann had observed her two superiors display consummate lifemanship. It was now her turn to feign unconcern in the British tradition.

"Very good, sir. Will there be anything else tonight?"

x

Valdemar looked around the small circle of solemn faces. They were gathered in the room of Svend Jacob Skern, Lund's namesake in the Ribe group. Marek and his uncle were also present, and so was Valborg. Circumstances had made her a participant in an aspect of her husband's activities he had hitherto kept her out of. Seeing Liz manhandled into the Gestapo car had instantly made her into a fervent partisan. Valdemar looked around the circle and decided that full disclosure was required. That way the SOE mission would have the best chance to succeed even if one or more of the group should be eliminated in the process. He cleared his throat.

"I have called this meeting because Svend Lund has come back after having escaped to England. He is engaged in an important operation and needs our help. The operation is the kind of thing we visualized taking on, when we organized and trained to start with. Here is the situation."

Starting with Lund and Hansen's recruitment into SOE, he described their task of finding and extracting Blum, their subsequent running fights with their German pursuers, the border crossing through the tidal flats. This aspect caused chuckles, for they were all familiar with Vadehavet, the coastal intertidal strip unique to southern Jutland.

He continued, telling about the impending pickup at Steensholt, the coded go-ahead Lund had already sent by radio, and he finally got to the coded reply they were now waiting for.

"Here is the way London will tell us the particular night the airplane is coming to pick up Marek and his uncle, Professor

Blum. You know how we have been puzzled by the girls' names the announcer rattles off every night on the Danish newscast from London?"

He was referring to a standard feature at BBC's evening broadcast to Denmark, which ended with the words, "And tonight we have greetings to Karen, Inger, Else, Anna, Caroline..." The nightly list comprised a dozen girls' names, randomly chosen except for one, which indicated that SOE was going to make a parachute drop of agents or materials on a particular field that night. To confound the Germans, a greeting list was articulated every night, even when no name had significance. A given location was code named by SOE, the name then dispatched to Denmark by a courier through Sweden. In the Steensholt case, the code name had already been included in McKinnon's instruction sheet to each of the *Dutch Treat* group.

"Well, one of the names tells a group like ours, someplace in Denmark, that the RAF is going to drop weapons and explosives to it by parachute that night." Valdemar paused to give the information time to sink in. "From now on, we will listen every night, and when our code name is mentioned, that will mean that the airplane is coming to Steensholt that night."

"What is our code word?" Several eager voices posed the critical question simultaneously.

Valdemar hesitated and suddenly looked unhappy, as his eyes sought Valborg's. He cleared his throat once more.

"Elizabeth."

Valborg gasped and broke into a subdued sob. Valdemar continued.

"And now let me tell you what happened today. Lund's group comprises three English agents; one of them is a young woman by the name of Elizabeth. She was staying with Valborg and me. This morning three Gestapo agents burst into our house, where Valborg and Elizabeth were talking in the living room. They grabbed Elizabeth and took her with them to

Copenhagen. They warned Valborg not to mention their visit to anybody, or our family would disappear.

"As soon as Valborg called and told me, I got hold of Svend Jacob. The two of us made a few quick inquiries, and as you all know, few things go on in town without everybody hearing about it. Well, Svend Jacob and I soon found out that the Gestapo people stayed at Hotel Dagmar last night, and that Lukas Frey had visited with them. We caught up with Lukas and scared him enough, so that he spilled all that he knew. The names of the two Gestapo agents are Jan Randschau and Dieter Braumüller . . ."

The telephone rang and Valdemar picked it up, answering with a non-committal, "Hello." He listened in silence before speaking, and when he did speak, it was in a tone of conversational chit-chat, in case the call was being monitored. "I understand, and I'll do my best to organize a nice welcome whenever our friends drop in. My wife and I have decided to move. By the way, my uncle visited this morning, you know, Jan Randschau, yes, Randschau, and uncle Jan had his friend Dieter Braumüller with him...yes, Braumüller. Well, I'm glad you called. And good luck with your project."

He hung up and faced the others. "We are going to handle the pickup on our own, without Lund and Hansen. They are going to try to get Liz out of Gestapo's headquarters in Dagmarhus."

The room fell quiet, as his listeners digested the full meaning of his words. Valborg said, "But...how can they...?"

Valdemar looked around the circle before answering.

"How they can, or how they will try, I don't know. But this I know: Lund was clear about his instructions, in case they don't show up at Steensholt, and that is what we must concentrate on. Getting Professor Blum to England takes priority over everything else. To that end, we must first of all prepare our arrangements for security, in case the Krauts should try to interfere. Tonight we will take our weapons to Steensholt, so that they are ready. And we will also take Marek and Professor

Blum there. It is a safer place than this town, where nothing can
stay secret very long."

The group listened without comment. This was the kind of
thing they had trained for and prepared themselves for, yet it
seemed a daunting undertaking, as the expected action
suddenly loomed close. And overwhelming.

At this point, Valdemar remembered that Marek and his
uncle had been unable to follow the proceedings, as they all
had spoken Danish. He looked at Skern. "Now, Svend Jacob,
you are the best German-speaker in the group. Please put
Marek and his uncle in the picture, so that they know the
plans."

x

Belying its modest canal side location, Kroghs was arguably
Copenhagen's best restaurant. And when it came to seafood, it
had no serious competition at all, even in this sea-girded
kingdom. In a secluded corner, Helge Lindbergh looked across
the table at Lund and Hansen, more than a little curious about
this dinner to which he had been invited, just as he was about
to leave the hospital and go home to his small bachelor flat.
Lund's voice on the telephone had carried an undertone of
urgency and, well, you had to be prepared for anything these
days. Lindbergh was an intern at Bispebjerg Hospital, one of
the city's largest and most modern medical facilities. He and
Lund were friends from high school days and had kept in touch,
despite their diverging career paths. In recent months he had a
couple of times arranged brief admission to a hospital bed for
someone awaiting passage to Sweden, and he had even on
one occasion removed a German bullet from the leg of an
unlucky saboteur. Lund was vaguely aware of his old friend's
activities, for whispers about such things tended to filter
through untraceable Underground channels.

Lund lifted his glass of Vouvray. "Cheers!"

They drank, savoring the vintage. Putting his glass down, Helge asked the natural question.

"So, what's the occasion for this most agreeable dinner, or shouldn't I ask?"

Lund smiled. "You might as well know the whole story. In a few hours many people will know, anyway, and your knowing will be of no consequence." He lowered his voice. "Helge, Hansen and I are part of a group of British agents, dispatched to rescue an important scientist from Gestapo's clutches and take him to England. We got our man, so our mission is being accomplished, but in the process, one of our group, a young woman, was captured by the Gestapo this morning. Tomorrow, Hansen and I are going to try to get her back. We are going into Dagmarhus, and we may have to shoot our way out."

"You are going to tackle Dagmarhus? Just the two of you?" Lindbergh sounded, and was, incredulous.

"Yes, just the two of us. Our plan is simple and it just may succeed. And we decided to treat ourselves—and you—to a real gourmet dinner and spend most of our Danish money, which we shortly won't need."

To Lindbergh, Lund's lighthearted, cheerful tone did not conceal the deadly serious prospect ahead, and he understood that Lund and Hansen's minds were made up. He took a bite of smoked eel and replied in the same spirit.

"Your plan sounds good, as far as I can see, particularly the part about not needing money after tomorrow. Now tell me what you expect from me in return for this bacchanalian spread."

Lund did not hesitate.

"I need to borrow your car. It has the MD markings, and I assume it has not been converted to generator gas. Hansen will alter the license plate, so that it cannot be traced. We will need it for our getaway. I figure we will go directly from Dagmarhus to Bispebjerg, unless we have pursuers close behind us."

Lindbergh did not ask what they would do if they did have a slew of Gestapo on their tail, howling for blood. The possibility staggered his imagination. He lifted his glass.

"You can have it. Cheers!"

They drank, and Lund looked relieved.

"Thank you. I really appreciate that. I couldn't come up with any other source for a gasoline powered car." He squeezed a wedge of lemon over some cod roe, grilled to perfection, and tasted it. "Oh, and one more thing."

Lindbergh laughed out loud. "I'm afraid to ask what."

"May we sleep on your floor tonight? We'd like to be well rested for tomorrow."

At seven in the morning, Lindbergh's old Adler convertible was parked across the street from the main entrance to Dagmarhus. At the wheel was Egon Sander, a saboteur Lund had worked with before. Next to him on the front seat, covered by a wind jacket, lay a Suomi M/31 machine pistol, its box magazine fully loaded with 50 parabellum 9-mm cartridges. Another Suomi lay on the back seat, also covered. Completing their armory the night before, Lund had scrounged silencers for their Walthers from one of his Underground connections.

Across the street from the entrance ramp to the Dagmarhus underground garage, Lund and Hansen sat at a table in a second floor Mælkeri, the city's most popular type of breakfast restaurant. Lund was observing the traffic to the garage through a small monocular. Hansen was reading a newspaper that discreetly concealed Lund from other restaurant customers. A Wehrmacht soldier was posted on the sidewalk at the ramp; at the main entrance another was checking people arriving at work.

By eight o'clock, three cars had entered the garage; none had left. At eight twenty-three an Opel Kapitän emerged from the garage and joined the morning traffic. Lund put his spy glass down. "There were two men in front and one in back of that Opel. I think that's our car."

200

Hansen put the newspaper down with a groan. "I sure hope so, for I'm getting a cramp holding this damn paper."

Lund poured some more coffee. "If they're getting her at Vestre, they should be back in about half an hour."

His prediction was not far off. At six minutes past nine, the Opel returned. As it disappeared down the ramp, Lund caught a glimpse of bronze-red hair through the rear window. His hand holding the monocular tightened involuntarily, throwing the image out of focus.

"That's Liz."

In the Dagmarhus basement, Randschau and Braumüller with Liz between them took the elevator, while Jensen parked the Opel. In his office, Randschau said, "Let's first put a gag on her to keep things quiet." Liz fought back, but the two men quickly gagged her with a handkerchief stuffed in her mouth.

Hansen paid the check, the two men went downstairs, passed the Adler with Sander watching them, and crossed the street. At the entrance they showed Hagen's and Wolff's IDs. The soldier acknowledged with a nod. Inside, Lund beamed his most winning smile at a passing clerk. "Excuse me, Fräulein, where is Mr. Randschau's office?"

She returned his smile.

"On the third floor, number 324, just to the right of the elevator."

He thanked her, and they joined two other people waiting for the elevator. When they got out, they first looked for the emergency stairway, which they located at the end of the hallway. Their plan called for using that–not the elevator–for their exit.

They now went to the office door marked 324 and drew the PPKs with the silencers. Lund opened the door, they stepped inside quickly, and Lund closed the door behind them, taking in the scene. Hansen was the first to fire.

Randschau, Braumüller and Jensen stood around a desk where Liz lay spread eagled, Braumüller and Jensen pinning her down, one on each side. Randschau had pulled her pants off and was dropping his own, when Hansen's bullet hit him in the back. The others let go of Liz and reached for their guns. Jensen went down as Lund and Hansen both shot him, but Braumüller ducked behind the desk, partly screened by Liz, who was rolling off the desk and getting to her feet. Lund ran left, Hansen right, both trying for a clear shot. Braumüller got his safety catch off and fired wildly at Hansen, but the bullet struck Liz, who staggered and fell. The report of the PPK without a silencer was deafening in the closed room, drowning out two cracks from Lund's gun, as he shot Braumüller in the heart.

Lund ran to Liz and lifted her in a fireman's grip, yelling at Hansen, "Throw away your silencer and take one of their guns." Hansen rushed to get Jensen's and Randschau's, handed one to Lund, and they ran out in the hall. Two doors were opening from the adjoining Gestapo offices, one man stepping into the hallway. Before he could jump back, Lund shot him at close range with his free right hand. They ran to the stairway, and Hansen fired a shot back down the hallway that momentarily discouraged others from pursuit. The main entry hall was almost empty, a couple of people fleeing at the sound and sight of the guns. The soldier checking IDs was unslinging his rifle, when Hansen shot him at close range, wounding him so that he dropped his weapon. They started across the street, dodging some cyclists and a truck. Sander had the engine running and his window rolled down. His eyes were fixed on the main entrance as he cradled the Suomi with the barrel poking through the open window. Lund pushed Liz into the back and Hansen jumped into the front seat, while three civilians with guns emerged in pursuit from the building. Sander picked a space between two passing cyclists and sprayed the front entrance glass doors, bringing two pursuers down and propelling shards of glass into the building. In a quick sweep he sprayed the facade of the building, ending at the garage ramp, where the soldier was trying to take cover.

202

"That'll keep those pissants inside," Sander sneered and nosed the Adler into the morning traffic.

Hansen shouted exuberantly, "We did it! We actually got away with her!" He let out a war whoop with Sander joining in. He turned, and looked at Liz, who was leaning against Lund with her eyes closed; blood oozing from her hip was forming a pool on the floor mat. His excitement at their escape abruptly changed to concern.

"How bad is it?"

Lund was pressing a handkerchief against the wound, but blood trickled through his fingers. "I don't know," he said hoarsely, "but when we get to Bispebjerg, go straight to the emergency entrance."

Sander maneuvered through the sparse traffic of the northern outskirts at maximum speed, racing toward the Bispebjerg ridge, where the hospital was situated with an unsurpassed view of the city. He braked to a halt at an entrance where a sign proclaimed Emergency, and Hansen dashed inside, returning seconds later with two orderlies pushing a gurney. They slid Liz onto the platform and wheeled her away, while Sander drove off to the parking lot before any of the hospital staff had time to recognize the Adler. An intern met them as they rushed toward the surgery wing, and a nurse with a gauze compress took over from Lund his attempt to stanch the bleeding. Liz was mumbling faintly, with her eyes closed, as they moved her onto the surgery table. One of the nurses bent over her, then straightened with a puzzled look, as the doors to the surgery closed behind them.

"She's speaking English and she keeps repeating, "Svend Lund, I love you."

As the anesthesia took effect, her whisper faded away completely.

Chapter 16

Jack Hawes was waiting for the morning messenger from Bletchley. McKinnon had left for a lunch appointment, a most unusual occurrence, but a lunch invitation from the Minister was in the nature of a command performance. Maybe Churchill would be there; he was always curious about SOE's work, taking a delight in anything clandestine. Despite his unruffled exterior, Hawes and Ann were both aware that McKinnon had been greatly relieved since the receipt of the request for the Lysander pickup. Their team had succeeded, incredibly, and the members would have much to tell upon their return. It was unclear just who would be on the plane, for the Lysander could not accommodate the whole group. Well, he would know when they arrived, as he would be there to meet them at Tempsford; then he would also discover the identity of the extra person.

Through the half-open window Hawes could hear the familiar sound of the Royal Enfield arriving in the street below. Ann Curtis would be logging any intercepts and would bring them to him in a few minutes. In fact, he could hear her footsteps in the hall. Surprisingly, it sounded as if she was running. A quick knock, she entered before he could answer and hurriedly put a single intercept before him.

It was from Jan Randschau, SD agent in Copenhagen, to SS-Brigadeführer Werner Best in Berlin.

"Have arrested the female SOE agent traveling as Elizabeth van Paassen."

"Good heavens! Not this late!" He fumbled for his cigarettes and lit a Players before looking at Ann, who had sat down on the other side of his desk. The fact of such an exclamation from Hawes was in itself a measure of the impact of the message.

She was shaking her head in despair, and when she spoke, her voice was not its usual, business-like normal.

"Shall I take the message to the Brigadier?" She knew the location of the luncheon party.

Hawes read the message once more and pondered the question for a moment, before shaking his head.

"There's nothing to be done just now. This would only ruin his appetite. Bring him the intercept with his afternoon tea."

X

As soon as she had logged the telegram, Giselinde Thöne rushed into Best's office with it. She was well aware that this was the news Best had been hoping for. He had been unusually hard to live with in the last few days. The atmosphere of RSHA headquarters was dismal in the best of times, but the fiasco in catching up with those British Commandos who had snatched that Jew from Westerbork had embarrassed several departments, making the lives of secretaries miserable. This should improve things.

"I thought you might like to see this right away."

She put the message on his desk and stood back to watch the reaction. Best picked it up and came to instant attention.

"*Endlich!* Finally we get results! Very good, Fräulein Thöne, you have done very well." He was talking absentmindedly, actually babbling, as if his secretary had personally taken part in the capture. In his mind he was already planning how to present it to Himmler for maximum effect or, rather more precisely, how to reflect most credit on his own rôle. He forced himself to think through what he would say, and to anticipate the Reichsführer's reaction. *Make it sound routine, although first-class SD work.* Something he had planned for and foreseen. He picked up the phone and dialed.

"Herr Reichsführer, Best here. May I take a moment of your time?"

When he marched into Himmler's office and saluted, he tried hard to make the matter sound low key, something he had expected all along.

"Herr Reichsführer, I thought you would like to be informed immediately that we now have preliminary results in dealing with the British Commandos and recapturing the fugitive Jew." He made a slight pause, lifting the telegram in his left hand before continuing. "My people in Copenhagen have arrested the female Commando agent, Elizabeth van Paassen. She may well be the most important person in the plot. I expect we shall shortly hear about further arrests." He handed the telegram to Himmler with a sweeping gesture.

Himmler read the short message before speaking with his customary non-committal detachment.

"I see, Werner, but this is just one person. The rest of the Commandos and our Jew are presumably now on the loose in Copenhagen. That is far too close to Sweden, where they would be out of our reach. Think of that, Werner, and do not let them slip away."

x

McKinnon looked aghast at the intercept Ann Curtis had placed on his desk next to his mug of tea.

"I say, has Major Hawes seen this?"

"Yes, sir. It arrived just before noon."

"Please ask the Major to come to my office, and please bring some tea for him." McKinnon was not about to let a disaster in the field rob the office atmosphere of courtesy and decorum. Moments later, Hawes was sipping tea across from McKinnon, who started cleaning his pipe with a pensive expression.

"Well, Jack, you've had more time than I to consider the ramifications of this bit of news. What are your thoughts?"

Hawes was lighting a Players. The click of his lighter snapping shut provided a full stop to McKinnon's question.

Hawes had in fact spent the last few hours thinking about the situation created by Liz's arrest, and his orderly mind had arranged facts and questions in a proper sequence of priority.

"As I see the situation, sir, the immediate problem is whether to dispatch the Lysander tonight as planned. In favor of going ahead as scheduled is the primacy of the mission, i.e., getting Blum here as soon as possible. Against proceeding is the risk that Liz under torture may have revealed enough to compromise our plans, in which case the Germans will be ready to capture the Lysander."

McKinnon nodded. "And cancellation will prolong Blum's stay in Denmark with a daily increasing risk of capture."

Hawes added, "If only Liz has been captured, sir, so that Lund and Hansen are still at large, they may be able to send a radio message to abort tonight's mission."

"Unless they have been killed." McKinnon reminded him.

"True, sir, but SD in Copenhagen would surely have included that, with glee, when they reported to Berlin about Liz."

The two men smoked in silence, each assessing the scanty information in their possession, each trying to visualize the current position of each of the three novice SOE agents entrusted with operation *Dutch Treat*. Each thinking of Liz.

At length McKinnon spoke.

"Let our plans stand, unless we get additional information to convince us otherwise before the Lysander's departure tonight."

x

The Ribe group was gathered in the room of Niels Larsen, one of their number. They were seated in a half-circle with the radio in the center on a small table. The evening news broadcast from BBC had become an evening ritual, gathering individuals and groups like this one from Norway to Greece, infusing hope and courage in populations otherwise reduced to perusing the official releases from Goebbels' Propaganda Ministry. The Germans had tried to suppress BBC's news by making listening illegal or by outright confiscation of radios. The most-used way to throttle the British broadcasts was simply to drown them out with a "noise generator" broadcasting an undulating howl on the same wavelength. This could be partly overcome by very careful tuning, and listeners soon found that household radio sets varied some in their selectivity. Niels Larsen's was an older set but quite good in this respect. He had patiently adjusted the receiver so that the BBC was fairly strong while the noise generator was reduced to a background nuisance.

BBC's Danish announcer reported on the fighting in Russia, where the Germans were on the defensive after a monumental battle in the Kursk salient; he had also reported on a meeting in Quebec, where the leaders of the Western Allies had gotten together to plan strategy. At the end of the broadcast, he finally got to the part the little group was impatiently waiting for.

"And tonight we have greetings to Laura, Maren, Edith, Ingeborg, Yrsa, Louise, Birthe, Elizabeth, Vera, Trine, Marianne, and Kirsten."

A triumphant "Yes!" escaped the group, when the name "Elizabeth" was spoken and obliterated any further interest in the announcer's words. There was a scraping of chairs, and Valdemar gave a final reminder.

"I will leave as planned in half an hour. I'll wait at Seem plantation. You will leave at ten minute intervals and join me there. Don't forget to bring a sandwich."

Leaving town one cyclist at a time made the group's departure as inconspicuous as possible. It was close to midnight, when they all finally arrived at Steensholt, where they were greeted with enthusiasm. Marek went with Valdemar to position each man to cover the landing strip most effectively against intruders, if necessary. Two were placed where the estate's driveway met the county road. Three were spaced out along the south side of the landing strip; this put one in the middle and one at each end, with the easternmost guard close to the hangar. Valdemar chose to stay at the hangar itself, to be at the expected center of activity and to be easy to find.

Shortly after midnight everyone was in position. Marek and his uncle were sitting together with Feldsted in the grass at the southeastern corner of the hangar. In the balmy summer night Marek was relating, piece by piece in response to Feldsted's quizzing, details of the Ghetto uprising. Also hearing it for the first time, Blum sat transfixed, as his nephew gradually unrolled the lengthy picture of the Ghetto's agony and death.

At the northeast corner of the hangar, Valdemar was peering into the darkness of the western sky, straining to hear engine sounds, but only the whisper of a gentle breeze and the slight rustle of leaves were audible. He was struck by the incongruity of this entire undertaking: a bunch of amateurs on bicycles pretending to challenge the world's most advanced military power. They didn't even know what or whom they were guarding against tonight. An off-beat German patrol? A stray night fighter? Was this what was meant by *Total War*, the new and novel concept of civilians taking part, rather than just leaving the fighting to the military? He had no answers, only questions.

Still, tonight they did have a clear-cut mission: to get this Professor Blum safely dispatched to England. Maybe that would help the Allied cause.

x

In Station Robbe on Rømø, the southernmost of the islands along the Danish west coast, Luftwaffe Oberfeldwebel Emil Bach and the rest of the second night shift were taking over the radar from the early shift. Bach was munching a cookie from the local baker, as he settled himself in maximum comfort at his scope. The output of Danish bakeries was superior, he thought, lighter and more delicate than anything he had enjoyed elsewhere, even at home in Bavaria. The Danish penchant for quality seemed to apply in many other ways as well: the Danes really knew how to live. Mind you, the people were perhaps too soft, lacking in martial qualities compared with the Master Race, but he surely preferred this posting to any other place he had been during his service so far.

His scope showed a plane on climb-out from Skrydstrup airport; he listened in on the exchange between pilot and controller: assignment of altitude, initial heading. It was a Bf-110 night fighter, now turning onto a southerly course that would intersect the track of RAF bombers destined for Hamburg. Bomber Command's onslaught against the city had kept most nightly activity south of his Himmelbett, the section of sky his radar covered, but stray bombers could be encountered in his area, often wounded and easy to pick off. His eyes swept the scope, which was fed by the big Würtzburg radar poised outside his concrete bunker: nothing, just the Bf-110.

He got up and walked to the corner where his coat was hanging among several others. There was one more cookie in the coat pocket, he was quite sure; fumbling around, he located it and strolled back to his chair. This one had a sugar glaze; he resolved to eat it slowly. He had put on a bit of weight in the fifteen months he had been stationed here, all due to the sinfully good food. Well, not to worry; his next posting might trim it right off, likely as not.

He got himself comfortably settled again, automatically gave the scope a searching look, and almost dropped his cookie. An intruder had entered his Himmelbett from the west, already well advanced toward the coast. Bach estimated its speed at about 180 mph, as he reached for the radio switch.

x

Luftwaffe Leutnant Ernst Weber nosed the plane over into level flight and checked the heading. In his first fifteen months of active service, he had racked up a spectacular performance as a fighter pilot: eleven kills, which had gotten him transferred to night fighters; the build-up of an effective night fighter force was

Reichsmarshall Göring's latest move to help strengthen the homeland air defenses and parry the blows of the British Bomber Command.

Weber was flying a Messerschmitt Bf-110, a versatile workhorse that was serving the Luftwaffe in several different configurations. This one was the G-model night fighter. It had been fitted with DB605 engines that each spun out almost fifteen hundred horsepower for takeoff and quickly lifted the fully loaded fighter to its optimum altitude of 18,700 feet. Tonight's sortie was another test to evaluate the plane's maneuverability after the latest engine modifications. He pushed the intercom button; it was time to get ready for action.

"Paul and Max, test your guns."

A brief burst from the twin 7.9-mm MG-81 machine guns in the rear cockpit was followed by Feldwebel Max Singer's voice on the intercom, "Rear guns tested and functioning."

In the front cockpit, Feldwebel Paul Schwarz tested his four MG-17s the same way, following up with a short tunk-tunk-tunk from each of his two 20-mm MG-151 cannons, reporting in his cheerful, boyish voice, "All forward guns tested and functioning." He had barely finished the sentence when the radio crackled, and the radar operator's voice conveyed the urgency as much as the message itself.

"Messerschmitt G-S-A, intruder heading zero-niner-two at 2,000 feet, bearing three-three-two, at distance four-six kilometers. You will intercept on heading three-four-seven."

As Weber was acknowledging, he was already hauling the plane around in a one-eighty to the left and starting a shallow dive that boosted his speed to almost three hundred knots. He made some quick calculations in his head and adjusted the Radar operator's suggested heading five degrees to the left. He should catch up with the target in just over six minutes.

Chapter 17

Heinrich Erhardt from the Gestapo section burst into Best's office without knocking and threw a telegram from the chief agent of RSHA Department IV in Copenhagen on his desk.

"What in flaming hell is going on with your SD people? You have been attracting Commando killers like we've never seen before, and you obviously don't know how to deal with them!"

He was so angry that his voice almost failed him. Best noted this as a good sign; whatever the news was, the Gestapo evidently felt involved and at least partly responsible.

"Calm yourself, Heinrich; we are doing very well against the Commandos, as a matter of fact. Now, let me see what upsets you so."

He took the telegram, read through its contents, and let out an expletive of impressive magnitude. He read it again, slowly, this time analyzing its implications. When he had finished, he waved the telegram dismissively at Erhardt.

"Listen to me, Heinrich, this is serious for both of us. I have lost some good men and, which is more important, a valuable prisoner. You have lost an agent, which is a serious matter as well. We must both point out to the Reichsführer that security evidently has left our people badly exposed. General Hermann von Hanneken is the Wehrmacht Commander in Denmark; he should bear full responsibility for the security failure in this case. How can your people and my people be expected to function under such conditions?"

A few minutes later, the two Brigadeführer jointly presented the telegram and their grievance to Himmler. The Reichsführer did not lose his composure, but his eyes narrowed into slits while he read the document, and his voice was colder than either of them had heard before.

"Are you telling me that two–just *two*–civilians can walk into our Copenhagen headquarters, remove a prisoner I consider very important, and walk out again, unhurt, while your people, armed and trained, stand by watching? Heinrich, how many agents do you have in Copenhagen?"

"Uh...eleven, Herr Reichsführer."

"And how many armed RSHA personnel at this Dagmarhus building all together?"

"Uh...about thirty-four, Herr Reichsführer."

Best had breathed a sigh of relief while Himmler was addressing the stammering Erhardt, but the Reichsführer now turned to him, and cold sweat broke on his forehead.

"This entire affair, taking one lousy Jew from Amsterdam to Hechingen, has been bungled at every turn. Your SD people have shown incompetence, Werner, much incompetence. Getting themselves killed is bad, but not executing my orders is far worse. Nothing like this ever happened when Heydrich was in charge, Werner."

The implication that he could not fill the shoes of the assassinated SD leader boded ill for Werner Best. While Himmler's two underlings stood at painful attention, he read the missive one more time before speaking.

"I am from this moment making the two of you jointly responsible for the swift recovery of the Jew *and* the immediate arrest or killing of the Commandos. Report to me with the resolution on this situation in twenty-four hours."

X

Facing west, Valdemar cupped his hands behind his ears to catch every bit of sound. There could be no doubt: this was definitely an aircraft engine approaching in the night sky. He ran to the gasoline filled bucket and threw a match into it, making the little beacon light up the darkness. On cue, Svend

Jacob Skern lit the bucket of gasoline at the far end of the runway, making the second improvised marker blossom.

At the controls of the Lysander, Flight Lieutenant Don Higgins saw the markers light up. He was somewhat to the right of the field and continued downwind, executed a one-eighty to the left for his approach final, came in low by the barn with full flaps, and touched down gently.

"Sweet airplane," he told himself, for the umpteenth time.

He turned around, taxied back to the barn, parked by the small group dimly illuminated by the marker, and climbed out. At that precise moment, the ME-110 came out of the south at an altitude of six hundred feet and flashed by perpendicular to the airstrip, guns blazing.

In the Messerschmitt, Weber had also seen the markers being lit, and he glimpsed the Lysander, as it taxied past the marker to park. Being left of his target, he tried to wrench his plane into an attack course, but too late. The Messerschmitt was going far too fast for a line-up. Realizing that his first pass had missed the Lysander, Weber started a 270-degree turn to the left, bleeding off speed, to line up on the two markers.

On the ground, Don Higgins yelled, "Douse the marker! Douse the Marker!"

Feldsted understood and dashed to the barn, returning with an empty steel bucket. Turning it upside down, he plunked it over the marker, instantly extinguishing the flames.

Weber had almost completed his turn, when the marker went out. He completed his turn, lining up on memory, came down almost to treetop height, and bore down on the airstrip, along which Valdemar had placed his group.

Svend Jacob Skern lay in a shallow ditch just beyond the upwind marker, armed with one of the group's two Schmeisser MP-40 submachine guns. They had foreseen protecting the airstrip against a chance German patrol—they hadn't really been too clear about the possible danger—but nobody had imagined a real German fighter showing up. Here it was, however, and the strafing run it had just made at the barn left no doubt about

214

the pilot's intentions. Skern readied the gun. He couldn't see the German, but it was easy to follow the plane's flight path, for the engine noise was deafening in the quiet summer night. Now the plane was heading straight in toward the marker. Skern's index finger rested on the trigger. The plane appeared as a black shadow against a slightly less black sky. Skern fired a long, long burst, the whole magazine.

At midfield, Johannes Styrup was stationed with an 8-millimeter Danish army rifle. He was ready to fire, and as the Messerschmitt came up the airstrip with its four forward machine guns tearing up the turf, he got off two shots at close range.

Close to the barn Niels Larsen was clutching the group's second Schmeisser. He stood up, resting the gun on a fence post, started firing when the plane was at midfield and nearly face-on, following it with a hail of bullets until it was almost overhead and too close to miss.

The cacophony of sounds from the powerful engines, the German's four machine guns, and the insistent ground fire, died down instantly, as the plane disappeared beyond the Steensholt estate. The ground party heard the German pilot gun the engines, followed by some faltering engine noises, and finally an impact explosion. In the sudden silence, the group by the Lysander all heard the low but clearly audible voice of Higgins.

"I don't think they'll believe this one at Tempsford."

Valdemar called out, "Is anyone wounded?"

There was no answer. Higgins said, "He plowed the airstrip for you, did a very precise job. I'm glad I parked on the side away from the marker. Now we have to hurry. Who's going with me?"

Valdemar pointed to Blum and Marek and replied in halting English, "These two men."

The two passengers shook hands all around, thanked Claus Feldsted, and climbed aboard. Higgins taxied into position, aimed at the far marker that was still burning bright, and gave the big 655kW Bristol Mercury XII engine full throttle. The Lysander was airborne before reaching midfield. When Higgins leveled off at two hundred feet and throttled back to cruising speed, he was already out of sight.

Valdemar sent Niels Larsen with the empty bucket to douse the far end marker and assemble the group. Then he turned to Feldsted.

"You and your wife had better get away and find some place where you can lie low; or perhaps you should go to Sweden. The Germans will be swarming all over here when they find out what happened."

Feldsted agreed. They returned to the main house and said good-bye. The Ribe group quickly strapped their weapons to their bicycles and left Steensholt in high spirits.

At Station Robbe, Emil Bach was waiting for the ME-110 to reappear on his scope. Both the intruder and the night fighter had been below his observational range for more than ten minutes. He called Skrydstrup, reported, and asked if the ME had landed.

It hadn't.

X

The anesthesia was wearing off, and consciousness stubbornly insisted on reasserting itself. Liz opened her eyes, slightly, as the pain in her hip welled through the lower part of her body and made her gasp. A voice called out, "Nurse! She's waking up." Quick footsteps approached in the hall, and she felt someone bending over her, checking her pulse, and poking a needle in her arm.

Her state again became more dreamlike. She remembered how, when as a little girl she went to sleep at night, her mother would be sitting on the edge of her bed, telling her that Morpheus, the god of sleep, would now take her away in his arms. It was so lovely to be a little girl again, immersed in total security, her mother watching over her. But wait, she was no longer a little girl. Dream and reality seemed joined in a friendly embrace. The pain was slowly subsiding, and she perceived that the nurse was talking to someone, "...and she'll sleep all night."

A man's voice answered, "Good, she needs it."

She turned her head a little and fixed an unsteady gaze on the speaker. It was Lund, sitting next to the bed. She tried to smile, but her facial muscles did not want to cooperate. As she was soaring away in Morpheus' arms, she remembered what she wanted to tell him, as soon as she got a chance. She saw in her mind exactly what she was going to say: "Svend Lund, I love you!"

Aware that she was floating away, she tried to say it out loud, and quickly, but her tongue was oddly inert.

"Svend Luuhhhh..."

Her voice trailed away.

X

McKinnon's telephone was ringing; it was probably the Minister. Before picking it up, he took a good sip of the tea Ann Curtis has just brought. He needed that, for the events of the night had left little room for sleep. Unwilling to wait passively, he had gone with Jack Hawes to Tempsford, where the Lysander arrived just after four in the morning, having been escorted by two Spitfires on the last leg of the flight. On the way back to London the essential piece of information had been extracted despite language difficulties: Blum was willing to go to the United States and work with Einstein's group. The preliminary information Marek had provided raised more questions, all of which would have to wait for an interpreter. After another sip, he picked up the phone.

"Yes, Minister, we have him...oh yes, he is willing, even eager, to go to the States and work with Einstein...no, none of our team was on the Lysander, only Blum and his nephew...a rather long story, and a rather tragic one, I'm afraid...there has not been time for a full debrief, so I can only say that it involves a sensational report on the Nazis' destruction of the Warsaw Ghetto...yes, Minister, if I may call you back later today, I'll then have a more complete report...thank you, Minister."

He looked at his watch. Hawes was due to bring Marek Blum and a Yiddish interpreter in ten minutes. He sipped more tea, leaned back and closed his eyes.

Punctual as always, Hawes arrived ten minutes later, shepherding Marek and Mrs. Yarona Rubin, an approved, confidential SOE interpreter of Yiddish. Debriefing Marek took up most of the day. His description of the Ghetto uprising alone lasted over two hours and caused Rubin to break down in tears. Marek's written report was sent to be photocopied. At four in the afternoon, McKinnon called a halt to the session and had Ann Curtis take Marek back to the hotel.

McKinnon took a fresh pack of Cremo from his desk drawer and began to fill his pipe. His eyes were fixed on the yellow tobacco pack without really seeing it, while his fingers mechanically performed their task. Hawes was looking through a sheaf of notes he had made during the interrogation. When he had arranged them in some kind of order, he lit a Players and shook his head in despair.

"I'm afraid, sir, that Marek's information has given us far more questions than answers. What we know is that Elizabeth van Paassen has been arrested; and Lund and Hansen did not return from Copenhagen after sending the radio signal."

"We also know," McKinnon added, "that the group Lund trained provided security for the pickup and in the process shot down a German night fighter. At Tempsford the scuttlebutt must be having a great time with that bit of news."

"Without doubt, sir. On the negative side, we have no clue to the whereabouts of Lund and Hansen, nor to their intentions."

"Right." McKinnon puffed on his pipe before continuing. "On the basis of their past record, what can we reasonably surmise or predict they will be doing?"

"Are you suggesting, sir, that they may try some desperate ploy to free Miss van Paassen?"

"I'm certain of it, Jack. These two are not going to just leave her in Gestapo's clutches and get themselves back here by the most expedient means. They will try something audacious and improbable enough to outdistance expectations, yours and mine and the Gestapo's."

x

Hauptman Helmut Peters together with six Luftwaffe technicians of Nachtjagdgeschwader 3, the Luftwaffe night fighters stationed at Skrydstrup, arrived at the wreck in the early afternoon. Danish police from Haderslev were present and had roped off the site which was in a rye field ready to harvest. Two Danish police technicians who specialized in crime site investigation had already made a quick survey and departed with their cameras and other paraphernalia well before the Germans could arrive and object.

When an aircraft impacts the ground at speed, it typically fragments and burns, leaving little evidence with which to reconstruct the cause of the accident. The Bf-110 was no exception. It had left an ugly burn scar through the golden rye and pieces of wreckage were scattered over a substantial area. When a human body is subjected to such an impact, it fragments even more than the aircraft structure and largely disappears. Such debris of the Bf-110's three-man crew as could be found was respectfully gathered, but no piece could be identified, and the whole collection filled less than two ammunition boxes.

The aircraft remnants were picked up and thrown in the back of a pickup truck, where Hauptman Peters carefully examined each of them. He paused over one piece of crumbled aluminum and called his chief mechanic.

"Carsten, what do you make of this?"

Luftwaffe chief mechanic Carsten Ludens carefully examined the crumbled remnant before giving his answer without hesitation.

"Herr Hauptman, that is from the door over the left wheel well."

Peters nodded. "Yes, and what do you make of these holes?"

"Bullet holes, looks like nine millimeter; we can determine that with more certainty back at the base."

Peters nodded again. The Bf-110 had been brought down with ground fire.

He looked around him. The tranquil pastoral beauty of the Danish countryside suddenly looked less friendly than usual.

x

Wearing well-used coveralls to blend with the shipyard workers, Lund and Hansen sat on the quay of Refshaleøen, a peninsula enclosing the entrance to Copenhagen's central harbor and accommodating a large shipyard. Two days had passed since their shootout at Dagmarhus, and Liz was recovering well, though still confined to the hospital.

The month of August was becoming a milestone in the occupation ordeal. German demands on the Danish government to introduce capital punishment for sabotage had been rejected with the result that the Wehrmacht Commander, General von Hanneken, had formally assumed power. Referring to the Hague Convention of 1907, he proclaimed a state of emergency, and declared the Danish King and Government to be superseded and replaced as functioning entities. As a second step, he decreed that the Danish government must first direct all civil servants to continue their work, and that it must then resign. The Cabinet patiently pointed out that the Hague Convention did not apply because no state of war had been declared or existed; that the powerless Cabinet was not inclined to order the civil service to continue working; and that there was no constitutional provision allowing the Cabinet to resign under these circumstances.

After further deliberation the Cabinet finally requested from the King permission to resign, but His Majesty chose not to reply. Incredulous at the idea of law prevailing in the face of raw power, General von Hanneken was for the moment stymied. In this unprecedented situation, workers in enterprises critical to the German war effort rediscovered striking as a means of expressing their dissatisfaction. This helped to spread a rebellious mood throughout the country, as typical, easy-going Danes finally put their collective foot down. The Germans reacted nervously.

Lund and Hansen were determined to stay out of the local fray and get back to England where they felt their efforts could be used most effectively. If they could get to Sweden, the British Consulate in Stockholm would take care of their further travel. The problem was how to get to Sweden with Liz in the safest and most expedient manner. They had considered going by kayak, but rejected that as placing them hopelessly at the mercy of a German patrol, should they be discovered on the way. Going with a fishing boat was out of the question for the same reason: should they be discovered, they could not shoot their way out. They had even considered hijacking a Belt ferry, which could not be stopped by patrol boats, but they had calculated that a ferry would take over ten hours to reach Sweden, more than enough for the Luftwaffe or some other German force to stop them. Out of ideas, they had combed the waterfront in the hope of finding new inspiration, ending at Refshaleøen's shipyard. The yard belonged to Burmeister & Wain, a large manufacturer of marine diesel engines for freighters. The engines, huge machines several stories high, with cylinders two feet in diameter, were produced at B&W's plant in the inner harbor and barged to the shipyard for installation.

Pulled by a small tug, a barge was moving sedately past, one of the diesels projecting high above its low platform. They watched the tug position its load below the shipyard crane and moor it securely. A worker on the barge cast off the towline, which the tug reeled in before proceeding to its own mooring nearby.

Hansen said, "How fast do you think that tug can go?"

"Oh, maybe six or seven knots," Lund replied. "Those things aren't built for speed, you know."

Hansen smiled.

"I know, but on the other hand, it could probably absorb all the bullets a German patrol could shoot at it, and still keep going."

They looked at each other and both started laughing.

"You have a point there," Lund agreed. "Let's have a closer look."

They strolled along to the spot where the tug was moored. The skipper was still in the wheelhouse, while his helper was cleaning up on deck. Lund and Hansen sat down again with their feet dangling over the edge of the quay, and looked down in the tug, where the helper had finished and was lighting a cigarette. They were level with the skipper in the wheelhouse and only a few feet away; Lund called through the open forward window.

"Hey skipper, what kind of engine do you have?"

The skipper was an older man, a semi-retired sea captain tired of being often away from home. He opened the small wheelhouse door and stepped outside on the narrow balcony.

"I have a Deutch diesel, 300 horsepower. Why do you ask?"

"Oh, we were just curious; we both work in the B&W engine factory, and we don't make them that small, you know. How fast can you pull a barge such as you just hauled here?"

"In smooth water such as we have in the harbor, probably four knots, but under the harbor regulations we are not allowed to go faster than three. No hurrying."

"I don't suppose you'd show us your engine room?"

"Sure. Climb down over there."

Captain Jacob Lorentzen pointed to a steel ladder embedded in the quay side concrete. He turned out to be gregarious and talkative. Without much prodding he proudly described his vessel and its engine in detail. The tug, *Samson*, had come from B&W's own yard eight years ago. The construction was riveted steel plate. Without load it had a maximum speed of almost eight knots and a range of 370 miles. This was its permanent mooring, where it was kept most of the time these days as compared with peacetime, when the harbor complex was bustling with traffic. Lorentzen had not taken the tug outside the harbor for more than a year. The Germans patrolled The Sound diligently; much paper work and many special permits were required for offshore traffic of any kind.

After their visit on board, Lund and Hansen reviewed what they had learned. In an encounter with a patrol boat, the tug looked like it could hold its own, at least for a while. Lund described to Hansen his previous experience and the outcome.

"We will need some means to douse their searchlight," Lund suggested. "If they cannot illuminate us, their marksmanship will be mediocre at night."

"Even so," Hansen said, "we'll need to be able to steer from a position below the wheelhouse. With its big windows all around, a machine gun will perforate it; but I think I can jury-rig remote steering, so that we can keep going, at least in roughly the right direction."

Lund laughed. "That sounds only roughly reassuring, but let's tell Liz our plans."

Chapter 18

SS-Reichsführer Himmler leafed through the sheaf of reports and memos in a folder before him. They had been assembled and brought to him by Jantz, his special aide. When transferring to RSHA to become Himmler's aide, Jürgen Jantz left behind him a long career with Kripo, where he had been trained as a case analyst to work on special projects. The work was sometimes in Abwehr's realm, but most frequently the cases straddled department lines in RSHA's all-encompassing activity to sniff out weak spots or threats to the security of the Nazi state.

The folder on Himmler's desk was labeled *Fall Blum* (Case Blum), and it was captivating reading. The Reichsführer did not possess a particularly analytical mind; he was just a borderline paranoiac with an ever-suspicious outlook. That mental makeup had stood him in good stead ever since he joined the small circle of followers whose uncritical devotion to Adolf Hitler had proven crucial in establishing the Nazi state.

The incidents in Case Blum formed a sequence of ruthless use of force that had proven impressively effective. Was this a new modus operandi for SOE? Up to now the agency had functioned only in a subdued, clandestine form, its agents training local Underground fighters to challenge German occupation forces, rather than doing so themselves. But this...? The SOE team had left a bloody track as wide as an Autobahn. He leafed through the summary once more: killing four at Amsterdam University; killing four at Westerbork; killing three at Buxtehude; killing four at RSHA headquarters in Copenhagen. And Jantz made a persuasive case that this Bf-110 was brought down by ground fire directed by the same SOE operatives. Moreover, the situation in Denmark had suddenly become tense, and Jantz was speculating that SOE might be instrumental in bringing this about.

Himmler leaned back in his chair, turning the problem over in his mind. If these incidents all resulted from some new policy initiative by the British SOE, as Jantz was suggesting, Gestapo and other agencies needed to know more about it in order to take appropriate counter measures. The only way to confirm Jantz' hypothesis was to catch at least one of their operatives alive and squeeze him, or her, to find out about the instructions under which they were functioning. RSHA's need to do so far outweighed the importance of catching that miserable Jew for Heisenberg.

The Reichsführer pushed the intercom button. "Fräulein Hofer, send in Brigadeführer Erhardt and Best, please."

Moments later he was giving his two underlings a frosty stare, as they verbally reported on their progress. Best had transferred six agents from France to Copenhagen. Erhardt had dispatched his most experienced agent from Berlin to take charge of the search efforts in Copenhagen. As to actual, tangible progress toward finding the SOE team, there was none.

Speaking to both of them, Himmler curtly issued additional orders.

"Find out who is in charge of patrolling the waterway between Denmark and Sweden, and tell him to double the patrols for the time being. In view of the Danish lack of cooperation with our forces, I will recommend to the Führer that it is time to collect and remove Denmark's Jews. Get in touch with Obersturmbannführer Adolf Eichmann and prepare, immediately, a plan for doing this, a plan to be ready for implementation on short notice."

"Jawohl, Herr Reichsführer." The two Brigadeführer saluted and left.

X

For a century and a half, Sweden had looked at Czarist–and later Communist–Russia as a greater menace than imperial Germany. Besides, the German national traits of order, symmetrical forms, achievement, veneration of the past, and Lutheran tradition appealed to the Swedes and stood in contrast to currents from England and particularly France, that curried experimentation and chaos. With such cultural baggage, it was natural for the Swedes, though neutral, to be German-oriented during World War I. Afterward Swedes bought into the belief, fostered by German propaganda, that Germany was being unfairly treated after the Peace of Versailles. This paved the way for helping Germany during the 1920s to avoid some of the military constraints imposed by the Versailles Treaty. It also led to German investment and influence in Sweden's superb arms manufacturers, Bofors and AB Flygindustri.

Hitler's seizure of power in 1933 made the rest of the 1930s an awkward period for the Swedes. The swiftness of the Nazi revolution left few doubts that Germany had taken a radical turn. Swedish Social Democrats and Liberals perceived that the dictator had destroyed democracy in Germany and was threatening it elsewhere as well. Conservatives, and even King Gustav, visited Paul von Hindenburg and other leading Germans to voice their alarm, succeeding only in annoying Hitler. The Riksdag, Sweden's Parliament, on its part took belated steps that ended the cozy relations between Swedish and German arms producers.

Early in World War II, liquidation of Lithuania, Latvia, and Estonia, their neighbors across the Baltic, had shown the Swedes what to expect from Soviet Russia. Without love or respect for Hitler's Reich, democratic Sweden now hoped for a German victory. England and America were so very distant, Russia so very close. Besides, Sweden's position vis-à-vis Germany looked precarious. Militarily, Sweden was better prepared than Denmark and Norway, yet far from looking formidable to an aggressor. The Swedes started a frantic buildup that boosted the military budget tenfold and raised their forces to a reserve strength of 600,000 by 1943.

Acting to avoid belligerence, Sweden devised her own expedient form of neutrality to change with the winds of war and with the country's growing confidence in her own strength. By 1943, the Nazi war machine had been fatally weakened; Sweden felt able to wage effective defensive war, if necessary, and fell back on Cromwell's dictum to "trust in God and keep the powder dry."

At the same time, Swedish industrial and commercial circles kept a keen eye on economic opportunities. The output of phosphorous-rich iron ore from the Gaellivare mines in northern Sweden and the high-quality ball bearings produced at the SKF plants were urgently needed by German armament manufacturers, and through most of the war, Sweden kept up a brisk pace of delivery. In August of 1943, an American air raid on the German ball bearing center at Schweinfurt sustained terrible losses: 60 Flying Fortresses downed out of 220. Public opinion in the United States became enraged at the idea of Swedish supplies making up for German losses—losses which American fliers had given their lives to incur. The American government ultimately aired the possibility of bombing the SKF plants. At this prospect, the Swedes at length agreed to cut the export by 60%, an action induced by economic compensation from the Allies.

Sweden's wavering policy had substantially hardened by August, 1943. The upshot was noticeable in The Sound, where Swedish naval patrols suddenly displayed firmer enforcement of the prickly concept of neutrality in the country's territorial waters.

x

McKinnon and Hawes had spent most of the afternoon reviewing SOE's manpower needs and training programs. The geographic extent of Hitler's aggression had placed twelve countries under German occupation, and now Italy was being added to the list. Led by Eisenhower, the armies of the Western Allies had jumped from Libya to Sicily and on to Southern Italy, their first actual foothold on the European Continent. This caused the collapse of Mussolini's Fascist state, Hitler's main ally, which virtually overnight changed Italy's status to become just another nation occupied by Germany. The demand for Italian speaking SOE personnel was immediate.

Hawes looked up from the list he was studying.

"Sir, did you read my note about Marek?"

McKinnon nodded. "You mean the one about his volunteering for SOE service? Yes, and I can think of few people better qualified."

"Indeed, sir, but I think he would be most valuable as an Arisaig instructor right now. The Jews of the Warsaw Ghetto found ways to fight against the SS, particularly street fighting against armor, that partisans elsewhere can greatly benefit from knowing about. Besides, instructing would force him to perfect his English very quickly."

"Hmm...good point. Yes, do send him up there in the Lake Country, and let's see how he gets along and develops."

A knock on the door was followed by Ann Curtis' quick entry with a Bletchley intercept. McKinnon took it, read it, and handed it to Hawes with a smile and a head shake.

"This is about what I expected them to do, but I admit to being in doubt about the outcome."

Hawes read the message twice, carefully, before answering.

"I wonder why the Gestapo in Copenhagen delayed sending this report."

McKinnon snorted. "Put yourself in the shoes of the sender. How would you like to report to Berlin that two SOE agents walked into Gestapo headquarters, killed four people, freed a very important prisoner, and got clean away? The message emphasizes that Liz van Paassen was wounded, but no matter how it is put, it is an enormous embarrassment."

X

The night had that absolute, all-obscuring darkness typical of August in Scandinavia. It was balmy, even on the waterfront, the last of the heat lingering from a perfect late summer's day. It was also silent except for the dull thumps of a few sabotage detonations somewhere in the city, that could be heard at intervals. Each explosion served powerful notice to the occupiers that the Underground never slept.

Helge Lindbergh parked his car behind a storage shed; it was near the tug's mooring but far enough from the shipyard to be out of sight and earshot of sabotage guards on watch at the gate. Lund and Hansen went to the tug and forced the locks to gain entry to cabins and engine room, while Lindbergh helped Liz out of the car, supporting her with a last admonition.

"I know it still hurts when you walk, but the exercise is good for your hip, nevertheless."

He took her arm and walked her to the tug. Hansen was already on board, rigging up a set of lines and pulleys to operate the steering mechanism from the cabin below deck level and testing a small telltale compass. Lund was preparing a firing position at a hawsehole in the raised railing, which was some eighteen inches higher than the tug's deck, enough to offer protection. He caught Liz, when Lindbergh handed her down, and helped her gently down the companionway to the small cabin.

They finished their preparations and gathered for a moment of farewell in the cabin. Lindbergh produced a small flask of Cherry Heering, filled four small glasses, and raised his.

"May you reach Sweden safely. Here's to a quick passage!" They drank the sweet liqueur and Liz said, "On behalf of the team, but mostly on my own behalf, thank you, Helge." They said goodbye, and Lindbergh climbed back up onto the quay.

After a couple of tries, Hansen got the diesel started and emerged from the engine hold. Lindbergh cast off the mooring lines, and they slowly pushed the heavy vessel free of the pier.

Hansen took the wheel, and with the engine barely above idling, *Samson* crept along the shipyard's dry docks toward the

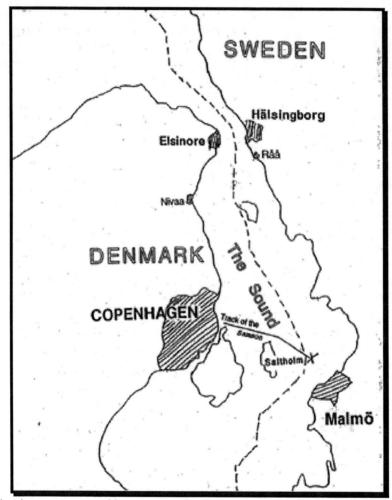

harbor entrance. Hansen gradually maneuvered into the middle of the harbor channel, and they passed the entrance between the two small beacon towers standing, unlit, one on each side of the harbor mouth. Hansen swung onto the course they had determined as the best and presently increased their speed to the maximum. The tug responded with an eight-knot surge, as Captain Lorentzen had told them it would, and the husky rumble of the diesel increased proportionately. The Sound was quiet except for a gentle breeze from the west, and the engine noise seemed earsplitting enough to alert every German patrol for miles around. Lund crouched at the railing with a Suomi, expecting searchlights sweeping in their direction any moment.

In The Sound between Copenhagen and the Swedish city of Malmö the island of Saltholm interposes itself about midway, a low uninhabited plot of meadowland deflecting sea borne traffic between the two cities slightly northward. They had measured the distance along the course line they had plotted to Malmö to be seventeen miles. About halfway they should enter Swedish territorial waters which, in theory, was off limits to the Germans. Well, in theory. In reality they had no illusions that a patrol boat in hot pursuit would respect diplomatic niceties or honor a neutral country's territorial integrity.

After one hour at full speed, they changed course twenty degrees to the right as planned. Fifteen minutes later, about where Sweden's sovereignty in theory should provide protection, it happened. On their port beam a searchlight stabbed through the darkness and swept the sea surface in their direction. Crouched behind the railing, Lund yelled to Hansen, "Get below, quick."

Hansen was already on his way. Kneeling on the cabin floor with his eyes fixed on the telltale compass, he tightened the lines of the remote steering. Liz was kneeling beside him, keeping the beam of a small flashlight on the compass. On deck Lund had his eyes and attention fixed on the patrol boat, waiting for it to get near enough to give him a good chance to shoot out the searchlight. The German was bearing down on them at full speed, at least thirty knots, he estimated. The distance between them looked to be a good two hundred yards, still much too far for the Suomi. A loudspeaker was screaming

German and, almost simultaneously, a machine gun let go a burst in the direction of the tug. Lund noted it as a warning salvo: the next one would be intended to stop them. He also noted that there was enough of a sea running to cause the patrol boat to pitch a fair amount, making it impossible for the search light operator to give the beam a steady aim. He realized that would make him only intermittently illuminated, when he sprang his surprise: poking the Suomi over the railing and with a burst put out the searchlight.

His train of thought was interrupted by another burst from the machine gun. It peppered the side of the tug, sounding like some giant beating a steel drum. The loudspeaker bellowed again.

"*Halt!* Stop! Or we shoot!"

Crouched on the cabin sole, Hansen with his eyes on the little compass mumbled, "Yeah, we noticed that, but did *you* notice that it didn't slow us down?"

For a split second, Lund popped his head up to estimate the distance. Still too far. The machine gun opened up again, this time riddling the wheelhouse. The glass windows shattered under the impact of the bullets, while binnacle, wall clock and barometer were torn to shreds, but *Samson* continued toward Malmö, oblivious and undaunted, at close to eight knots.

The patrol boat turned parallel to the tug, slowing down to keep abreast, and closed in. The protective railing still gave him cover, but Lund realized that he would have to kill the search light in order to even the odds somewhat. Otherwise, the Germans would get close enough to sweep the deck of the tug from either side, leaving him no cover, and in the end enabling them to board. He readied the Suomi, but another long salvo from the machine gun hammered the tug from stem to stern, followed by another order to stop from the loudspeaker. The tug was now too well illuminated; an attempt to show his head above the railing would be almost certain suicide. From the companionway came Liz's voice.

"Hansen wants to know the situation on deck."

Before Lund could answer, a larger searchlight suddenly lit up the entire scene, bathing both tug and patrol boat in its glare. The light was mounted on the Royal Swedish Navy's torpedo boat V48 *Polaris*, towering over the two smaller vessels. The Swede turned on his deck lights as well, thereby illuminating his forward guns, which were trained in the direction of the intruders. A loudspeaker bellowed in Swedish-accented German, "You are in Swedish territorial waters. Stop your engines. Do not shoot. If either of you shoots, I will sink him!" Hansen cut the tug's engine and came bolting up the companionway to join Lund and Liz, as the Swede repeated the order.

The German sensibly reversed his engine before shutting it down, keeping the patrol boat from running on momentum too close to the "Polaris."

For good measure, or perhaps to irritate the Germans, the Swedish captain repeated his order in English, while a crew of his sailors launched a boat to take a boarding party to the intruders.

Epilogue

WAAF Lieutenant Ann Curtis was waiting on the tarmac when the SOE *Dutch Treat* team descended the portable stairs from the DC-2 just arrived from Stockholm, and the three SOE agents filled the Morris Minor with no room left for baggage. As it happened, the team traveled without any. The little car was abuzz with animated conversation, notably different from the reserve Ann had displayed when she picked up Lund upon his first arrival on British soil.

In McKinnon's office they were greeted as old friends, or nearly so, as both McKinnon and Hawes dropped a bit of their habitual reserve. Ann served tea all around, while the initial debriefing was taking place in an almost lighthearted atmosphere with questions flying in all directions. McKinnon was curious about the Swedish Navy's rôle.

"I am surprised that the Swedes are patrolling The Sound with such powerful ships."

"They aren't," Lund said. "They are patrolling with smaller craft, and I managed to find out that the *Polaris* ran into us by sheer chance. She was discreetly on her way to a Göteborg shipyard for maintenance. It was simply our good luck that the Captain stretched his orders by revealing himself and interfering. He may be reprimanded for doing so, but I thanked him, needless to say."

Hawes wanted to know whether the shooting and killing could have been avoided, and Lund described the scene in Blum's office at the University, when he and Hansen had been Hagen and Wolff's prisoners at gun point.

"Oh...so it was Miss van Paassen who opened fire?" Hawes was taken aback at this piece of information and did not further pursue the matter.

There was particular interest in the Dagmarhus shootout. Although brushes with the Gestapo had occurred in other places, the clean getaway after inflicting losses on the Germans was without parallel in SOE records. Lund, Hansen and Liz all had to describe their individual impressions, observations, and actions in the brief period between their entering the building and spraying the facade when they drove away in the Adler.

The team members on their part were eager to learn about the Lysander pickup. Lund was silently proud of the Ribe group's performance, and there were both incredulity and cheers when Hawes told about the group's downing of the night fighter. This was news to them, as Lund had refrained from trying to contact the Ribe people.

Liz had to tell about her time as a prisoner and the SD's rape intentions.

"I am certain," she said, "that the bullet in my hip was meant for Hansen, but I am happy to have taken it. I owe him more than that for killing Randschau."

It was late afternoon when McKinnon broke off the conversation and told Ann to set up for each of them an appointment for a more thorough and official debriefing the following day. Before the team left his office, he impressed on them the necessity for total secrecy about every aspect of Operation *Dutch Treat*.

"I should tell you," he added, "that Marek has gone to our Arisaig training facility as an instructor in urban insurgency. When you come in tomorrow, I will discuss with each of you some other possible assignments for SOE. Between now and then, think about whether you will consider further work, now that you have tried it."

They left, Liz for her mother's apartment, Lund and Hansen for the modest hotel SOE used for its people.

An hour later Liz was enjoying the feeling of security by being in the heart of London. Already when leaving Sweden, she had succeeded in putting the memory of the Continent and its perils far back in her mind. Very far back. While waiting for her mother to come home, she heated enough water for a bath in their bathroom's small sitztub. Relaxing and luxuriating in the hot tub, she was, as always, thinking of Lund. Strangely, it seemed as though there had never been any opportunity to speak with him alone. On the way in the plane from Stockholm, she had been thinking that the closest they had ever come to being alone was in the haystack. Maybe it was intentional on his part, but she refused to believe so.

She was getting out of the bath, when her mother came home.

"Oh, you're back, dear! How nice. Come and tell me all about your trip."

The two women were having tea in the kitchen, when the telephone rang. After taking it, her mother handed it to Liz.

"It's a Mr. Lund, dear, for you."

Her heart leaped uncontrollably, as she took it.

"Yes?"

"Oh...uh...Liz?...I was just wondering, uh...if you would care to have dinner with me. In town."

She suppressed a giggle.

"Svend Lund, I cannot see your face, so how can I know what your intentions are?"

"Why...but what...how do you mean?"

She broke into peals of happy laughter.

"Never mind. Pick me up in half an hour."

Printed in the United States
80453LV00002B/379-402